Akel Dama

J.C. Simmons

iUniverse, Inc.
New York Bloomington

Akel Dama

Copyright © 2008 by J.C. Simmons

All rights reserved. No part of this book may be used or reproduced by any means, graphic, electronic, or mechanical, including photocopying, recording, taping or by any information storage retrieval system without the written permission of the publisher except in the case of brief quotations embodied in critical articles and reviews.

This is a work of fiction. All of the characters, names, incidents, organizations, and dialogue in this novel are either the products of the author's imagination or are used fictitiously.

iUniverse books may be ordered through booksellers or by contacting:

iUniverse
1663 Liberty Drive
Bloomington, IN 47403
www.iuniverse.com
1-800-Authors (1-800-288-4677)

Because of the dynamic nature of the Internet, any Web addresses or links contained in this book may have changed since publication and may no longer be valid. The views expressed in this work are solely those of the author and do not necessarily reflect the views of the publisher, and the publisher hereby disclaims any responsibility for them.

ISBN: 978-1-4401-0382-7 (pbk)
ISBN: 978-1-4401-0890-7 (cloth)
ISBN: 978-1-4401-0383-4 (ebk)

Printed in the United States of America

This book is for
Pauline Matthews

Acknowledgments

Carolyn Matthews Simmons: Without whose help this book could never have been written.

Lisa Jones: My "Editor in Chief." Finally, the one you've waited for.

Jeanne Kroker: My "West Coast" editor who always makes the work better.

Rick Shackelford: For being the "Shack" of this novel and for bringing the reality of country life to the fore.

Debbie Bennett: Whose insight into the book is amazing, and for keeping the characters true to themselves. Your hard work on a raw manuscript is much appreciated.

(Now this man purchased a field with the wages of iniquity; and falling headlong, he burst open in the middle and all his entrails gushed out.
And it became known to all those dwelling in Jerusalem; so that field is called in their own language, Akel Dama, that is, Field of Blood.)
Acts 1: 18-19

Prologue

The aged, ex-airliner crossed the shoreline a mere one hundred feet above the ground a mile or so west of Bay St. Louis, Mississippi, and passed abeam the John C. Stennis International Airport. It was shortly before daylight and still dark. Fog and rain obscured forward visibility. The weather had been bad since departure from Belize in Central America.

The pilot, the lone occupant in a cockpit that normally required three crewmembers, checked the hand-held GPS receiver and turned twenty degrees to the right altering his course. His hands moved over the controls like a concert pianist, adjusting throttles, mixtures, changing fuel tanks, checking dials, gauges, and switches. His destination was a newly graded, but yet unpaved, roadbed near the town of Union, Mississippi, in the central part of the state. Ground crews were standing by to offload the cargo. If his luck held, and the dirt road supported the weight of the DC-4, he would be airborne within an hour of landing. He had been assured all would be well by the one who hired him. But then dope dealers were hardly known for their veracity.

He looked out the windscreen. The night was formless and everything seemed to have no purpose. The damp air pushed him into the seat and felt heavy on his face. The thought was that now all he had to do was fly, to decide on an optimal course. That was what a pilot did. It was an aviator's way. You just got it done because you had to. Otherwise you would fall out of the sky.

. . .

Five miles west of Union, Rose English walked out the back door of her farmhouse holding an eight-month-old kitten that had been fighting with his sisters. It was six a.m. on a Sunday in December, and a cold misty rain fell from a low overcast sky. Her intentions were to calm the kitten, then gently scold him, teaching that fighting with his siblings was not a good thing. The ground began to shake beneath her feet followed instantly by the roar of four fourteen hundred and fifty horsepower radial engines straining to keep a huge, old, ex-airliner aloft. Passing a hundred feet above her head, the Douglas DC-4 quickly disappeared below the treetops beyond her view headed in a westerly direction. She waited for the sound of the crash that never came. The smell of exhaust fumes and unburned oil settled down around her like a noxious fog. Inside the farmhouse, Rose dialed not 911, but the number of her neighbor, Jay Leicester, who lived a few miles to the south. The kitten left claw marks on her shoulder that oozed blood, staining her white blouse.

Chapter One

I lay in bed, staring at the dark, in the little cottage in the wild woods. I felt like one of those nocturnal animals in a zoo, revealed in the darkness, who growls or bites his fellow creatures and eats their offspring. In spite of my desire for an ordered universe, my life felt scattered, full of small moments, without great purpose. Perhaps it is because small things repeat their importance on a farm and make them indelible in my memory. What is most untrustworthy about our nature and self-worth is how we differ in our own realities from the way we are seen by others. But then I could care less what others thought about me.

Maybe I have spent too much time alone at this cottage conversing with just myself. These were private words, as if collected from birds, or cows, or the cats and dogs. I spoke a few sentences to myself about wine, or a rusted gate, or a windmill that refused to pump water or a coyote's nervousness as I watched him through the scope of a rifle. It seemed I had protected myself with words, with the small and partial clarity they brought. I seem to live by retrievals from childhood that coalesce and echo throughout my life. I live permanently in the recurrence of my own stories, whatever stories I tell. Darkness has many potent hours. It is a shame I was wasting time dreaming through it.

The phone rang, startling me so that my heart seemed to race out of control.

"Jay, a huge airplane just skimmed over my head. I think it may have crashed."

"Who is this?"

"You s.o.b. I'm serious."

"Okay, slow down and tell me exactly what you saw."

"It was big, it flew low, right at treetop level, and had engines like what's on your little airplane, four of them. It went behind the trees and then disappeared. I never heard it crash, but I think it did."

"Rose, the timber company may be using an old airliner to spray nitrogen fertilizer. The forest service uses them to drop fire retardant, and they are used to haul freight all over the country. Maybe it wasn't as low as you thought."

"I know what I saw and I know how low it was. Get your butt out of bed and check on it."

"Yes, mother."

Lying back in bed, I laughed. Rose English was my closest neighbor and long time friend of over ten years. When I first met her, she spoke sparingly in a low-pitched monologue, mostly to herself, as if language was uncertain. It seems that all of us loners do this. Her expression back then was the quizzical and knowing looks an animal can give, as if she already knew what I would or could provide. I once saw her dance in a field with a cat, and I remembered that. It has become for me this delicious witnessed example of who she is.

In the kitchen, I plugged in the coffeepot and heard a strange bird outside the window. The song of an unseen bird was a great mystery I had come to love. I align myself within its vast architecture, which contains all forest life and life in the sky. Coyotes howled close by, then further away, like crying souls descending into the depths of hell.

While the coffee brewed, I took a hot shower and thought about the airplane Rose saw passing low over her head. A call to Paul Bradford, the tower chief at the Meridian airport would probably solve this quickly. One thing I did know about Rose, she was not an alarmist. She thought it warranted calling me, so I felt it prudent to follow up.

As I finished the first cup of coffee, the phone rang again. Come on, Rose, I said I'd look into it. "Jay Leicester."

"Bob Morgan, Jay. Sheriff over in Scott County."

"Hello Bob. What can I do for you early on this cold, dreary morning?"

"I have the front end of my car parked up against the nose wheel of a big old airliner. All four engines are idling, the pilot refuses to shut them down. We caught a crew off-loading ten thousand-pounds of marijuana. We have twelve plus the pilot in custody. The pilot says the airplane belongs to him personally and he doesn't want to leave it here to be dismantled and ruined. He wants me to fly with him to any local airport where the airplane would at least be safe until his case is disposed of. I informed him we would confiscate it anyway, but he's insistent. I knew aviation was your business, so maybe you can offer some advice."

"Bob, listen to me carefully. Do not under any circumstances let that pilot takeoff with you aboard. Once airborne, you are at his mercy. Even though you've got the gun, what are you going to do, shoot him? You can't fly the airplane. You'd both be dead."

"You have any suggestions?"

"Tell me exactly where you are."

"They are building a new road, comes out of Neshoba County into Scott, supposed to connect to highway 21."

"I know where that is. I'll be there in twenty minutes."

"Thanks. I was hoping you'd come."

Pulling on my old leather flight jacket, I checked to be sure the model 66 S&W magnum was in the pocket and walked out the front door of the cottage. The sky was gray. The trees bare and black. Each biting gust of wind tightens my face. The sweet, seasoned scent of cow manure and wood smoke fills my nostrils. The icy cold chills me to the bone. Behind the cottage I watch a bobcat drink from the pond, then bound up the slope of the dam with an almost surreal grace and vanish into the woods like some creature wholly of the imagination. As I close the door to my truck, I think that Rose is really gonna enjoy this.

. . .

It has been almost twenty years since I'd flown a DC-4. To see one sitting out in the woods on an unpaved dirt roadbed with the engines running seemed, at the very least, an odd apparition. A remarkable thing I noticed about this airplane was that there was not a speck of paint anywhere on the wings or fuselage. It was all polished aluminum and clean, no corrosion or oil streaks. It was as if it came out of the factory last week.

Parking off to the side, I walked up to a deputy who pointed to a ladder leaning against the wide double cargo door opening at the rear of the plane. Over the noise of the engines, he shouted that the sheriff and pilot were aboard. Climbing the ladder, I entered the cavernous, oval-shaped fuselage, empty except for a strong odor of cannabis sativa. The last DC-4 I flew had sixty seats. Making my way forward, I entered the cockpit. The pilot was in his seat. Sheriff Bob Morgan stood behind him, his hand on his pistol. He shook my hand.

Glancing at the instrument panel, I said to the pilot, "The cylinder head temps are at the redline."

"I know. We need to take off now."

"Sheriff, tell your men to clear the road and shut the cargo doors. We'll meet you at the Philadelphia airport."

Sitting down in the copilot's seat, I donned a David Clark headset, adjusted the volume, and reached for the checklist hanging in its familiar place.

"So, you're a DC-4 pilot?" The Captain asked without looking at me.

"Flew them for the Matson Line for six months before they went belly up. Oakland to Hawaii."

"I heard about them. First class operation. Too bad."

"Yeah, too bad. I'll run the checklist."

"Name's Amos Dudley."

"Jay Leicester." We did not shake hands.

As we went through the litany of the pre-takeoff checklist, I watched Dudley. He was a big man and heavily built, although his sallow complexion and baked-potato physique gave no suggestion of either good health or strength. His eyes were gray and distant. About my age, his face was wrinkled with time and had peculiar indentations, which were more like rotting pine bark than a souvenir of some childhood disease. The minute craters gave his features a crumpled, indefinite look, as if he could change their meaning by molding the skin with his fingers. He had a long scar that extended from the lobe of one ear to the center of his chin.

"Checklist complete."

Dudley fingered the scar, kneading his tactile face and muttering something about his luck, which I found easy to ignore. "Okay, here we go."

Whatever I thought of Amos Dudley as a person was irrelevant to the fact that he was an excellent pilot and flew this old bird as if he were a part of the machinery. We landed twenty minutes after liftoff from the dirt road. Neshoba County deputies and Philadelphia police surrounded the plane with guns drawn as we went through the shutdown checklist. I hoped one of them didn't shoot me by accident.

Bob Morgan arrived and, along with the Neshoba County sheriff, took Dudley into custody. He gave me a furtive glance, rubbed the scar on his face. "Nice to fly with you."

"Same here." I would never see him again, but would often wonder what misfortune could befall such a talented aviator to make him resort to hauling illegal drugs. It didn't somehow seem fair. However only fools and little children think the world's fair.

A deputy had been kind enough to drive my truck to the Philadelphia airport. He handed me the keys. "Wow, that's a big flying machine. Could I see inside?"

"Sure, come on, I'll give you the fifty cent tour."

He sat in the Captain's seat and listened intently as I told him the history of this wonderful old airplane. It was designed by Douglas Aircraft, whose DC-3 was an instant success and moneymaker for the airlines, for United, who wanted a four engine long range airliner. As fate would have it, the DC-4 was developed under the darkening clouds of WW2 and after the USA's entry into the war all DC-4s then on the production line were requisitioned for the military. The result was that the first DC-4 to fly was in February of 1942 in military markings designated as the C-54 Skymaster. Some 1162 were built during the war with another 76 built to new orders for the airlines postwar. Over the years the airplane has been passed down to charter and freight airlines, and today small numbers survive in service attesting to the successful design by Douglas.

"Wow," the deputy said. "And to think I've been afforded the opportunity to sit in the cockpit of one." I couldn't have put it any better myself.

Driving from Philadelphia back to Union, many thoughts ran through my mind: illegal drugs, old airplanes, good pilots gone bad, Rose, and what I was doing living in the middle of the woods in rural Mississippi. Jay Leicester, aviation consultant, former NFL linebacker, former medical student, former airline pilot…former, former, former. Too many formers, and not yet fifty years old. It seemed a winter of storms. I felt something taking shape in the cab of the truck. It seemed to be a dark, cauled form that floated off to the side and watched me with hooded expressionless eyes. It scared me.

Parking in Rose's driveway, I thought that I have been a secretive man for most of my life, and now was disconcerted by the secrets I had kept from myself. Succinct histories tell us something…that anything peaceful has a troubled past. The past is always carried into the present by small things. Maybe flying the old DC-4 was the cause of this unrest in my psyche. Maybe I wasn't going insane.

Rose sat the coffee cups on the kitchen table, poured them full, and handed me a jar of honey that was so old a half inch of crystal had formed in the bottom.

"You can heat this in the microwave for thirty seconds and the sugar crystals will dissolve."

"I can also use the microwave to measure the speed of light. If you'd come by and visit more often maybe the honey wouldn't get old."

Point taken.

I placed my hand on top of hers. "I already know the speed of light. You want to hear about the big old airplane that almost landed on your head?"

She had turned into a woman who was differential and old-maidish, but pleased beyond good sense when I placed my hand atop hers. "I do."

"It was carrying ten thousand pounds of marijuana. Seems you were not the only one to see it flying low. Someone called the sheriff and he caught them offloading the drugs. Bob Morgan, from Scott County, called me and we flew the airplane to Philadelphia."

"Who in this part of the country is a big enough drug dealer to bring in ten thousand pounds?"

"Probably not local, but whoever it is, they were smart enough not to be there this morning. I'm sure one of the men arrested will roll over for a light or suspended sentence. Maybe the pilot, he stands to lose the most."

"Well, this has been a great morning. I get scared half to death and you get paid to fly an old airplane from a dirt road to Philadelphia."

"I won't bill them for that. Maybe I can get a break on my next speeding ticket."

"Then you are a fool."

"Been told that before, more than once--by you."

She laughed, took the cups and sat them in the sink. "Go away, I've got work to do, and I'm late for church."

"Heaven forbid the Bluff Springs Church of God hold a service and you or Pauline Matthews are not there. The world would tremble and God would get up from his throne to see what was the matter."

"You should go to church."

"I'm not much into organized religion, but if I was, your little church in the wild wood is where I'd go."

Back at the cottage, I spent the afternoon doing paperwork for my aviation consulting business, billing, filing, and catching up on things long neglected. As dark approached, I sat in front of a slow burning fire reading and sipping a glass of vintage Graham Port. It is always a pleasure to rest in a soft chair and hold a book in my hands. Later, after the fire had burned down, I stood, gathered my senses into almost clarity, and went through the darkness to my bed, not knowing that plans were underway that would change my life forever. Plans that would demonstrate the truth that this world holds mysteries you do not want to know. Visions that would steal the very light from your eyes and leave them sightless.

Chapter Two

I spent the next two nights and three days in Jackson, the state capital, working with a small advertising agency that was expanding its business into surrounding states. The agency was owned by a man I'd gone to college with. He was an offensive lineman on the football team. I played linebacker, so we had little in common, but roomed together during training camp and road games. He wanted to purchase an airplane to facilitate the growth of his company. My job was to advise him on which aircraft to purchase, make the acquisition, hire and train the flight crew, and project an operating budget for the newly formed flight department.

Walking into his office located not far from the Jackson International Airport, I was greeted by a pleasant woman who could have been Rose English's sister but, thankfully, not of the same temperament. She informed me that Mr. Verinis was waiting and to go right in.

Jim Verinis was standing behind his desk, all six feet five inches of him. Trimmed down from his college playing weight of three hundred pounds, he looked slim, healthy, and much younger than his forty-five years. Sandy hair, cropped short, his broken nose (a wound I inflicted during practice one day), fit his rugged face and clear blue eyes.

Coming around from behind his desk, he stuck out a massive paw. "Jay Leicester, good to see you. How's life in the country?"

"The armadillos still irritate me, but other than that, wouldn't be anywhere else."

"You need to let us do an ad campaign for you, put Jay Leicester, Aviation Consultants on t.v., newspapers, and radio. We're expanding into five states. Do your business a lot of good. Make you some money."

"I've got more business than I need at the moment." That was a lie, but to advertise like some ambulance chaser, no thanks.

He offered a chair. "So what do we need to do to get us up and flying?"

"We'll start with what destinations you plan to visit, how many people will be aboard, how often you need to make the trips, and how much money you want to spend. Plus, how many days a year I can use the airplane free of charge."

He looked quizzically at me for a moment, reached up and fingered his crooked nose as if remembering a hot August practice and a misplaced elbow. Then he broke into a big smile when he realized I was kidding. "You haven't changed a bit."

"How much have you spent on charter aircraft over the last year?"

He opened a folder and slid me a sheet of paper. Out the window behind his head, I watched a C-17 military cargo plane take off and climb steeply into the clear winter sky. The local air guard received this advanced plane to replace aging C-141s. I had watched the development of the C-17 and thought that with its four turbofan engines, long range, and short field performance, it would be even better than the venerable old C-130 turboprops, and that's saying a lot.

Looking at the figures on the paper, I said, "It is time to consider your own company airplane. Should be less expensive and more convenient."

After getting the answers to all the pertinent questions, my recommendation for the type of aircraft was made much easier. "Jim, I want you to look at three different planes. You've been chartering King Airs, which are fine turboprop machines designed for short haul, multi-stop trips, but I want you to consider going with jet engines, simply because I think the most dangerous thing on an airplane is a propeller. Let me make some phone calls and we'll get demo airplanes here tomorrow and the next day. We can fly them, I'll give you the pros and cons of each, and you can make a decision. After that, we'll talk about hiring a crew, getting them trained, deciding where you want to be based, and all the other hundreds of things involved with starting up the Verinis Advertising Agency Flight Department."

"Sounds like a plan. I see now, why you get paid so handsomely for what you do. I had no idea it was so complicated."

"This is easy. Try starting up a charter company or a scheduled airline. Now that is complex."

Jim led me to a vacant office and I started making calls.

One would think that with the country headed toward the brink of a recession that the aircraft market would be flooded with good deals from backlogs of factory new and used airplanes. Not true. Like the book business and the liquor business, sales increase when times are hard. Companies have to travel more to make money. Prices have actually increased, especially in the used aircraft market. My business, like most, survives on networking, having contacts across the industry. I make two phone calls and had three airplanes scheduled to arrive for demo flights, two tomorrow and one the next day.

With the budget Verinis Advertising had to work with, I decided a used, low-time, well-maintained small corporate jet with short field capability would be the best for the agency. Later, if business continued to expand, new aircraft with more seats and longer range could be purchased. A friend in Dallas had available a one-owner Cessna Citation 1SP with 1400 hours and a Dassault Falcon 10 with 2100 hours currently owned by a Fortune 500 company that was trading up. Both would arrive in the morning. The third airplane I wanted Jim to look at was an older Saberliner 40A. A broker in Orlando had one with a low-time airframe, recent engines, new interior, upgraded avionics, and no damage history. He promised to have it here day after tomorrow. All three aircraft were in the 1.5 million-dollar range. With an estimated annual flight time of three hundred hours, either of these aircraft would serve Jim Verinis and his agency for years before major overhauls were due, and by then it would be time to trade.

Deciding not to drive back to the cottage, only to have to return in the morning, I got a room in a motel near the airport, and phoned Rose. She promised to see to my cat, B.W., and check on the farm. I spent the rest of the afternoon going over a checklist of items for the startup of the Verinis Advertising Agency Flight Department, and arranging for a pre-buy maintenance inspection of the airplane Jim decided upon. This is a hard and fast rule I insist on. Mechanics carefully go over logbooks to see that all airworthiness directives have been complied with, and the aircraft itself is pulled apart, inspected, and put back together. It is an expense a buyer must be willing to pay. Hundreds of thousands of dollars can be saved in unknown, unsuspected, and needed repairs. *Caveat emptor.* Discrepancies can be negotiated between buyer and seller. It makes me sleep well at night knowing I have bought the safest and most airworthy airplane for my client.

. . .

Another clear, cold winter day brought perfect flying weather. We flew the Citation 1SP and the Dassault Falcon 10. Both impressed Jim Verinis, but he fell in love with the Citation. That was the aircraft he wanted.

"Jim, I really think you should look at the Saberliner 40A before you make a decision."

"No, I want that Cessna. Is there any thing wrong with it?"

"I wouldn't have shown it to you if there was."

"Then my mind's made up. Start the pre-buy inspection, let's go to my office and we'll talk about hiring a pilot."

Offensive linemen!

Back at Verinis Advertising Agency, I called and canceled the demo on the Saberliner. The Citation pilot flew back to Dallas on the Falcon 10, and my friend, the aircraft salesman, remained in Jackson to negotiate the price of the 1SP after the inspection was completed, which should be tomorrow afternoon.

Jim propped his feet on his desk, laced his huge hands behind his head. "So, you got anyone in mind for my pilot?"

"You're going to need two pilots, Jim."

He put his feet on the floor, sat up straight. "I thought the SP stood for single pilot? I flew with one pilot on the King Air."

"The SP does stand for single pilot, but I think anybody's a fool to fly a jet airplane into high density airports like Dallas, Memphis, Atlanta, or Chicago with only one set of eyes, not to mention the possibility, however remote, of a stroke, heart attack, or a brain bleed. Whose gonna fly the plane then? An extra person at the controls is a small expense compared to the safety it offers. You will not argue with me on this point, understood?"

He looked at me hard for a moment, then broke into a grin. "I guess that's why I hired you for advice. I would be a fool not to take it." Sitting up, he put his elbows on the desk, stared at me intently. "How much for you, Jay Leicester?"

"You know my fee."

"How much for you to work for me and fly my airplane? Name your price."

"Thanks, Jim. I appreciate the offer, but no."

"Why not?"

"Jim, I've done everything I ever wanted to do, accomplished every goal, but every step of the way, there has always been another flight test to pass, another standard to meet. I was tied into the machinery of aviation; complex, unyielding, and while not without its rhythm, keeping that beat always seemed to come at the cost of some measure of self. Where I'm at now, I never have to alter routine, never get caught in traffic, have to stand in the rain, bumped into on a sidewalk, jostled on a subway in some crowded city, tied to a desk. Never rushed. Never late. I know the freedom without the anchor, have my routine without the drudgery."

He sat back, looked at the ceiling. "Then hire me somebody that's as good a pilot as you. I checked. You're considered one of the best."

"No, not the best, but I was taught by the best. The pilots we hire will be even better."

I spent the rest of the day at the maintenance hangar observing the inspection of the Cessna Citation 1SP.

· · ·

That evening, the aircraft salesman and I dined together, and then I retired early. Back at my motel room, the message light on the phone was blinking with an evil red glow. Rose had called.

"What's up old woman? B.W. acting ugly?"

"I am not an old woman and no, B.W. is much more of a gentleman than you."

"He's had his balls cut off."

"Maybe we should consider that for you. Smooth your temperament."

Laughing, I said, "Enough chit chat, Rose."

"Are you expecting visitors at the cottage?"

"I am not."

"There's been a strange car coming out of your drive twice today. I met them as they were leaving once, then later saw the car pass a couple of times in front of my house. Gray sedan, two suit-type, clean cut occupants."

"I have no idea, but thanks for the eyeball."

"When you coming home?"

"Late tomorrow afternoon, if all goes well."

"Plan on having dinner with me. I want to discuss a letter from Alella."

"I'll call when leaving Jackson."

Alella was Rose's adopted daughter. She was originally from Spain, now attending college at the University of Madrid. I had saved her from a bad situation in Mexico, had introduced her to Rose, so I felt an obligation to listen to news about her. Plus, I adored her, and would have adopted her myself if Rose hadn't. As for the men in the car, I didn't have a clue, unless it had something to do with the DC-4 sitting on the ramp in Philadelphia.

· · ·

At noon the next day, the chief mechanic for the Fixed Base Operation at the Jackson International Airport, approached me.

"Leicester, we haven't found a single squawk on this Citation. It's like it rolled out of the factory last week. It's been well maintained. We'll have her back together and ready to test fly within an hour. I want to ride along."

"I'll round up the salesman, and we'll be ready whenever you say."

We filed an IFR, round robin flight plan, up to Little Rock with a requested altitude of 35 thousand feet. I flew in the captain's seat, the salesman as copilot, and the mechanic behind us, observing. With an unrestricted climb, we reached altitude in 28 minutes after liftoff. Leveling off, I let the Citation accelerate until I heard the "ding, ding, ding" of the over-speed warning, then pulled the power back to cruise. It was a halcyon day to fly. Visibility was forever. Over Little Rock, we turned and headed back to Jackson. The airplane performed beautifully, and I knew it would serve Jim Verinis and his business well. A hundred miles from the airport, I pulled the power back to flight idle and started our descent. Things were quiet, with only the noise of the wind on the windscreen. I felt in my soul the wearing away of the calluses of life on earth. It was as though my skin had been stripped off and replaced with a fresh pink layer. What I experience in the air is the petite life on earth, with only the essential notes of humans reaching me through that distant air. An angel seemed to tug at my shirttail. Flying does this to me.

Back on the ground, the aircraft salesman and I reported back to Jim Verinis. Leaving them to finalize the purchase, I went to the office space provided and made a few phone calls. The search for a flight crew would not take long. Training them to my standards would take a little longer.

An hour later, Jim Verinis walked into the office. "I now own the Citation. What's next?"

"Where do you want to base the airplane?"

"What's wrong with where it is? It's only a five minute drive from where we are."

"Nothing's wrong with the FBO at the Jackson International Airport, except it's three times as expensive to base there than Hawkins Field, five times more expensive than Madison County. Just wanted you to know."

He scratched his wide, square chin, seemed confused.

"Look, Jim, keep the plane where it is for six months, see how things work out. You may want to build your own hangar later on."

He smiled. "Good idea. I want to interview the pilots before you hire them. When can we expect to be operational?"

"If I can find a crew current on the Citation, a week. If not, then they will need to attend Flight Safety or SimuFlite for training."

"We won't hurry this. I want the best, and I want them up to speed. I'll leave it up to you."

"I'll let you know as soon as I have a crew to interview."

"How much do I owe you?"

"Let's wait until we hire the pilots. I'll send you a bill then."

We shook hands, and I headed back to the little cottage in the wild woods and dinner with Rose.

Chapter Three

I drove straight to Rose's house, bypassing the cottage, a choice I would later regret. December darkness fell like a curtain, without a warning--light, then black. The smell of frying chicken permeated the kitchen, and I knew that somewhere in or on that stove, a pot of turnip greens with a piece of ham hoc simmered away. Rose was stirring a batter for a pan of cornbread. I think the woman could live off of peas, turnips, and cornbread. Always had a hankering for them, myself. I was, however, the only boy ever raised on a dairy farm that detested buttermilk, still cannot drink it today.

My big cat, B.W., a name he ignored more often than not, jumped upon the table and looked at me with an expression that seemed to say, "Where have you been for the last three days?"

"None of your business."

Rose turned from the stove. "What?"

"B.W. wanted to know where I've been."

She looked at me as if I should be committed to the nearest psychiatric ward. "The letter from Alella is on the table next to the couch. Read it while I finish up with supper and we can discuss the contents while we eat."

Her voice emanated from the neatly printed hand-written letter. A voice deep and resonant, smooth and melodious, as if she were sitting beside me on the couch. I could visualize her shoulder-length ebony hair, large, round, black eyes, unsurpassed and depthless, her olive skin and bare feet. Alella hated to wear any kind of shoes, even in cold weather. Born in Cataluna, Spain, she had come to Ciudad Victoria, Mexico, to live with a rich uncle who tried to turn her into a whore. It's a long story, but we ended up bringing her out of Mexico to the USA and Rose adopted her.

Now twenty-one years old, she attended the University of Madrid, and from her letter, I learned that she had fallen in love with a medical student and wanted to bring him home for the summer. He would have the time off before starting his first year residency program.

"I poured you a glass of buttermilk."

"Why?"

"You need to learn to like it."

"Never."

"I learned to like your cognac crap."

"No you didn't."

"So what do you think?"

"About the buttermilk?"

"No, not the buttermilk. Alella and the boy."

"It sounds to me like she's fallen in love."

"Ha! More like she's fallen in heat."

"Easy, Rose. Remember her past. It took you two years to bring her out of that horror. I doubt that she's being hormonal. Maybe she's making beautiful music with the young doctor."

"I'll bet it's a lot more than music the two of them are making."

"You have the stubbornness of an incorrigible nonconformist."

"It's more than music they're playing. Didn't you read the letter?"

"Mozart said it's the silence between the notes that makes the music. Creates the rhythm."

She lay her fork beside the plate. "What in the world does that have to do with Alella and that boy being in love?"

"Love isn't an emotion, but a deliberate decision to do what is best for someone."

"What---Leicester, you are insane."

"Maybe, but I'm still not drinking this buttermilk."

She took the buttermilk and sat the glass on the kitchen counter.

I love to play with Rose's mind.

In the living room, over coffee, I told her I thought it a good thing Alella was involved with a serious relationship. It would give her stability and prove that she was once again trusting men. There was a long time when it was doubtful if she would regain her self-respect or trust any human being again. But Rose had succeeded, almost single-handed, in bringing her back from the brink.

. . .

Tired, but in a good mood, I left Rose and drove slowly the few miles back to the cottage. B.W. sat beside me, his eyes staring out at the darkness, looking for a way to escape into the night. Parking beside the cottage, I held the big cat in one arm, fished for the door key, and walked upon the porch. B.W. growled, and I told him to hush. He was not getting down so he could traipse off and chase coyotes.

"Are you Jay Leicester?"

The voice emanated from the south end of the cottage. I have always been a careful man, aware of my surroundings. Tonight, though, something went terribly wrong with the built-in mechanism that had always protected me. Not even the warning from B.W. worked. Fingering the magnum in my coat, I eased the cat down on the porch, turned and faced the figure silhouetted by the dim light of the doorbell.

"I am aware of the Smith and Wesson in your coat pocket, Mr. Leicester. You have nothing to fear from me, sir. I'm with the federal government and wish to speak with you on a matter of national security. Here is my I.D." He carefully and slowly held out a leather case. "If you will turn on the light--"

Opening the door, I flipped on the porch light. B.W., to my surprise, bolted inside. I held onto the magnum and took the I.D. case. It looked official and identified the man as Alec Aardwolf, CIA.

"Why would the CIA want to talk with me? A phone call, a letter, an e-mail, any of these would have done the trick, however, standing on my porch in the dark of night doesn't cut it. And how in God's name do you know about my magnum?"

"We know everything about you, Mr. Leicester. Can we go inside?"

"Sure."

The man was small and dark. He had the look of a rat about him. His beady eyes were set too tightly in his narrow face, his nose twitched upturned and sharp. Atop his wide ears sat a grimy football cap with an Oakland Raiders logo, its brim ragged with use. I detest Al Davis and the Raiders. Aardwolf, if that was his real name, was off on a bad foot.

"Have a seat."

I watched him closely. He seemed one of those small men who find it especially hateful to lose at anything he attempts. Disgust hangs smothering above him, black and indecent and dangerous. Serves him right--rooting for the Raiders.

"This have something to do with the DC-4 sitting on the ramp in Philadelphia?"

"We want you to fly the airplane to a clandestine runway in south Florida. Some work will be performed on the fuselage, cargo will be loaded, and then you will fly to a jungle strip in Venezuela, where the cargo will be off-loaded and new cargo put aboard. You will then return to Florida. After landing you will be driven to Miami, put aboard a private jet and returned to this little cottage in the woods."

"All under the watchful eye of the CIA?"

"Yes."

"What's the cargo?"

"Diamonds going out, classified coming back."

"It must not be drugs or it wouldn't be hush-hush."

He took his cap off, ran a hand over close-cropped gray hair, reset the cap. He seemed to make some kind of decision. "Mr. Leicester, we have a terrorist cell that is attempting to, for the lack of a better word "construct" a nuclear device and detonate it somewhere in the US. We have a deep-cover agent who thinks the diamonds are payment for components whose shipment has been tracked from Iran to Venezuela. One of the components is enriched uranium that we know was sent from Iraq to Iran just before we invaded the country. The WMD (weapons of mass destruction) we could never find. Now, al-Qa'Ida and Osama bin Ladin, having given up on a biological attack, have focused on nuclear."

"Does not make sense to me that someone could build a nuclear bomb and just transport it around the country unnoticed."

"The big bag you carry around with all your flying gear--a small nuclear device could fit inside it."

"What about radiation exposure to me and my crew?"

"There's a risk, but a small one."

"Why me? There have to be hundreds of pilots in the government who can fly an old DC-4. Use the pilot who flew the dope and owns the airplane. He'll do it to get out of jail."

"Had planned to, but he's dead. They got to him in jail. You haven't read a newspaper in the last few days, I gather."

"The dope dealer got to him. Didn't want to risk being ratted out. Too bad."

"Yeah, too bad. You were recommended. An anonymous source who has worked with you before."

"And you are going to protect me and my crew?"

"We always protect our operatives."

"I can name a couple who were outed."

"Wasn't our fault."

"The CIA, whose work force has been slashed by 25%, five directors in seven years, no recruiting of new people, and an intelligence community that has lost billions of dollars in funding. From what I hear, the FBI has more special agents in New York City than the CIA has clandestine officers covering the whole world. You're going to protect me while I'm flying into and out of foreign countries hauling nuclear components."

"You have an invidious character, Mr. Leicester, and you read too much. Our agency is in good shape. We need your help." He fingered the brim of his cap.

"I don't like the Raiders, or the owner."

"What? Oh, the cap. John Madden gave it to me when he won the Superbowl."

"Really. How you know Madden?"

"We were teammates in college."

"What position did you play?"

"Defensive Back. I believe you were a linebacker?"

I wondered that if in every life there came a moment when you realize just how little you have actually escaped from whatever it was you'd fled. "I'll need to hire a copilot."

"Of course. Mr. Opshinsky, I presume?"

The guy was good, I'll give him that. "When do you want to depart?"

"Day after tomorrow. We have a plane on the ground waiting to fly your copilot to Philadelphia. Call me by noon tomorrow with your decision and after you talk with Mr. Opshinsky." He handed me a card with only a telephone number and walked out the door. I never learned how he'd arrived, or why a man nearing seventy years of age was working as an operative for the CIA.

. . .

Still in Key West since hurricane Katrina, Hebrone Opshinsky would be at one of two places on the island, the boat yard, where he was rebuilding his beloved Wheeler sportfisherman or Captain Tony's bar. Noting the time, I tried the bar.

"Get Opshinsky to the phone, and do not hang up on me. Tell him it's Leicester."

"Ah, Leicester. Well bugger off, Leicester." The line went dead.

The bartender knew Hebrone, without a doubt, for he was one of those men who attract attention by making an effort to attract none. People had a sense of his presence before seeing him. Without fail, every time I've called Captain Tony's for him, the bartenders have ignored me and hung up. Anonymity seemed a courtesy on the island.

Five minutes later the phone rang. "The wolf welcomes you."

"If you look around there should be one or two people watching your movements. Could be female."

"Yeah, for two days, now. Amateurs. Figured they'd make contact sooner or later."

"They're CIA, waiting to fly you here."

"What if I don't want to go?"

"Then they would walk away."

"What's the deal?"

"DC-4 to South America, back to Florida, then we are flown back to normal lives."

"Is it dangerous?"

"It is, and I need you on this one."

"Count me in." He hung up.

That was Hebrone Opshinsky, one of the most deadly men on earth. Trained by our government, and then deserted by our government. A man I called a friend. A man who saved my life on more than one occasion, and someone I would not hesitate to die for. Strangely, I knew little of his life before Vietnam, where he was an assassin. A member of the pajama gang, he wore no uniforms, carried no I.D., and his existence was denied by the government. He was always laconic and silent about the landscape of his past before the war. The only thing he ever said about his childhood was that he hailed from a family so poor that his father slopped the children at a hog trough. I almost believed him. He was not one of those men who went to war and never came back. It took awhile, but he made it--all the way back.

A year or so after I met Hebrone, I taught him to fly, and he went on, with the help of the GI Bill, to attain his Airline Transport rating. He spent several years working for freight hauler's gaining vast experience in many types of aircraft while flying mostly at night and in all kinds of weather. He is now one of the finest airmen I know. I would fly with him anywhere in any airplane, under any conditions.

I lay in bed, trying not to think about flying an aged ex-airliner to South America, and the cargo we'd be hauling, or the people involved. Instead, I thought about living in the country, this rural part of the state. What I liked most was that nobody in this area cared if you came or went. Mostly they were coming or going themselves. Having spent a lot of time in urban areas, I found the anonymity of the country blissful. The freedom of conversation with an affable farmer, a man who was only talking to you to kill a little time. Someone who wanted nothing and offered nothing in return. You would probably not see each other for months, if ever. The exquisite silence of the country at night. To hear your voice echo across the hollows or to catch sight of the distant moonlit woods. This was what I loved about this area.

Sleep came easy and welcome.

Chapter Four

An apricot dawn spread through the eastern sky heralding a glorious winter day and illuminating the trees in front of the cottage a rust color. Alec Aardwolf phoned early, informing me Hebrone would be arriving at the Philadelphia airport at noon. We would plan on a dawn departure tomorrow in the DC-4 for the isolated landing strip in Florida. Aardwolf would ride along with us.

Rose made me promise to bring Hebrone for dinner. The two had become friends over the last few years. I was glad, for I loved them both. Hebrone had been with me when we brought Alella from Mexico.

It is a half-hour drive from my cottage to the Philadelphia Airport. During the trip, I thought about al-Qa'Ida cells in this country. After the attack on nine-eleven, our government implemented surveillance programs to root out these people, by monitoring the local and overseas phone traffic and the money trails. Immediately critics started bitching about the abuse of our rights as Americans. I guess they would prefer the terrorist blow up another city rather than provide us with the speed and agility we needed to protect this country. Terrorism in itself is the stuff of everyday nightmares, but now the specter of a nuclear-capable terrorist group operating within our shores is cause for everyone to have sleepless nights.

Standing in the waiting room of the Fixed Base Operation at the Philadelphia airport, I spotted the speck in the sky to the south that would be Hebrone's plane. The Westwind jet landed, taxied to the ramp, and shut down the engines. At the controls was my old friend. How he managed to do that aboard a government aircraft would be interesting to hear, though for some reason I wasn't surprised.

Hebrone deplaned and walked straight to the DC-4. A deputy sheriff, guarding the aircraft, confronted him. A few heated words were exchanged. Then Aardwolf appeared and the tension relaxed. Hebrone continued to walk around and examine the aged airliner the way a grandmother would a child. Satisfied, he looked toward the FBO, and headed this way.

"Hello, Jay."

"I see you are still courting danger. I believe that deputy would have shot you."

"He was merely doing his job."

"You met Aardwolf."

"Is he our point man?"

"Yes, I'll fill you in on the way."

"I'm sure you will."

"Rose is expecting us for dinner."

"It will be a pleasure to see her. Is Alella at home?"

"She's still in Madrid. Has a new boyfriend."

"That's good."

"Rose is having trouble with it."

Aardwolf walked up. "See you in the morning."

We drove toward the cottage.

Hebrone stared out the windshield of the truck. We passed a herd of black cattle grazing in a field that was green with grass, even in December. "I haven't seen a cow since I was here two years ago."

I made no comment.

"Smash is upset you didn't invite him along on this adventure."

"Had no need for his services."

"CIA--?"

"It's Rose's fault."

He turned, shot me a skewed grin. "I can believe that."

"The DC-4 almost landed on her head. She called me, thinking it may have crashed. Turned out it was delivering five tons of cannabis. Some other early rising citizen saw the plane and called the sheriff. The pilot and I flew it off the dirt road to Philadelphia, after he'd tried to entice the sheriff to let the two of them do it."

Hebrone laughed. "Smart lawman. If he hadn't called you, he'd be in Mexico by now, or dead. None of this explains the CIA?"

Come to think of it, I didn't know how they'd become involved with the DC-4, either. It was a question we'd pose to Aardwolf. "Whoever owned the confiscated dope whacked the pilot in jail. The old agent appeared out of the night on my porch at the cottage with this proposal."

"Which is?"

"You and I will fly the DC-4 to a strip somewhere in south Florida where extensive work will be done on it. I assume sound and video recorders installed, along with any other 007-type gadgets. We then depart with a cache of diamonds bound for a secret landing strip somewhere in Venezuela where the stones will be swapped for components used to "construct" a small nuclear device supposedly which will be used to blow up some high profile US target. We return the goods to Florida and we are done. The "Company" will arrange for our transportation home."

Hebrone stared straight ahead out the front window of the truck. "This is why I exist. Thanks for the invite. Would not want to miss this."

"You're welcome."

We stopped by the cottage, unloaded Hebrone's ditty bag. He rekindled his friendship with B.W., a wary one at best because the cat smelled Savage, a full-bloodied wolf Hebrone raised from a pup. We spent the rest of the afternoon reviewing the flight manual for the DC-4. It had been years since either of us had spent much time in the cockpit of one. We wanted to be sure, needed to be sure, that we were familiar with all the systems and emergency procedures. If something were to go wrong there would not be time to read the book.

Rose phoned and said dinner would be served promptly at six. If we were late, she'd cut us out of her will. I promised we'd be on time.

As we left the cottage, clouds bricked overhead and were brindled pink, then crimson and violet. The wind blew and leaves sailed like scattering birds and the air carried the tang of decaying foliage, cattle, and chimney smoke.

Rose met us at the door, gave Hebrone a hug that was sincere, and maybe even tender. "It's so good to see you. Have you been taking care of yourself?"

"You look good, Rose, even prettier than before."

Hebrone, when he was around her, had the qualities of a little boy, which made you want to love him. His eyes were close-set and unwavering, his head broad browed and perfectly centered over square shoulders. He exuded a magnetic amiability that made most people want to please him. This was the same man who, in the Vietnam War, tied enemy NVA combatants belly to back in a row to test bullet penetration of various weapons. The most powerful weapon would kill ten. I imagined the horror felt by the last man in the row. "I wish I hadn't done that now," he told me. "They did worse to our people, though."

All cats are gray in the dark, I thought.

"Since Hebrone is here for dinner, I assume you're grilling ribeyes. I brought a couple of bottles of wine." Both were 1982 Chateau Villemaurine from the Saint-Emilion region of France. Not great wines, but decent and from a good year. I had bought a case years ago for four dollars a bottle.

At table, Rose asked me, "Is your steak rare enough?"

"I've seen cows worse off than this get well."

"I'll put it back on the fire."

"I'm kidding. It's perfect. I've never eaten anything you've ever cooked that wasn't delicious."

"So tell me about this adventure you two are taking off on."

I've never lied to Rose, but somehow telling her we would be hauling highly radio-active components to be made into a nuclear bomb did not seem wise. Hebrone looked hard at me wondering what I would say.

"We are going to deliver that big old airplane that almost landed on your head to Florida."

"I thought the sheriff confiscated the thing. Why is it going to Florida?"

"The government has a use for it. They paid the county a fair price."

"This have anything to do with that pilot getting killed in the Neshoba jail?"

"Not that I know of."

I saw a sudden, nearly volcanic agitation in her eyes. The candle light on the table flickered and Rose and the room seemed to be in motion.

"You do not have a gift for evasion or misdirection or lying. The two of you are going to do something dangerous."

Hebrone sat back in his chair, swirled the wine in his glass, and seemed immersed in what he saw.

"There are some things you just don't need to know, Rose. This will be a government run operation and all precautions are being taken. The risk to Hebrone and me will be related only to flying that aged aircraft."

I saw her face was grave and strangely probing, eyes that held you dangling, as from a noose. "I'll have to bury you both if things go wrong, and you don't want to tell me the circumstances. You want me to hear it from some government weenie?" Her eyes flared visibly with quick and oddly violent flames that were deep and scary.

"Tell her, Jay."

Putting both elbows on the table, clasping my hands together, I looked her straight in the eyes, and said, "The CIA wants us to deliver a cache of diamonds to Venezuela as payment for parts to build a nuclear bomb which we will return to Florida. The government will arrest the bad guys and prevent a national disaster."

She seemed subdued and oddly weakened, like someone at the end of a long journey. "Terrorist--oh, my God. The men I saw coming from your cottage while you were in Jackson--?"

"CIA."

"In the course of human events, I wish we'd never had love. Then we would not feel the death of others."

"Our only involvement is to fly the plane. We'll be fine."

Rose got up from the table, went to the door leading into the kitchen, stopped, and turned around. "You both have to promise me you will be careful. I don't know what I'd do--?"

"Why, Rose, I do believe you care."

"Piss off, Leicester." She hurried through the door.

Hebrone laughed. We moved into the living room for coffee. Here, the conversation was less serious. We talked about Alella and her upcoming arrival home with the new boyfriend. Soon it was time to go and we left Rose with tears in her eyes, something I'd seldom seen except when it involved injury to one of her animals. I did not know it then, but it would seem like a lifetime before I saw Rose English again.

It was almost nine o'clock when we drove up to the cottage. As we exited the truck, Hebrone said, "Wait, Jay. We got company."

"How--"

Alec Aardwolf.

"You are going to get shot sneaking around my cottage. Why are you here?"

"We have a problem you can help us with."

"That would be?"

"Can we go inside?"

"Sure."

"We do not need the information on the DC-4 to get out to the national media. The publisher of the *Neshoba Democrat* has been handled. It is known that you are friends with the man who owns the *Union Appeal*."

"You are afraid that the wire services will pick up the drug running story and might expose the DC-4 and jeopardize the Venezuela thing."

"Exactly. There are many eyes watching. There was a reporter from the *Union Appeal* who took photos and interviewed a lot of people at the airport."

"Jack Tannehill is a friend of mine. But you do not order him to do anything. He is his own man. I know him to be fair, but he needs to know the truth."

"Can he be trusted?"

"Beyond a shadow of a doubt."

"Then call him, now."

Jack answered his phone on the first ring. I told him everything. He did not hesitate. The story was front page for the current edition due out tomorrow. He would kill it, but for a week only. He made me promise to give an in-depth interview on the terrorist-nuclear threat after the CIA was finished with the operation. Quid pro quo. I promised.

Alec Aardwolf look relieved when told Jack Tannehill would corporate.

"How did the CIA get involved with this marijuana deal?" Hebrone asked the little man, who at the moment looked his age.

"It's complicated. This Florida terrorist cell is using many means to raise the money necessary to carry out various attacks. Amos Dudley was one of our agents."

My mouth dropped open. "Then why didn't he just tell the sheriff? He'd still be alive."

Aardwolf bowed his head. "I wish he had. He didn't want to blow his cover. It took him years to gain their trust."

Hebrone sat up in his chair. "So you don't know why he was killed?"

"No. It could have been because of getting caught and losing the drugs, or--"

"Or they found out he was a government agent."

"Yes."

"My, God," I said. "Our job just got a lot more dangerous."

"I would not blame you two if you wanted to back out now."

I looked at Hebrone. He had that deadly grin on his face that told me all I needed to know.

"We'll see you at daylight, Aardwolf."

Chapter Five

Sleep was fitful. Too many thoughts running through my mind. Pilots needed to be hired and trained for the Advertising Agency in Jackson, a DC-4 had to be flown to Florida, then to South America, radioactive materials dealt with, radical Islamic terrorist and al-Qa'ida operatives, the CIA. At least B.W., the cat, was safe with Rose. I could hear Hebrone snoring in the other room. The man could sleep through a firefight--come to think of it, I think he told me he had.

Turning over, I saw that the bedside clock glowed three a.m. The alarm was set for three-thirty. I got up, plugged in the coffeepot, and took a hot shower. When I dressed and got back to the kitchen, Hebrone was scrambling eggs and frying country-cured ham. He slid me a plate across the table piled high with the steaming food.

"Thanks," I said, pouring coffee.

"Remember this, Leicester, when you eat a breakfast of eggs and ham, the chicken was dedicated, but the pig was committed."

It took me a minute to figure this one out, but then it hit me as funny, and I laughed out loud. Looking at Hebrone, I saw that he wasn't smiling.

"We need to be alert. We do not want to be the pig."

Point taken.

Checking the weather, we found it to be clear all the way to south Florida. At least we had that in our favor. It was still dark when we left the cottage. The stars were out, and there was enough light that we could make out the steep banks through which the road ran and at the top canted pines leaned out like indecisive suicides silhouetted against a fading moon. During the drive to the airport, we decided that I would act as Captain during our flights in the DC-4, not because I was the better pilot, but I had the most time in type as pilot-in-command. Hebrone would serve as copilot.

Alec Aardwolf was already at the airport when we arrived. He had a ground crew going over the aircraft.

"Good morning, gentlemen. Your plane is full of fuel and oil. My people have conducted a pre-flight and assure me that it is airworthy. An auxiliary power unit is plugged in and we await your order for engine start."

Hebrone looked at him with a diffident expression. "You don't mind if we walk around and look at things, do you? Just so we can be sure the tail is still attached to the airplane."

"I would expect nothing less."

The two men eyeballed each other.

Settling into the cockpit, with Aardwolf buckled into the jump seat between us, we went through the checklist. The engines on a four engine airplane are numbered one through four starting on the left wing. We always start number three first, because it is nearest the batteries and located on the opposite side of the fuselage from the passenger boarding door, followed by numbers four, then one and two. With a power cart attached, it does not matter the sequence, but as with most other systems on airplanes, it is best to do everything the same way all the time.

We taxied out at first light and lined up on the five thousand-foot runway. Aardwolf tapped me on the shoulder, handed me a GPS receiver.

"This is your heading. You are cleared up to eleven thousand feet. There is no need to talk with anyone on the radio."

Hebrone turned and looked at the little man. He seemed impressed. I know I was.

We advanced the throttles and accelerated down the runway. The airplane performed well, and we climbed out into a sky so blue one wanted to swim in it. I gave thumbs up and Hebrone raised the landing gear, retracted the flaps, and adjusted the throttles back to climb power. We were once again airborne and in control of our fate.

We pass through eleven thousand feet and for a moment climb another hundred feet so we can descend back through it. By doing so, the DC-4 can be set flying in a slightly nose-down position. Thus "on the step" we will add ten knots to our airspeed and satisfy our sensual appreciation of flight. To any dedicated pilot a mushing airplane, regardless of its speed, becomes a miserable collection of nuts and bolts flying in loose formation. A good pilot absorbs this unhappiness through the seat of his pants. I have concluded this will only change with "fly-by-wire" aircraft design. By then my time will be done. For now, pilots become morose or irritable unless his plane is "on the step." We will work endlessly to achieve that delicate angle. When the instruments finally admit additional speed, the pilot is doubly content, for he has proof that the instruments are not his absolute master and he is not as yet altogether a mechanical man.

We slide back down to exactly eleven thousand feet. Hebrone eases the propellers and engines into cruising power, slowly and gently. If you had been a passenger in the back of the plane you would not have noticed any change. Now, he moves the mixture controls into cruising position, one at a time. We are on the step and I am well pleased with the cramped little world over which I am to preside for the next five hours. I bend forward and set the autopilot in operation.

Now I have time to look at the landscape below us. A pilot, because of what he knows about the planet's architecture and weather will see more than most people might. He can see all of the geological features that others might miss: channels, alluvial fans, glaciers, crater lakes, forest devastation, and human expansion. He can watch clouds of every shape and combination. He can see how clouds over cold water look different from those over warm water. He can see first-hand that storms do spin in different directions. He can delight in lightning flashes, bands of dark clouds illuminated by fingers of spark, reaching out to each other across miles. He can see brown rivers spilling into blue ocean. He can watch long, solitary waves rise up in the middle of a calm sea, giant walls of water that build up until they break over themselves, having come and gone, wondrous, and having been invisible to everybody but him. He can watch light scattering and corona haloes. He can see how farmland absorbs the sun's rays. At night, he can see stars, suddenly seeming close enough to touch. In the evening hours, he can watch dusk's waves wash over the earth. In daylight the cities look like gray, indistinct smudges, similar to the fingerprints on the windscreen in front of him.

I remember when I saw my first airplane. I trembled at the invisible order behind that chaotic reality. Airplanes, water, and God became intermingled in me in a complexity of feelings, a moral unity, the trace of which has never vanished. The first time I flew solo, alone and unaccompanied, I discovered the alchemy that turns fact into fiction, poverty into plenty, history into art. Bread was flesh, and wine was blood. I had found my true vocation.

I look over at Hebrone. His eyes are attentive to the reading of the gauges on the instrument panel. He often gazes out into space as we fly. Today he has a look that is not exactly sad, yet it is the look of someone who is comprehending sadness. I want to ask him his thoughts, but decide against it.

Our heading is southeast. We will pass over Meridian and east of Mobile, across Panama City, out over the Gulf of Mexico, finally across Tampa and on to a secret landing strip somewhere in the swampland of south Florida. Mobile Bay was prominent in the morning sun and I remembered Watkins and Lippincott crashing into the water just north of Fort Morgan enroute from Ponce, Puerto Rico, with a cargo of Don "Q" Eldorado rum. They were flying an aircraft like this one, a DC-4. The weather was terrible, with embedded thunderstorms and low ceilings. They flew into an unseen tornado from which there was no escape. I thought about the moments before the crash. Had they felt the sting of their own inadequacy, painfully understood the fatal consequences of their own failure to comprehend the horrible danger before it was too late? I looked down at the water of the bay with an unsettling sense of how naked to the elements we remained, how helpless before fate. A similar feeling of inadequacy passed through me as I turned back to the instruments in the cockpit.

Snodgrass and Bamberger were lost under similar circumstances a hundred miles to the south of our position in the gulf. Their plane was never found. Today our fortune is better than theirs.

We entered the Gulf at Apalachicola, and Tampa was already visible on the far horizon. The weather offered a dark sapphire sky dappled with cirrus trails pilots refer to as Mare's tails. Colors were harsh and dry. Far to the south cumulus clouds built in towering battlements, intensely defined yet somehow ghostly, like hallucinations.

It remains a mystery to me, the true order of things. I had yet to learn how the universe works. Some Astronauts become the first men to walk on the moon, and others burn to death on the launch pad, or seventy-three seconds after leaving it or sixteen minutes from returning to it. Airplane pilots, more skilled than Hebrone or me, crash on takeoff, or minutes after leaving the runway or moments before landing.

Aardwolf tapped me on the shoulder. "After Tampa, descend to one thousand feet."

"That's low."

"Yes."

We started a slow letdown, five hundred feet per minute, abeam Fort Myers. Lake Okeechobee appeared off to our left like some giant Inland Sea. Ahead, we could see Everglades Parkway, better known as Alligator Alley, slicing across the land like a surgeon's scalpel.

Aardwolf handed me a slip of paper with a radio frequency written on it. 131.75. "Descending through two thousand feet, key the mike and say, 'Thirty north.'"

We were crossing into the Miccosukee Indian Reservation. At two thousand feet, I keyed the mike and said, "Thirty north." Instantly a voice replied, "Cross mid-field, left downwind, landing south."

Leveling off at one thousand feet, we looked ahead for the strip. Suddenly it was there. A long, shell runway carved out of scrub pine and swamp. Two huge hangars sat midway the strip painted in camouflage to match the surroundings. We did as instructed, crossed over the runway at mid-field, turned north for a left downwind. Hebrone completed the landing checklist and we turned final.

"That runway must be two miles long."

"Full flaps."

As we rolled out, Aardwolf said to taxi to the northern most hangar and shut down the engines. A crew would hook a tug to us and tow the airplane inside before we deplaned.

We went through the shutdown checklist and sat listening to the silence, smelling the odors of an old airplane, of hot oil and gasoline, and the sweat and fear of countless crewmembers that sat in the worn seats we now occupied. Ten or twelve men moved around the airplane. A tug was hooked to the nose wheel.

Hebrone looked at me. "Did you know that Ponce De Leon named Florida in 1513 because they discovered it in the time of the Easter Flowery Festival--Pascua Florida: Flowery Easter? Not discovered--as rumored--on Easter Sunday, nor was the coast flowery. They landed somewhere--north or south--of Cape Canaveral."

Before I could make some snide remark about the discovery of Florida, the tug jerked the DC-4 so violently in motion, that we were concerned about the safety of the nose strut. As soon as the tail cleared the hangar, the doors slammed shut.

"We can get out now."

Hebrone and I followed Aardwolf back to the double cargo doors where a metal stand had been rolled into position for us to climb down. Already mechanics were working on the engines and fuselage. Cowlings were being removed, inspection plates were opened. Whatever was being done to this old bird, it was extensive.

Aardwolf pointed to an exit door at the rear of the hangar. "You will be here for two days. We will take you to a nearby motel where you will be secure."

"Two days?"

"Maybe longer, depending on how the work goes and the arrangement for shipments arriving in Venezuela. It's complicated. I will go into greater detail at the motel."

Hebrone looked at me. "Maybe I should stay here and watch what they are doing to the airplane?"

"That will not be possible," Aardwolf said.

"I didn't ask you, old man." Hebrone was angry.

"Why would it matter if he stayed and watched, especially to what they are doing to our engines and control surfaces. He's an aircraft mechanic and inspector. We need to be sure all the electronics being installed will not interfere with our radios and navigation equipment."

"I can assure you both, these men are the most expert in their field. All will be well."

"Fine," Hebrone said. "As long as your ass will be aboard."

"No, I will not accompany you to South America. We have an agent better suited to deal with the people there."

It was a tense moment.

Hebrone glared at me. "You okay with this?"

"When in Rome---"

He shrugged his shoulders and we headed for the exit door and the motel.

Motel was a misnomer for the place Aardwolf took us. It was a new structure, built like a two-story motel, but there were no signs indicating it was open to the public. It seemed a place designed to house people like Hebrone and me. We were assigned adjoining rooms. There was a separate building that served as a reception office and small restaurant. We seemed to be the only occupants. Aardwolf told us that as soon as we were settled to come to the restaurant and we would talk.

Hebrone knocked on the door between our rooms. "There are no phones, Jay. These rooms are probably wired for sound and video. I don't like this."

"Neither do I. Let's go see what the man has to say."

Aardwolf was seated at a table with a man who could have passed as a twin brother to Tariq Aziz, Saddam Hussein's Deputy Prime Minister. The man we saw "ad nauseam" on t.v. before and after the first Gulf War. He appeared the same age, with silver gray hair, mustache, and round, dark-rimmed glasses. Neatly dressed in a white suit and blue tie, he seemed out of place in this south Florida swamp.

"Gentlemen, Mr. Muhib Bahri. He will be flying with you to Venezuela and handling all transactions. He will fill you in on the details. I will excuse myself. Have a good trip. I'll see you when you return."

"I have some business calls to make, Aardwolf. There are no phones in the room."

"I'm afraid that will have to wait, Mr. Leicester. I'm sure you understand, the delicacy--"

Hebrone looked at me and smiled. "When in Rome--"

I did not find it funny.

Muhib Bahri spoke perfect English with no accent. He turned out to be a very pleasant companion. A man not shaken by circumstances.

"Mr. Opshinsky, I have read your dossier. You are a very brave man and have served your country well. It is a pleasure to work with you."

Hebrone nodded, but made no comment.

"Mr. Leicester, excellence in aviation. It will be an honor to fly with you."

"This cargo we'll be bringing back, how much danger will we be exposed to?"

"Not much, as long as everything stays encased in its containers. There is no danger of detonation, if that's your worry. Many steps must be completed before a fissionable event would occur. The main danger to us would be from radiation if something happens."

"Fill us in on the destination."

"As far as anyone is concerned," Bahri said, rubbing a well-manicured finger along his mustache. "We are delivering a cargo of food stuff to the earthquake ravaged area around the Cordillera Merida Mountains. Our destination is Valera, a hundred and thirty miles southeast of Maracaibo."

"Jesus Christ," Hebrone muttered. "That's over a thousand miles."

"Thirteen hundred, to be exact."

"It will be over seven hours flying time, if we go direct."

"What about over-flight permits for Cuba?" I asked.

"All arranged."

"Will fuel be available at Valera?"

"Everything will be taken care of, gentlemen. We will unload, refuel, have our cargo stowed aboard and depart as soon as possible."

Hebrone scratched his chin. "It's going to be a long day."

"How are you going to get your diamonds through customs?"

"Mr. Leicester, do not be naïve, and do not fret about things that do not concern you."

Muhib Bahri said this in such a pleasant manner and with such a convivial smile that I was not offended.

"So what do we do all day tomorrow?" Hebrone asked.

"I would suggest you get some rest. We will have dinner, here, tomorrow night. Your plane should be ready and we can put the finishing touches on our departure. In the meantime, gentlemen, I have things to do. It was pleasant meeting you both."

Hebrone and I went back to our phoneless rooms in the middle of the south Florida swamp. We were up to our asses in alligators and the CIA.

Chapter Six

Hebrone was waiting in the small restaurant reading the Miami Herald when I arrived for breakfast. There were two other people sitting together in a corner. One was an old man who looked as if memories were his only future. His skin was brown and wrinkled and I thought he could be Cuban. I paid special attention to his eyes. They were absorbed, empty, and fixed on some indeterminate spot, contemplating something I couldn't see but could intuit. Eyes that looked without seeing, familiar in a man about to enter combat. Hebrone Opshinsky eyes. He sipped on a cup of coffee and seemed not to notice the woman who sat with him. She was young and ethereally beautiful despite the horizontal scar that marred her forehead. Her lips were cracked and dry as if from illness or extensive exposure to the sun. She too was of Spanish descent with an unflinching and hopeless resignation. She looked at me and smiled or maybe it was her lips that smiled, while her eyes, fixed on me, remained uninvolved. There seemed a geometry of chaos in her serene face. I wondered what use the CIA had for these two opposite types.

Hebrone, without saying good-morning, slid a section of the paper across to me. The headline read: *Heiress to Brach's Candy fortune feared missing north of Puerto Rico. Contact lost with yacht during violent winter storm. Emergency beacon signal received by Coast Guard in vicinity of missing craft. Search launched.*

"Yeah, so?"

"Smash was supposed to deliver that boat to St. Thomas. I've got to make a phone call."

"Let's go to the front desk."

Hebrone slammed a fist on the counter. "You got a phone back there?"

The startled clerk, a small man about thirty, said that there was one, but guests were not allowed calls.

"You get someone in authority here, now, or this is not going to be the best day you've ever had."

Muhib Bahri and Alec Aardwolf came out from a back office. I explained the problem. Aardwolf handed Hebrone a cell phone.

"One call, Mr. Opshinsky. It is being monitored."

Hebrone dialed a number from memory. "Skinner, did Smash leave with that candy woman?" There was a short, one-minute reply. "Thanks, Skinner. I'll be in touch." He closed the phone, handed it back to Aardwolf, and looked at me. "Smash was aboard."

There was nothing I could say.

We went back to the restaurant. Bahri joined us, uninvited. Aardwolf disappeared.

"I'm sorry about your friend. We will update you with the latest news. I promise."

"Thanks," I said.

"Here is the cargo manifest for our departure tomorrow. There will be thirteen thousand pounds of food, sixteen thousand pounds of fuel, and three passengers, including myself."

Hebrone wrote some figures on a napkin. "That will put us at gross weight for takeoff. Seventy-three thousand pounds."

"How much reserve fuel?"

"If nothing goes wrong--hour and a half."

"Good enough."

"I would like to land at Valera precisely at three p.m."

Hebrone looked at me, then Bahri. "Precisely at three p.m., you say. Then we need to take off at precisely eight a.m."

Bahri did not appreciate the humor.

"Gentlemen. A car will be waiting to take you to the airport. Get some rest, you will need it."

After he left, the two people in the corner got up and walked by our table. The woman ran a hand over my shoulder. "I hope your friend on the boat is safe." Then she was gone.

"Smash is probably bobbing around in a life raft singing salty songs to the candy lady. Try not to worry. There's nothing we can do."

"Yeah--nothing we can do."

. . .

At six o'clock there was a knock on my door. Muhib Bahri stood there impeccably adorned in a tuxedo.

"You didn't have to dress for dinner."

"I am going to have to cancel. Some important business has come up. I must go to Miami. I'm sure you understand."

"What happened? DeBeers decide not to issue you the diamonds?"

Bahri looked around as if someone might be listening to our conversation out in the middle of a south Florida swamp. "It does concern the stones. It is imperative that I go to Miami tonight."

"If you are unsuccessful, the trip will be canceled?"

"No, we will depart at the planned time. Goodnight, Mr. Leicester."

"Who are our passengers?"

"None of your concern. Two people who need to get to Venezuela."

"We're smuggling diamonds and people out of the country and bringing nuclear bombs back. You CIA operatives are something else."

"Goodnight, Mr. Leicester."

. . .

Hebrone and I left for the airport at six-thirty a.m. We wanted time to go over the DC-4, see what had been altered. We also needed to check the fuel load and cargo.

Everything appeared in order. After a half-hour of searching, Hebrone came to me. "I can not find a thing. If cameras are aboard, they are so tiny as to be virtually undetected."

"That's what they strive for."

Muhib Bahri arrived. He was not wearing the tux. The DC-4 was still housed in the hangar and Hebrone and I were standing at the nose. "Everything is arranged, gentlemen. We are ready to depart. I'm afraid there is no word on your friend, Andrew Bullard. The Coast Guard informed us they found debris, but no survivors. I am sorry."

"Thanks for checking."

"We can move the aircraft out now. Come, I want to show you something."

In a room off to the side of the hangar was what appeared to be a command headquarters. Consoles and monitors manned by men and women covered every square inch of space.

"This is what we did to the airplane." He pointed to a bank of screens. A 360-degree view around the DC-4 was depicted. Ground crew could be observed opening the hangar doors, a tug being attached to the nose gear strut. "This is all digitally downloaded via satellite in real time. Outside and inside the airplane is fully covered. With the stakes as high as they are, we cannot afford to miss anything."

Even Hebrone was impressed. I sure was, without a doubt.

Someone handed me a weather report for the route and destination, and a flight plan with the necessary overflight permits and radio frequencies. I handed the folder to Hebrone. We boarded the airplane and settled into the cockpit. Six airline type seats had been installed just behind the flightdeck. Our two passengers had not arrived.

Hebrone and I went through the prestart checklist. I turned to tell Bahri we were ready for engine start and saw that our passengers were seated. It was the old man and woman from the restaurant. Bahri nodded.

All four engines started without difficulty. Hebrone signaled for the powercart to be disconnected, and we taxied out to the end of the runway for a departure to the south. It was a glorious morning with little puff ball cumulus clouds already forming in the Florida heat--even in December. With the exception of one small area of squalls south of Jamaica in the Caribbean, the weather would be benign all the way to Valera with favorable winds.

The take-off was normal until just after the landing gear had been retracted. Suddenly the number four engine quit abruptly. More chagrined than concerned, I immediately began the necessary trim corrections. We passed over the end of the runway in good order at some four hundred feet. The scrub pines of the Florida swamp were below.

The DC-4 flew beautifully on three engines in spite of the full load of fuel and cargo--for some thirty seconds. Then the number three engine lost power, caught again, subsided, and after much nursing ran in a rough fashion with about one third power. Two engines out on the same side is nothing to be trifled with even in a DC-4, but there was still no reason to believe we could not make it back around and land. We had lost altitude, settling to two hundred feet. We gingerly turned downwind and in thirty seconds were alongside the hangars trying everything we knew to keep the two ailing engines on the right wing running. We had lost more altitude and were barely able to hold one hundred and fifty feet without approaching a stall. The old airplane was shaking in vicious spasms.

Suddenly the number two engine failed in exactly the same manner as had the others. It would quit for approximately five seconds, then unexplainably catch again and return to full power for fifteen seconds. The resulting surge of power over-revved the propeller until I was certain it must tear itself from the mount. Now engines two, three, and four all joined in this mad scene of running and quitting, backfiring and howling like an angry den of rattlesnakes. At moments all would quit simultaneously and then separately return to life.

Only the number one engine, far out on the left wing, held absolutely steady at full emergency power. I had not touched its throttle since we first rolled into the take-off. We had lost an additional fifty feet of altitude and I banked as much as I dared, trying to line up with the final approach.

The flight deck was a shambles as wayward engines posed a constantly changing dilemma. Throttles, mixture controls, and propeller controls were all so out of kilter as we sought to coax the last bit of power from each engine, or prevent its over-revving when it decided to run again, that it was impossible to perform our standard emergency procedures with any degree of efficiency. Hebrone and myself were a stiff, erratic ballet of darting hands.

Two minutes after the first engine faltered my left hand and both legs were entirely engaged in trying to satisfy the physical demands of mere flight. The DC-4 weighed over thirty tons and composed a mass that must be kept in motion at an absolute minimum of one hundred and ten miles per hour. If this speed was not maintained, flight would cease and the laws of gravity prevail.

In a DC-4 there are sixteen engine controls. There are also thirty-two switches and knobs by which various other functions of each engine may be controlled.

There are thirty-two instruments to inform on the health or ailments of each engine. In an emergency, all of these must be given instant and correct attention. An inaccurate reading or wrong movement can compound an already serious difficulty.

All instruments except the set concerned with the number one engine were now frantic with pernicious readings. They screamed spite and intermittent betrayal. At moments the plane was shaking so violently that we simply could not absorb their messages quickly enough to relate intelligence with action. Yet my one free hand and those of Hebrone's, moving swiftly in fright, somehow united to pull or push the right lever at the right time and so maintain an average speed that was enough to aim the airplane at the runway.

It was less than a mile to the edge of salvation. We limped, porpoising with each explosive surge of power as the engines revived. When they failed we sank toward the swamp again. At the precise instant that I had lost all hope, a final surge of power occurred. It lasted perhaps ten seconds. Hebrone slammed the gear lever down and the wheels locked as we touched the very edge of the runway. The flaps were still in the process of extending when the nose wheel banged down on the shell strip. I had not touched the throttles to reduce power. We landed with everything we had.

Our total airtime was less than four minutes, something of a record in a four-engined airplane. Relief soon changed to bewilderment. Taxing toward the hangar at normal speed, all four engines ran perfectly.

Stopping in front of the hangar, I stood on the brakes and separately ran each engine up to full take-off power. Number one behaved perfectly, as it had all through our brief misfortune. Our affection and respect for that engine was that reserved for an old lover. The others backfired outrageously and threatened to jump off the wing when full power was applied. The noise was so clamorous that I considered it a rude public display of our difficulties. So we shut down all the engines and waited while the gyros whined down. A group of men had emerged from the hangar and were trotting anxiously toward us.

The first to appear on the flight deck was the lead mechanic who oversaw the modifications on the DC-4. He was stocky, black-haired, and his almost crimson cheeks contrasted so spectacularly with his olive skin that his face seemed more of an oil portrait than real. I felt that I was growing older at a pace that was not to my liking, and my manners were sorely lacking as I asked him if he would please tell me what was wrong with all but one of these engines.

I was surprised when he waved one hand wearily toward two young men who had followed him onto the flight deck. They wore bow ties and white shirts with pockets sprouting pencils and pens clearly marking them as engineers. I had always regarded aeronautical engineers as curiosities, probable geniuses, and therefore special people politely avoided lest their erudition prove my shallowness.

One of the young men said to me, "Captain, we're very sorry about this and frankly cannot understand it."

"Can't understand what?"

"The plugs."

"What plugs?"

"You see, Captain, we have been experimenting with this new type spark plug. They are supposed to withstand powerful microwave bursts and extreme radiation exposure. They proved out perfectly on the test bench so we believed they were ready for a service check. The new plugs are in three of your engines, but there wasn't time to install them in the fourth."

"What a shame!" Hebrone's eyes showed that he shared my dismay.

"Apparently these new type plugs broke down under the heat of full power take-off, which leads us to believe our test bench data must be in error. We'll have to analyze it further."

I wanted to beat their brilliant heads together. The fright and adrenaline racing through my system would have resulted in murder and I knew Hebrone would have to be restrained. So I said, "Gentlemen, we are not qualified, nor have we recently received any pay as test pilots." I suggested they conduct their own test flights in the future and recommended an empty airplane with a minimum of fuel aboard for such projects.

We waited the rest of the morning while the old and reliable type plugs were installed in the engines. Our take-off at noon for Venezuela was so without incident that I found time to brood upon man's technological progress and remember that he often stumbled before gracefulness was attained.

We leveled off at eleven thousand feet and pointed our nose toward Kingston, Jamaica, our next radio fix before aiming for the South American coast. I turn the flying over to Hebrone, sit back in my seat and relax, staring at the waters of both the Gulf of Mexico and the Atlantic Ocean as we headed across the keys toward Cuba.

It has been well documented that timidity untempered by judgment can exact a heavy price in a cockpit. Thank God Hebrone was up to the task today. Our near disaster this morning made me think that eternity is accomplished in split seconds. Having lost many engines, made hundreds of missed approaches, I recognized that the near defeat of today carried annealing and even salutary properties. In these instances the incompetent becomes competent, the fearful courageous, the unlucky lucky. The more one commanded an airplane, the faster it would happen.

Hebrone and I worked well together in the face of sure disaster. During our short time aloft, something miraculous happened. There was no thinking, no emotion, no wonder or dread. Instead, we slipped into a kind of trance, quiet, serene, tuned into only the sound of our breathing, our minds wiped as clean as those last, brave members of a flight crew. The calm is a by-product of our years of training. It also springs from some small remarkable part of us that we were born with. Writers have extolled it in poetry, but there is a lie in the words, because it makes that "something special" sound more exclusive than it is. It's in all of us. Millions of people tap into "it" whenever they are trapped in extraordinary situations, whenever they might have otherwise seemed done for. When the engine on their plane's wing starts belching smoke, or a soldier waiting for combat, suddenly, all that's left is their faith. Their bodies give them no other choice but to believe that everything will work out. They think of everything that brought them to this moment, every step and movement in the history of their lives, and they see reason. They see, looking back at that long, crooked course, an artful conspiracy. Each of them comes to accept that in some profound way, we're all just passengers, and in the end, it's the universe that lives in us, not the other way around.

It is hard to believe that in all the centuries behind us we could, in a few short decades, have learned to fly. It is too heady a thought that from 1903-1969 we went from a flight of 112 feet to the moon. We fly, but we have not conquered the air. Nature presides in all her dignity, permitting us the study and use of such of her forces as we may understand. It is when we become complacent that the harsh hand slaps us on the back of the head and we rub the pain, staring upward, startled by our ignorance.

Flying is my passport to what's real. In the cockpit things cannot be embellished by stupidity, rhetoric, or money.

Hebrone looks across at me and nods as if he understands what I am thinking.

Chapter Seven

As we approached the coast of Cuba, I turned and motioned for Bahri to come forward. He came and sat in the jump seat between Hebrone and me. A fly circled the cockpit and landed on his arm, once again proving Einstein's Special Theory of Relativity, that the basic laws of physics remain constant regardless of their state of motion.

The sun suddenly shined through the cockpit, illuminating Bahri's face, and his pupils looked lighter behind the lenses of his glasses. The trace of a smile evaporated from his lips as if the light had erased it. His eyes revealed their true dominion, giving the impression that the smile had never existed.

"Show us the diamonds."

"You want to see the diamonds?"

"Captain Opshinsky is a true connoisseur of rare and precious gem stones."

Bahri reached into a side pocket and retrieved a black case not as big as a clipboard and an inch thick. He unlocked and opened it. There were no more than two dozen round cut diamonds sitting in their own little individual holes.

"That's it? These are worth enough to purchase nuclear bomb components?"

"Captain Leicester, you obviously do not know the industry."

"I know it generates eleven billion dollars a year and is controlled by DeBeers in London. I also know that these "rare stones" are as plentiful as grains of sand on a beach and that the Oppenheimer family who controls DeBeers are the marketing geniuses that keeps their sale price high. Pretty smart of them, don't you think?"

"Yes, I would think."

"So what's the value of this pile of rocks?"

Bahri looked fondly at the brilliant diamonds. "There are 24 grams of the most perfect, flawless stones in the world. These would sell for one hundred thousand a carat."

"How many carats in a gram?"

"Five."

Doing some quick math, I said, "You're telling me there are twelve million dollars worth of diamonds in that little case?"

"Jay--" Hebrone pointed to the right wing.

A Mig 29 fighter jet was positioned a hundred feet off the wingtip. Hebrone pointed out my side of the window. Another Mig 29 was alongside. The pilot was frantically gesturing.

"I think he wants to talk. What was that radio frequency for the overflight of Cuban airspace?"

Hebrone looked in the folder we had been given. "121.25."

We tuned the radio to the frequency and heard the Mig pilot saying in broken English that we were to follow him and land immediately at the Jose Marti International Airport in Havana or we would be shot down."

Hebrone looked at me and grinned. He keyed the mike. "My name--is Jose Jimenez. I am an ass-tro-not. We are headed for the moon, Senior." He wrapped his tongue around the English language like an enchilada.

The Mig 29 pilot shook his head and pointed down with his thumb. He wanted us to land.

Bahri spoke up. "The delay with the engines must have caused our permit to expire. Tell them we have an overflight permit under ARINC 1009, authority RC-02."

Repeating to the Mig pilot what Bahri said, I watched him apparently consult with someone on the ground. He wagged his wings and banked sharply away, as did his wingman.

"I'm impressed, Bahri. I'm familiar with ARINC (Aeronautical Radio, Incorporated), but what is RC-02?"

Nonchalantly he replied. "The new president of Cuba."

We crossed the Cuban coast midway of the island. I strained to see Havana to the west, but the sun blocked our vision. I was hoping to spot Hemingway's farm, La Finca Vigia, thirteen miles east of Havana near the small village of San Francisco de Paula. Fidel maintained the house as a museum. In fact, it had not been altered since Hemingway left in 1961, except for bringing "Papa's" boat, the Pilar, and installing it on the grounds of the property. Castro had used Hemingway's book *FOR WHOM THE BELL TOLLS*, as a model for his overthrow of Fulgencio Batista's government.

Bahri asked, "What are you looking for?"

"Hemingway's home."

"Hemingway--he wrote books or something."

"Yes, books--or something."

Bahri returned to his seat next to our passengers.

I looked at Hebrone staring out the side window. "You know you could have got us shot down with that "Right Stuff" crap."

He looked at me with one of his enigmatic half-smiles. "Any Cuban fighter pilot flying a Russian-built Mig 29 would have a deep appreciation for our space program. It is rumored that the movie is as popular with foreign airforces as the "Godfather" series is with the Mafia."

I laughed. He was probably right.

"I'm going back and talk with our passengers. Do you think you can keep this airplane straight and level until I return?"

"I can manage, but I don't think she's your type."

"I simply like to know who's aboard."

"Sure."

"Besides, you have no idea what my type is."

"Depends on what "is" is--quotes the ex-president."

Sitting down beside the old man, I watched his eyes veer warily as if he were unable to decide what to do. He merely nodded when I spoke to him, said nothing.

The woman sitting across from us said, "He doesn't speak much English. Have you had any word on your missing friend aboard the boat?" Her ebony hair was parted in the middle and pulled tight so that a perfect line ran from her brow to the back of her head. Her eyes were like black ice. She was smoking a cigarette. She put it out in the built-in ashtray in the armrest of the seat, coughed, then drew in a long breath and exhaled. Even above the drum of the engines, I hear her mortality in the wheeze at the end. Another lung cancer death approaching. Far off still, perhaps, but coming nonetheless.

"We have heard nothing more, thanks for asking. You are returning to Venezuela?"

"My father and I are part of the deal. Did you not know?" Her eyes dulled inexplicably into a kind of sullen pewter, the puffy half-moon beneath them offsetting the flatness. I have seen such eyes sunken within the skulls of crack-whores roaming the filthy streets of big cities, in the oft-raped, and in soldiers who have killed more men than they have lived in years.

Looking at Bahri, I saw that his expression was noncommittal. "No, I am unaware of your circumstance. The other pilot and I are merely hired to fly the airplane. That is our only involvement."

"Then you are lucky, Captain, for the only feeling more powerful than hope is lost hope."

"I can assure you, Miss--?"

"My name is Marina Cicogna Pineiro."

"Miss Pineiro, you don't have to stay in Venezuela if you don't wish to. We'll see that you and your father are safe."

She smiled. "It is not that simple, Captain. There are things of which you do not understand, things that are beyond your control. Do not worry yourself."

I realized the inescapable fact of how thin it is, the line between clarity and confusion, correctness and error, and that it is this cloudy, insubstantial thread that alone supports the weighty illusion of control. It is a perilous illiteracy, the failure to read the motives of men.

Getting up and starting back to the cockpit, I said to Bahri, "We need to talk."

"Let it alone, Mr. Leicester. It does not concern you."

Buckling my seatbelt, I said to Hebrone, "I think the woman and her father are being forced to return to Venezuela as part of the deal."

"So?"

"She seems resigned, but not a willing participant. We can't allow this."

"Jay, we do not know the players. Iraq, Iran, Columbia, Venezuela, Israel or, for that matter, any of the mid-east countries. Maybe we should stay out of what the CIA has working and just fly the airplane."

"I'm not in the slave trade."

"I understand, but we're talking nuclear--"

"Take a break, Hebrone. I'll keep us on course for Kingston."

Listening to the steady drone of the engines, I could hear nothing out of order. The gauges on the instrument panel confirmed the health of Pratt & Whitney's four 1,450 hp, 14 cylinder twin row radial piston engines driving three blade constant speed propellers. This was comforting, for when we left Jamaica behind there would be nothing ahead of us but six hundred miles of Caribbean Sea.

Thinking of Marina Cicogna Pineiro and her father, I wondered what would cause them to return to a situation from which they had fled. Having flown enough CIA personnel, I knew they believed they could break anyone, turn anyone, if you knew their weakness. It was usually sex, always number one, then money or power. Now and then pride and vanity. But this old man and his daughter--? Hebrone was right, we knew little of the operation other than some radical Islamic group wanted to acquire, build, and set off a small nuclear device in the US and kill Americans. Still--

As we approached the island of Jamaica, I could see Montego Bay, on the north shore. Soon Kingston came into view and to the west, Spanish Town, where a close friend was killed foolishly taking off in an overloaded Beach 18 filled with bales of marijuana. He was a good family man who was trying to fix some severe financial problems in the wrong manner. How long, I wondered, had he been dead inside before he finally flew that aircraft into the side of that hill?

The ADF (automatic direction finding) needle swung around to the 180-degree position, indicating passage of the Kingston beacon. Our next radio fix would be Maraciabo, Venezuela. Up ahead, I could see the area of thunderstorms that were forecast on the weather report we were given on departure from Florida. There were some high clouds and as the sun started to set, the world turned a rust color, and twilight's lengthening shadows ran like black paint across the cockpit.

Smash flashed into my mind, but I did not want to think about him, would not think about his fate until there was conformation. Instead, I looked over the approach plate for the Valera airport. Its 6,800-foot runway was plenty long for the DC-4, and we should be well below maximum takeoff weight on departure. Yet, it would be a night approach into an unfamiliar area with high terrain all around. I thought of landing at familiar airports. How intense the pleasure of the familiar can be, how welcome and reassuring the old, safe, comforting places of the world and self.

Hebrone returned, settled into the seat and buckled up. "I see some bumpers ahead. Too bad we don't have a weather radar aboard."

"Drug runners would never spend money on such luxuries. They are going to fly in a straight line from point A to point B, anyway. Let the fates do what they will."

Up ahead we could see white-heaped Caribbean clouds, colored by afterglow's of the sun, standing like Alps of pure rose and violet and ice gray against the darkening blue, and harried by the upper winds. White streamers blew from their tops, veils from their sides, and they themselves are pushed and scuffled and beaten down into long moving snowy sheets or rolls of gray, yellowish gray, lavender-gray, greenish-gray--until they smash down in long marching, continuous reverberating downfalls.

We had learned that these storms are rather benign this time of year, and do not pack the punch of summer storms or squall lines that occur across the US. Still, we must pay attention for there is always that potential. Complacency has no place in a cockpit.

Except for some heavy rain and light turbulence, we flew through the area of weather without consequence. An hour from the South American coast, we contacted Maricabo Approach Control on the radio frequency we had been given and were instructed to descend and maintain six thousand feet. We would be radar vectored to Valera. Simple enough. The weather was clear, we were fat with fuel, and the airplane was behaving nicely.

In the darkness we could see the outline of lights as they surrounded the shore of the Gulfo de Venezuela as it narrowed into a neck that opened into the Lago de Maraciabo. On the other side of this body of water was our destination, Valera, which was surrounded by thirteen thousand-foot high mountains.

Hebrone ran the checklist, and soon we were on final approach. The landing, while not my best, was acceptable, and we were instructed to taxi to an area designated as the freight ramp. An ancient jeep, belching smoke, met us with a sign mounted on the rear that read, "Follow me." Other aircraft were parked on the ramp unloading cargo for the victims of the terrible earthquake that had struck this region a few weeks ago. There were DC-3s, a C-46, and several older jets, a Boeing 737, two DC-8s, and a 707. We were the only DC-4.

We followed the jeep to a parking area and shut down the engines. I was suddenly tired, and we still had the return trip before us.

An unloading crew opened the cargo door and two men climbed aboard from the ramp. They came forward and were met by Bahri. There was a short conversation, and one of the men walked to where Marina and her father were sitting. The expression on his face in the dim light of the cabin made me focus on him. He was a big man, about my size, with bushy black hair and a mustache. His forearms were hairy and massive, hands wide with fingers as big as sausages. It was hard to tell his nationality, but I guessed he was of Spanish origin. He stood in front of Marina. Snarling, he yanked her up by her hair, then twisted his fist in it and pulled her head back. He put his face close to hers. He was detached, his eyes empty looking. They might have been shards of glass on a sand beach. He slapped her and she began to cry.

I started forward, but Hebrone bumped me out of the way. It was so fast. He had the man on his knees and subdued within a second. The woman moved away toward me. She wiped the tears with the tail of her blouse, smudging it with eye shadow.

Someone hollered, and the unmistakable sound of an automatic rifle having a round ratcheted into the chamber echoed throughout the hollow fuselage. Two men with AK-47s were aiming at Hebrone's head. Bahri stepped in and the tension eased.

"Let him go, Mr. Opshinsky. If you do not, they will kill you."

Hebrone turned him loose.

Marina Cicogna Pineiro looked up at me. She possessed a special talent that I've seen in only one or two other people, the uncanny ability to look right at you and then, without appearing to shift her gaze, peer at some point over your shoulder. The change was so subtle that the only conclusion you could come to was that she'd never been looking at you in the first place.

"It's okay," she said, head tilted back with dignity. "He is my husband. I will go with him. Come, father."

It is amazing how effortlessly hate slipped into the space reserved for love and vice versa, as if these two things had been made compatible by design. How satisfying a substitute each was for the other. Who cares about a single life beyond the one whose task it is to live it? In the end, what difference does it make?

The men left the cabin with Marina and her father.

Bahri walked up to me. "I have to say, Captain--"

"Have you ever noticed that when people use the expression, "I have to say," what follows usually needn't be said?"

Bahri shrugged, walked away.

The crew finished unloading the food crates within an hour. The DC-4 was fueled and Hebrone had checked the engines. We were ready to depart, but nothing had been loaded aboard. No nuclear bomb parts.

A catering truck rolled up and delivered some welcome hot food and fresh-brewed coffee. Bahri paced the inside of the empty fuselage. I could not imagine what was going through his mind, or the pressure he was under.

Soon, a black limousine pulled alongside the airplane, followed by a pickup truck with a camper shell. No one emerged from the limo, but four men got out of the pickup and began bringing small wooden crates aboard. There were ten of the crates, and from the way the men handled them, I estimated their weight at around a hundred pounds each. Finally, the men unloaded a large crate from the truck. It was heavy, for they struggled mightily getting it up the ramp and secured in the airplane. The men returned to the truck and drove away.

Five men exited the limo and climbed aboard. Bahri greeted each man with a hug and a kiss to each side of the cheek. There was no doubt as to their nationality. They were mid-east, probably al-Qa'ida. These were our "bomb" people. One of them was Maria Cicogna Pineiro's husband. This was going to be a fun flight back to south Florida.

The cargo doors were secured, and Bahri came forward with a flight clearance and load manifest. It showed we were empty, no cargo listed.

"How much does our, umm, cargo weigh?"

"Fifteen hundred pounds."

"Can you keep these "passengers" under control?"

"Yes, if you can contain Mr. Opshinsky."

"Buckle up, Bahri. We have seven hours of flight time ahead of us."

Chapter Eight

"Douglas 98541, fly heading 340, climb and maintain 14 thousand. You are cleared out of our airspace."

"Roger, Douglas 98541, up to 14 thousand, heading 340. Goodnight, Maraciabo." Hebrone took off his headset and hung it on a hook next to his head that served as a latch for the side window. Adjusting the number four propeller, which was surging fifty rpms and thereby causing us great irritation, he looked at me, but said nothing.

"Probably some sludge in the prop governor," I said, hoping this to be the case, for out the windscreen in front of us was blackness, and the now familiar six hundred miles of Caribbean Sea.

"Yeah, sludge."

We leveled at fourteen thousand feet and Hebrone set our engines to cruise power. The number four propeller settled down and the surging ceased. We were on the step, the DC-4 was performing beautifully, and all was well on the flightdeck. Hebrone tuned the ADF radio to Kingston. I turned the cockpit lights as low as possible so our eyes could adjust to the dark.

"The crew oxygen bottle is fully charged. We have about two hours for both of us, plus the small portable bottle is available."

I thought it strange, even though the DC-4 is an unpressurised airplane, for Hebrone to inform me of the supply of oxygen, as we had no reason to expect a climb above breathable air. There was no severe weather along our route, and no restricted airspace. He is not given to foolish observations, so I acknowledge that we have oxygen and search unexplored crevasses in my brain for an explanation. I find none, and we fly on into the night.

A half an hour later, Hebrone peers into the darkness, and without looking at me asks, "You remember back in the seventies a couple of your colleagues at Southern Airways, Billy Bob Haas and Harold Johnson, being hijacked on a flight out of Memphis?"

"Sure. I flew with Haas. Good pilot, smart man. As I remember they were flying a DC-9. Three black guys, ten million in ransom. One of 'em shot Johnson in the arm. Talked about diving the airplane into the Oak Ridge nuclear power plant. Ended up in Cuba after three days of terror. Hell of an odyssey. Heck of a crew. What brought that to mind?"

"Just doing some thinking."

We droned on through the night as if suspended in a black void. Our only indication of movement was the airspeed indicators holding steady at 197 knots. We had heard nothing from our passengers since departure from Valera.

"You want to talk about Smash?" Hebrone turned slightly in his seat.

"No, not until we get back and find out the facts. I will not concede to his demise. Making concessions only puts me into the habit of conceding. Never have I found that to be a good thing."

It was now past ten p.m., and we were both tired. Our day had started early and, to say the least, had been eventful. I glance at the instruments. All was as it should be. Hebrone adjusts the ADF receiver ever so slightly, seeking a signal from Kingston, but we are still too far away. He is a good pilot, this man of few words. His reserve is not cold, but borne of his past. A past that I would not want.

From somewhere I know not, a poem comes to mind:

> *Out of the night that covers me,*
> *Black as the Pit from pole to pole,*
> *I thank whatever gods may be*
> *For my unconquerable soul.*
> *My head is bloody, but unbowed,*
> *Beyond this place of wrath and tears*
> *Looms but the horror of the shade,*
> *And yet the menace of the years*
> *Finds, and shall find, me unafraid.*
> *It matters not how straight the gate,*
> *How charged with punishments the scroll,*
> *I am the master of my fate:*
> *I am the captain of my soul.*

If memory serves me, this was written by William Henley in the 1800s.

Hebrone reaches up and turns the cockpit lighting even lower until we can hardly see any of the instruments. I start to say something for it would be nice to see if we lost a cylinder or the oil temps rose to the redline, but he beat me to it.

"You remember that Hickson/Parker thing in Pascagoula back in the seventies?"

"Hickson/Parker--you mean that UFO abduction incident? Yes, I recall it well. In fact, I was Chief Pilot for Gulf Coast Airlines when that occurred. We were flying from Gulfport to Pascagoula to New Orleans and Baton Rogue using BN-2 and BN-3 Islanders. I had the unique opportunity to have Dr. J. Allen Hynek, representing the Air Force, and a man named Harder from the Aerial Phenomena Research Organization, on board one night. They'd been sent to investigate the incident. Both Hickson, who was 42 years old and Parker who was 19 at the time, passed lie detector tests. Whatever happened to them, both believed it occurred. Hynek and Harder thought the two men were telling the truth. Hynek told me that this was definitely something not terrestrial. What in the world brought that to your mind?"

"Because for the last half hour we have been followed by an object off and slightly behind our right wing. It is definitely not a Mig 29."

"You conclude it is a UFO?"

"It does not have lights. It just glows."

"Could be something on the sea, or a planet. Where's Venus this time of year?"

"Rises in the morning."

Leaning across Hebrone, I peered out his window. There it was, looking like a glowing golf ball the size of a pumpkin with a definite solid metallic surface. Sitting back in my seat, I thought of what the light could be.

Hebrone said, "Well, it's gone."

Leaning forward and looking around, I said, "No it's not. It's sitting close off the left wing."

It sat there for five minutes and then, with incredible speed, the object shot out in front of us at our altitude and sat there matching our speed exactly. It remained there for another five minutes and just as suddenly vanished. It did not speed away, it simply disappeared.

We were baffled.

"You want to report this?"

"To who, and tell them what? That we are smuggling a load of atomic bomb parts along with people we think are radical Islamic terrorist intent on blowing up an American city, and that we are being followed by a UFO?"

Hebrone grinned. "Well, you are the Captain."

"Let's just hope that whatever this thing is, it doesn't come back."

"You've seen UFOs before. Remember the one over Chandeleur Island? The one coming out of Chicago? After the lightning strike on the way to Houston?"

"Yeah, but those were unidentified lights. This thing was different."

"We'll never know."

"Hopefully."

Muhib Bahri came forward. "What was that light following us? Some of the men are getting nervous."

"We don't know what it was, but it's gone now. Tell them it was a military plane curious as to who we are. Tell them all is well."

"When do you think we'll land back in Florida?"

Hebrone looked at me and smiled. "Precisely at 4:30 a.m."

Bahri failed, once again, to get the humor and returned to the back of the airplane.

For the next half-hour we fly on through the night uninterrupted by unidentified flying objects, enigmatic questions by Hebrone Opshinsky, or mechanical malfunctions on the venerable old DC-4.

As is usually the case, just as I became totally relaxed and had found a comfortable spot in the lumpy, well-worn seat, Muhib Bahri stuck his head in the cockpit.

"We have a serious problem. They are unpacking the crates and assembling the bomb."

Hebrone jerked around. "How long will it take?"

"Four hours."

"Jay, I'm going back."

Hebrone followed Bahri out of the cockpit.

My mind raced. Why would they want to assemble the atomic weapon now? It was at that moment I heard a muffled explosion. Turning the lights up in the cockpit, I scanned the gauges, looking for anything out of the ordinary. All was well with the airplane.

Hebrone entered the cockpit, escorted by Marina Cicogna Pineiro's husband. He had an automatic pistol pointed at Hebrone's head. There was an ugly smirk that raised one side of his mustache at an odd angle reminding me of the hackles on a cur dog.

"I want to deal with your copilot personally, Captain, but at the moment there are more important things. I figured you might need his services. I will kill him later."

"What do you want, Pineiro?"

"For you to plot a course to Orlando, Florida, Captain."

"Orlando? We don't have enough fuel to reach that far inland."

"Yes, you do, Captain."

Pineiro disappeared back into the darkness.

"He shot Bahri in the head. He's dead."

"Why?"

"This is a suicide mission. They want to dive the airplane into the ground, setting off the atomic explosion."

"Killing what? Thirty thousand families? Men, women, and children at Disney World?"

"I don't know, but Orlando is the intended target. Bahri tried to stop it, identified himself."

"We can't allow this. We'll have to crash this airplane into the sea."

"Easy, Jay. Let's think this through. We have options."

Setting back in my seat, it all suddenly became clear. Hebrone's questions about the Haas/Johnson hijacking. His comments about our oxygen supply. This man of few words, this trained assassin, was thinking like the enemy. We didn't have to crash into the sea. We had something better--altitude and hypoxia.

Hebrone raised his thumb upward. "Slowly, gently."

I put the airplane into a gentle climb, one hundred feet per minute. It would go unnoticed by the terrorists. Hebrone increased the power as needed so succulently that even I could not detect the change. Passing through eighteen thousand, we donned oxygen masks. At twenty-five thousand, we were as high as the DC-4 would go.

Hebrone took the portable oxygen bottle and went into the back. Returning shortly, he said, "They're all out. I collected the weapons and found some plastic tie-wraps they were using to assemble parts and bound them."

"Good. We can descend back to breathable air."

We leveled at fourteen thousand feet and Hebrone went back to check the terrorists. Soon, he stuck his head back in the cockpit. "They are all awake. I'm going to have a talk with Mr. Pineiro, settle some things."

I concentrated on flying the airplane. We were near enough to Kingston that the ADF was receiving a strong signal. Bahri played his hand well, but he was in a war and war treats the merciful no better than the unyielding.

If circumstances had turned out different would Hebrone and I have flown this airplane into the Caribbean Sea? Yes, we would. I realize, now, I am neither coward nor hero, but simply this, a series of impressions leading to a series of actions. Life has taught me that men desire most to know only themselves. Few ever arrive at such knowledge, though they awaken each day to attempt and fail to gain that knowledge. I stare miserably into the night and draw my leather flight jacket tighter around me. The world has grown too cold.

A cargo door warning light flashes on. Then a few seconds later it goes out. An electrical anomaly, I think. The number four propeller surges fifty rpms again. Moving the prop lever slightly settles it down. The governor for that propeller needs to be checked upon landing. I write it in the maintenance log.

Hebrone returns and buckles into the copilot's seat.

"You have a talk with Pineiro?"

"I did."

"And?"

"He wanted to be a martyr."

"A martyr--?"

"Yes. You know, if they die in martyrdom they get all the virgin girls and all that other crap they believe."

The cargo door light--

"Tell me."

"He jumped."

"Hebrone--"

"He jumped, Jay. Let it alone."

"The cameras--"

"Yes, the cameras."

"We need to try and call Florida. What was that frequency for the landing strip?"

"131.75"

Tuning the number one radio to those numbers, I keyed the mike hoping they had rigged the radio signals to bounce off a satellite. "Six hundred south with a problem."

Instantly there was a reply. "We have seen. Understand in control. Continue home. Call thirty south."

We fly on through the night. I again think of Bahri. The luckiest of us are insulated against failure, just as it is the unavoidable destiny of the luckless to remain thwarted. I do not allow myself to think about Hebrone throwing Marina Cicogna Pineiro's husband out of the airplane into the Caribbean Sea.

Chapter Nine

We crossed the Island of Cuba at 3:30 a.m., this time without interference from their Air Force. However we knew many eyes followed our progress through the night sky. Our government keeps a KC-135 aloft, orbiting, along the southeastern coast electronically monitoring both air and sea traffic twenty-four hours a day, seven days a week. The DEA and Coast Guard operate interdiction aircraft and sea-going vessels to monitor traffic, and there are satellites that can read a license plate number on an automobile from twenty-five miles above the earth. Yet drug traffickers still manage to get their evil product onto our shores. It is comforting to know that at least we are trying.

When our GPS radio showed we were at the correct position, I keyed the mike. "Thirty south."

An unknown voice, in a bored and monotonous tone, answered. "Cleared straight in to the north. Lights are coming up now."

We saw a thin line of bright lights suddenly appear out of the blackness of the south Florida swamp. Hebrone carefully went through the landing checklist. We were tired, and did not want to make an error like forgetting to lower the landing gear or extend the flaps.

Taxiing up to the hangar, we were met by at least thirty heavily armed men who were aboard before the propellers stopped turning. Hebrone and I were instructed to remain in our seats. I slumped forward, head bowed, eyes closed. It had been a long two days and I knew we had to be debriefed before we could rest. I feared for what could or would happen to Hebrone.

A hand gently touched my shoulder. I looked up into the scraggly old face of Alec Aardwolf. His expression is one I'll never forget. It was sadness, compassion, and sympathy. It said "I'm sorry we got you into this, sorry that Muhib Bahri had to die, sorry that your friend killed a man and will have to face justice." Or maybe his expression said none of these things. Maybe I saw only what was running through my mind.

"Let's go get this over with and you can get some rest."

We followed Aardwolf onto the ramp where a caravan of military vehicles was lined up behind the aircraft. Hebrone and I were put into separate SUVs and driven to a building away from the airport that I had not seen before. The lobby was paneled with dark wood and furnished in expensive-looking leather couches and chairs. The room was small with low ceilings. I was led down a long hallway and into an interrogation/debriefing room. The walls and ceilings were heavily padded and certainly sound proof. Anechoic, is the word they use for these rooms. The furniture was military issue. A young man dressed in a white shirt and black tie sat at a table. Aardwolf and I sat across from him. I had not seen Hebrone since we left the airport.

An hour later we were done. Hebrone was waiting in the lobby when we emerged. Aardwolf said he would drive us to the motel. We could rest as long as needed, then we would be flown home.

At the motel, Aardwolf said, "When you are ready, I'll be in the motel office. We can talk."

I wanted to ask him what he wanted to talk about. I'd already talked enough. But I was too tired. False dawn lightened the Florida swamp as my head hit the pillow.

. . .

I awake with a gasp, though promptly wish that I had not. My head feels glutinous, as if clotted with the stuffing's of a shotgun shell. My ears ring. I look about me and see Hebrone sitting at the foot of the bed. Dimly, I recall the last two days. "You okay?"

"Couldn't sleep. Sometimes it's the sounds. Sounds I can't stop, or forget. The buzzing of flies among bloated bodies. The noise a bullet makes as it bursts a skull. Or the insane laugh of a grunt who just won a twenty dollar bet from his buddy for correctly guessing the sex of a fetus he pulled from the belly of the mother he'd just disemboweled with a bayonet."

"How did the debriefing go?"

"No problem."

"I'll get a shower. We'll go talk to Aardwolf."

. . .

The sun was setting when we left the room. The day was cold, with a northwest wind. Rising and falling in flight along the tops of the scrub pines, a flock of gulls picked up the last ambient light from the red glow in the west. The silent birds, undulating on the wind, shone bone white against clouds massed somber gray and low over the land. A cloudbank looked dark and ominous, like waiting winter.

Aardwolf appeared from behind the counter wearing the worn Oakland Raiders cap. We went into the empty restaurant.

"So, how does Hebrone stand with the Pineiro thing?"

"There was a glitch in the camera pointed at the cargo door. The video was distorted. We could not see exactly what occurred, only that Pineiro went out the door. The matter has been put to rest. Do you understand, Mr. Leicester?"

"Yes."

"Now, I'm afraid I have some bad news. The search has been called off for your friend Andrew Bullard. All aboard are presumed dead. I am sorry."

"Thanks, we appreciate you checking on it for us."

Tears formed in my eyes. I am six feet three inches tall and weigh two hundred and fifty pounds, played linebacker in the NFL and was, at one time, considered so mean that my own mother admonished me for ferocious actions on the football field. But right now, I was unashamed, as tears rolled down my face. Even Hebrone took a napkin and daubed his eyes. Smash Bullard was a part of our family.

"There is a plane waiting at Miami International Airport to fly you back home. I will personally drive you there when you're ready."

Back in the room, while I was packing, I asked Hebrone his plans.

"I'm going to take the DC-4 to St. Thomas. There's a freight hauler who wants to buy it from the CIA."

Looking long and hard at him, I knew he was lying to me. "St. Thomas--?"

"They own me, now, Jay. I saw the video. There was no distortion. They saw it all and they want to collect. Tit for tat. It's the way they operate."

"I'll stay. We'll do whatever it is together."

"No. I'll be fine. It's nothing complicated. One of their men will fly as copilot. A couple of runs, then they'll tire of me and it will be over."

"Rose and I will plan a memorial for Smash. I'll let you know the time. Maybe we'll put a marker in that cemetery up on the highway where she has all those plots. Next to where we buried John Belkin, that old biker we brought out of Mexico."

"That sounds nice. Let me know. I'll be there."

We shook hands. It would be a long time before I saw Hebrone Opshinsky, and after that, never again.

. . .

The drive to Miami was mostly in silence. The weather had turned rainy and cold and Aardwolf kept the heat in the car too warm.

"I have some tough questions."

"I welcome tough questions. Tough questions should never be a problem, so long as you don't change the answer from what you believe to what you think the inquisitor wants to hear."

"How long are you gonna screw with Opshinsky?"

"Till they have no further use for him. I have nothing to do with it anymore."

"He did you a favor, you know, throwing that terrorist out of the airplane."

Aardwolf looked at me. He seemed older, more tired. "Yes, he did us a favor, but he didn't do you one."

"What do you mean?"

"You left four men alive. It would have been better if all of them--" He hesitated. "Went out that cargo door."

"How high up was Pineiro in the group?"

"Second in command of all North American operations. Sent personally by Osama ben Laden's right hand man, Dr. Ayman al-Zawahiri, to see that the bomb was assembled and detonated."

"But he would have died anyway."

"They will come after you and Opshinsky."

"Why? And how would they ever find us?"

"I had no trouble. They can't come after the CIA. You and your friend, they can make an example of, save face."

Point well taken.

"You know, Mr. Leicester, you can never reveal the details of this operation. It is highly classified, and would be extremely dangerous to you and other people."

Jack Tannehill came to mind. I'd promised him an exclusive.

We parked in front of an obscure hangar. Waiting on the ramp was a Westwind jet, painted ebony black, its right engine running, the copilot standing beside the entry door.

"You did a good job for us. Good luck, Mr. Leicester, and remember this, history happens in the first person but is written in the third. This is what makes history a completely useless art."

We shook hands, and I climbed aboard the airplane. The copilot was a young woman with a ponytail and she smelled wonderful.

While the copilot secured the door, the Captain started the left engine and we taxied out in a heavy rain. Lightning flashed out over the Gulfstream.

"We'll have a little turbulence for the first few minutes during the climb, but we should be over the weather pretty quick. The destination weather is clear with calm winds. We are aware of who you are, Mr. Leicester. Feel free to come forward whenever you wish."

Thanking her, I said that I was tired and would rest for awhile.

We climbed into a dark sky. A little black bird reaching for the stars. An old Beatles song came to mind:

Blackbird fly, Blackbird fly
Into the light of the dark black night

Blackbird singing in the dead of night
Take these broken wings and learn to fly

You were only waiting for this moment to arise, oh
You were only waiting for this moment to arise.

Blackbird fly, Blackbird fly
Into the light of the dark black night.

Feeling the airplane level off and start to accelerate, I kept humming that tune. I knew, though, that music, in its very ability to calm, betrays a man's disquiet like little else in the world.

. . .

A power reduction on the engines of the Westwind woke me. Looking at my watch, I saw that over an hour had passed. We would be starting our descent. Unbuckling my seatbelt, I went forward and knelt in the cockpit between the two pilots. I was surprised to see the Captain was also a female. I guessed her age at around thirty-five. The copilot seemed younger, but not by much.

"Ladies. Where might we be?"

The Captain looked at me and grinned. "Hopelessly lost, Mr. Leicester."

"How's the weather in Denver?"

"Clear and cold this time of the year."

The copilot spoke up. "I hear there's twenty-six inches of fresh powder at Aspen."

These were my kind of pilots. Quick-witted, professional.

We landed at Philadelphia shortly after midnight. The airport was deserted.

"You need fuel?"

"No, we are going back to Mobile and dropping the airplane there. It's been sold to a dealer. We are being reassigned to non-flying field duty. Some funding cuts."

"Either of you ever fly a Citation?"

"We both are Flight-Safety type-rated in the Citation. I flew one for an oil company in Lafayette, Louisiana, and Wendy was an instructor pilot on the Citation for SimuFlite in Dallas. Why do you ask?"

I gave them both my card. They promised to be in touch in a couple of days. Jim Verinis Advertising Agency may have just found a flight crew.

My truck was parked in the airport lot. As I turned onto the highway heading south toward Union, I thought of Rose and how to tell her about Smash. He was on that dark shore, now, where shadows spoke with the barking of dogs and the howling of wolves. A line from a poem by Andrea de Chirico came to mind: Taci & reposa: Qui se spegne il canto. *Be quiet and rest. The song ends here.*

At least I would not have to look at him lying in some over-priced casket. Every dead person I've ever seen looked terribly alone. No solitude was more perfect, absolute, and irreparable than death. Slamming a fist on the steering wheel, I thought that we lose ourselves in the weeping.

Parking beside the cottage, I walked upon the porch, carefully checking the south side, halfway expecting Alec Aardwolf to appear out of the darkness. He did not. It was good to be home. Though I'd only been away for a few days, it felt more like a year. I planned to see Rose first thing in the morning.

Chapter Ten

Something was smothering me. It smelled like fish. Opening my eyes, I looked into the face of B.W., whose mouth was up against my nose. "Hello, ol' boy. How did you get here?"

"I brought him. Now get up. You can't sleep all day. I want to hear all about your trip and the Atom Bomb, which I assume will not explode over my farm today."

"You assume correctly. All is well."

"After you get a shower, and I assure you you need one, because I can smell you from here, we can have breakfast, which I've prepared in your kitchen while you slept the morning away."

Scratching the big cat behind the ear, I said, "Aren't you glad I'm home? You don't have to put up with her anymore."

B.W. jumped from the bed and ran to Rose's feet. She picked him up and went into the kitchen. So much for loyalty.

After my shower we sat at the table and, during my third cup of coffee, I looked at Rose.

"What's the matter? I can tell by that look there is something wrong. Is it Hebrone? Did he get hurt?"

"It's not Hebrone. He's fine. It's Smash."

"What has Andrew gotten himself into, now? It has to be a woman. Tell me."

"He's dead, Rose. He was delivering a yacht. There was a terrible storm. The Coast Guard found no survivors."

"Oh, my God, Andrew--you're sure?"

"Yes."

Rose looked out the kitchen window. Tears formed in her eyes. "We will bury him here."

"No bodies were recovered."

"Then we must have a memorial service, get a headstone. I'll pray for his soul."

"I'm sure he would appreciate your prayer. We talked a lot about science and religion. His college major was Electrical Engineering. His soul is fine. He had a strong belief in God, but a somewhat different view than you and me."

"How different?"

"He believed in a creator. He just didn't think that God, who reveals himself in the lawful harmony of all that exists, would concern himself with the fate and doings of mankind. He had a feeling of utter humility toward the secrets of the universe." I laughed, remembering something he'd said. "He thought the "Big Bang" theory correct, but said that it was a misnomer because it was neither big nor a bang. It began with something smaller than an atom and couldn't have been a bang due to the fact there was no air to vibrate. Couldn't argue with that."

"Then I'll pray harder for his soul. He had no other family?"

"None."

"I will take care of organizing the memorial and ordering the marker. You write the epitaph to go on the marker."

"Rose, I'm not too articulate when it comes to things like that."

"You knew him best of us all. It's your job."

"Okay. I'll get it to you in a couple of days. Hebrone said he'd come for the service."

"Good. We'll wait until we get the marker. It'll give us plenty of time."

Rose smiled, but if one played much poker, you would know nothing shows a person's mindset more than false cheer. I have come to the conclusion that humans are a notoriously sentimental group, disposed to bouts of fierce regret and nostalgia, particularly as we ascend into the twilight of our years.

After Rose left, I thought about what could be written for Smash's epitaph. It takes a bold man to contemplate a human being realistically touched by death. The sad thing about memories is that they can turn you into a Prophet. However, we all are obedient to the inescapable threads spun by the fates.

I suddenly remembered a book I'd read years ago that had a wonderful epitaph written for one of the characters. Pulling a copy of Larry McMurtry's *LONESOME DOVE*, from the bookcase, I searched for the passage. A young Indian boy killed one of the characters, Deets, who just happened to also be a black man. Woodrow Call, Deets' boss, carved on a cross placed at the head of the grave these words:

JOSH DEETS

SERVED WITH ME 30 YEARS. FOUGHT IN 21 ENGAGEMEENTS WITH THE COMMANCHE AND KIOWA. CHEERRFUL IN ALL WEATHER, NEVER SHERKED A TASK. SPLENDID BEHAVIOR

These words fit Smash perfectly. With some minor changes, I would use them. I hoped McMurtry wouldn't mind.

There were two things I needed to do today, one, contact Jim Verinis, and two, set up a meeting with Jack Tannehill. Before I could do either my phone rang.

"Mr. Leicester, we'd like to interview for the Citation job."

"Outstanding. Where are you?"

"In New Orleans. We're waiting for a flight to D.C. for reassignment."

"Stay where you are. I'll pick up the Citation and fly to New Orleans with the owner. Meet us at General Aviation, three p.m."

Hanging up, I called Verinis. He was delighted with the idea.

By six p.m., I was driving from Jackson back to Union. The Jim Verinis Advertising Agency Flight Department now had two ex-CIA agents/pilots hired to fly the Citation. They would start the first of the week, and I had a fat check in my pocket for services rendered. Now all I had to do was make a decision on the newspaper interview. When I parked my truck beside the cottage, my mind was made up.

Jack Tannehill answered his home phone, and we agreed to meet in his office at nine a.m. I was tired, and went to bed early.

.   .   .

The *Union Appeal* is typical of all small newspapers. Located downtown, its office is plain and functional. It reminded me of the *Magnolia Gazette* in the town where I grew up. I worked there during high school. That was back when type was set by hand using lead plates. My job was to melt the lead from previous editions for linotype machines *(so complex as to baffle the mind)* could reform the lead into words, sentences, and paragraphs. I still have scars on my arms and chest from hot metal popping out of the melting pot, and I can still smell the odors of molten lead and black, thick ink used to cover the plates after they were set.

If the *Magnolia Gazette* and *Union Appeal*'s offices could be set side by side they would be identical and appear as if designed by the same architect. Entering the *Appeal* was like walking back in time, except for computer terminals that now occupied space where the frantic hustle and bustle and click-clack of manual typewriters and deadlines used to face harried reporters.

Jack Tannehill's office was in the back of the building. It was plain, with desk, two chairs and a small couch. He sat behind the desk and Bill Graham, his managing editor, sat across from him. I occupied the couch. Pulling no punches, I told them everything except Hebrone throwing Pineiro from the DC-4. Jack listened intently. Graham took notes. When I finished, Graham filled in the blanks with the Holy Grail of reporters: who, what, where, when, and why.

"I was advised this was top secret, not to be divulged, but if a terrorist cell wants to get even with me for their botched operation, the more it's exposed, the safer I'll be and the people around me."

Jack looked at me. "You are a man of your word, Leicester. You gave us the story. We won't publish it if you ask. But, be warned, if we do, count on it to go national. This is big."

I leaned back into the comfortable couch. "Publish it."

.   .   .

Nearing the cottage, I observed a huge dump truck in my field. "Oh no, Shack and his chicken shit," I thought. It was that time of year, again. Shack Runnels, a friend, neighbor, and cattle farmer, who lives a few miles to the north and cuts the grass from my farm for hay, is fertilizing the fields with chicken shit collected from local growers. It stinks horribly, floats in the air for days, permeates clothes, houses, noses and eyes, but is a necessary evil. Liquid fertilizer would be much preferred, but its cost is prohibitive.

Riding into the field, I parked my truck in front of Shack so that he had to stop. I needed to tell him about Smash. He had become friends with him and Hebrone over the years. Shack is a tough man. A hard environment and hard times make hard men.

"I'm sorry to hear about Bullard, Jay. You gonna do some sort of service for him?"

"Rose is planning one. Maybe put a marker in the cemetery up on the highway."

"That'll be nice. Let me know the date. We'd like to attend."

"Will do. I hope you know," I said, waving an arm around the field, "that if it doesn't rain in the next day or two I will hunt you down and shoot you."

He laughed. "This from the man who said he could sit on a week old corpse and eat a baloney sandwich, and now you're bitching about the sweet smell of a little chicken shit?"

We parted with a wave of hands, and a smile. Good friends are comforting.

It was almost noon, but I wasn't hungry. I sat on the porch, thinking of Smash's death, ranting and raging at the world. Crows, feeding at the base of the post oak where I put out birdseed, watched as though they found me strange. The poet, Milton, wrote, *"The mind is its own place, and in itself can make a heaven of hell."* He was right, though I wasn't having much success. I have always tried to express my thoughts, having learned early on in life that you always pay for what you suppress. Mental costs accrue.

It took me a half-hour to realize that I was so cold my teeth were chattering. Going inside, I built a fire, fixed a tuna sandwich, and fed B.W. Making a pot of coffee, I took a cup, sweetened with Fireweed honey and sat in front of the blazing oak logs. It seemed illogical to me that radical Islamic terrorist, al-Qa'ida, or any other religious zealots would waste time and money looking to retaliate against a lowly aviation consultant living in the woods in central Mississippi. It wasn't me or Hebrone who screwed up their nuclear project. It was, thank God for them, the CIA. We were simple pilots. I dismissed any reprisals and decided to get on with my life, but promised to keep them in the back of my mind. If I saw someone wearing a turban and a robe wandering around my property, I'd get Shack to spray them with chicken shit. That would make them jump on their camel and head for the desert.

At five o'clock, I opened a bottle of 2005 IO, Upper Bench Syrah, a red wine from California, so fruity and spicy you would think you were eating grapes, picked up a book by Arturo Perez-Reverte, titled, *The Painter of Battles*, and settled in front of the fire. B.W. was curled up on the hearth, looking like an old panther.

Andres Faulques, a world-renowned war photographer, has retired to a life of solitude on the Spanish coast. He spends his days painting a mural on the curved, inside walls of a tower overlooking the sea. The mural pays homage to history's classic works of war art that incorporates a lifetime of disturbing images. One night, an unexpected visitor arrives at Faulques' door and explains he was the subject of one of his photos taken in a war zone years ago, and that he is there to kill him.

I am over a hundred pages into the work and find that this is a stunning composition on morality and the chaos of war. Tautly written, it is a deeply affecting literary thriller about life and art, and I have fallen in love with one of the characters, Olvido Ferrara, who oddly seemed a cross between Alella and a young Rose. This book is exactly what I needed to take my mind off the last few days.

After a while, I put the book down, got up and added two logs to the fire, poured another glass of the Syrah, and walked to the back door of the cottage. The December sun was beginning to descend in the sky and the intense light gave the trees, winter grass, and the water in the two ponds a precise clarity, a special beauty, like a glaze that instead of making colors more dense, clarified them, gave them an incomparable transparency. I wanted to shout with joy at the sight.

By eight o'clock, I had finished Perez-Reverte's little masterpiece. It was only 211 pages, and he truly was master of the literary thriller. I must introduce this work to Alella, for the writer lives in Madrid. Maybe she could meet him.

Buttoning everything up in the cottage, I prepared for another early bedtime. Closing the screen on the fireplace, I decided to walk out on the front porch and view the winter sky. The night was clear and cold, with no moon. My breath formed a wispy cloud with each exhalation. Walking further out into the front yard, the first thing I noticed was the quiet. It was as if everything had paused to honor the silence. Above the drive from the tree line to the cottage, the Big Dipper was perfectly framed in the opening. The familiar constellations jumped out at me. Cassiopeia, near the north star, looking like an "M" or "W" depending on one's perspective; Auriga, with its bright star Capella; Gemini, with the twins, Castor and Pollux; Taurus the bull, with Aldebaran; Orion, with its four corner stars, Betelgeuse, Bellatrix, Rigel, and Saiph, and the three stars of the belt that few know the names: Alnilam, Alnitak, and Mintaka. The Milky Way ran through all of them composed of the light of so many closely crowded stars that they cannot be resolved by the naked eye.

The night sky has always been an awesome, awe-inspiring phenomenon that produces a feeling of peaceful permanence. Starting to shiver, I took another look across the brilliant vista and went inside, not knowing that at the end of this night my life was going to change drastically.

Chapter Eleven

I woke to the sound of an engine running. Then there was a pounding on the front door. Grabbing my magnum and looking at the clock at the same time--it was seven a.m.--I pulled on a pair of pants and went to the living room. "Who is it?"

"It's me, Shack."

When I opened the door, he said, "There's a problem. Come with me."

"Let me get a shirt and shoes."

"You'll need a coat."

Climbing into the passenger side of the cab, I saw that the truck was loaded with chicken fertilizer. It stank terribly. We drove down through a hollow and up to the field south of the cottage.

Approaching what looked like a pile of discarded cloths, Shack said, "I almost ran over them."

"Them?"

"Two bodies. They are handcuffed together with those plastic cuffs and have not been in the field very long."

Shack stopped the truck and we got out to look. As we neared them, I noticed that the dew was still on the grass and there were no footprints except Shack's and no vehicle tracks other than the truck.

Bending down, I turned one of the bodies over so that the face was visible. "Jesus Christ!"

"You know them?"

A wave of nausea swept over me. "Yes, Shack. I know them." Pointing to one of the bodies, I said, "This one's name is Marina Cicogna Pineiro. The other one's her father."

"How did they get out in the middle of this field? There are no tracks. Look at all the blood. They were alive when they were left here."

Standing up, I scanned all around where we stood. Our breaths could be seen in the cold, and steam rose from the bodies. Looking up into the clear blue sky, I said, "Rigor has not set in. These people were tossed out of a helicopter or airplane. Someone is sending me a message. Shack, you better come back to the cottage. There's something I need to tell you."

. . .

The sheriff and the state forensics team spent the entire day going over the farm. Shack was interviewed for almost two hours. He told them how he'd found the bodies, then came to get me but, true to his nature, mentioned nothing of what I'd told him about Hebrone or the CIA involvement.

Sheriff John Quincy Adams was an old friend. He had worked a murder case with us last year that involved a missing woman and her airplane. Both were found buried on my farm. He was also familiar with Hebrone Opshinsky. They both served "in-country" during Vietnam and had things in common. I trusted Adams and decided to tell him everything. The *Union Appeal,* due out tomorrow would reveal most of it anyway.

After Shack finished his interview, he took his truck and left to fertilize another field. Mine was cordoned off indefinitely. Sheriff Adams walked him out of the cottage to the truck. Returning, he said, "Let's go out back."

Outside, Adams looked across the valleys at the two ponds. "I see you cut the hanging tree."

"Yes. Too many daytime nightmares." He was referring to a small post oak that leaned awkwardly to one side. Shack hung a man from it one night while trying to extract information. It worked, but brought out the animal in a lot of us. I burned the tree in the fireplace this year.

Adams looked at the hole left by the tree. "I thought Runnels and Henderson would have settled their differences by now. Figured one of them would be dead."

"Henderson is not dumb enough to push Shack. If he did, my money would be on the cattleman."

The sheriff looked at me with a wry grin. "Mine too. Okay, Jay, start at the beginning."

"Sheriff Bob Morgan called me that morning about the DC-4 with the load of marijuana. I flew the plane off the roadbed to Philadelphia, then spent the next three days in Jackson on some business. Arriving back here late at night, I was met by a CIA agent. Turned out the pilot of the airplane hauling the dope was one of their own under deep cover."

"Now that is information I did not know. Neshoba County took a lot of heat for that killing in the jail."

"Well, the CIA wanted me to fly the DC-4 to a clandestine strip in south Florida, then from there to South America, where nuclear bomb parts were to be loaded aboard by radical Islamic terrorist and flown back to Florida. The CIA was going to end their little operation there. I asked Opshinsky to fly with me. During the flight back from Venezuela things took a turn for the worse--they started to assemble the bomb with the intention of forcing us to crash into the city of Orlando, detonating the nuclear device."

"Jesus, Jay."

"They were not smart people, John. We were able to overcome them and Hebrone threw their leader out of the airplane somewhere over the Caribbean Sea south of Jamaica."

"That sounds like Opshinsky."

"The man Hebrone tossed was named Pineiro. The woman in the field was his wife. The old man she's cuffed to is her father."

"What am I missing? Why did they end up in your pasture?"

"John, from what I gathered, Pineiro's wife had fled from him, along with her father to the US, probably with the help of the CIA. However complicated the deal was for the nuclear parts--we were not privy to any of the details--the wife and her father ended up as part of the swap. They flew back to Venezuela with us. We only knew that twelve million dollars worth of diamonds were part of the payment."

Adams took off his Stetson hat, ran a hand through thinning gray hair, reset the hat. "Let me see if I got this straight. The CIA infiltrated a terrorist cell that was raising funds to buy nuclear components from Iran or Iraq. They were going to strike somewhere in the USA. Along the way, plans changed and they decided to dive-bomb Orlando. You and Opshinsky thwarted the plans and now the terrorist are going to retaliate against you both. They dump two people from the sky into your field for what reason? To say, "Here we come?""

"Doesn't make sense to me either."

"I'm getting a headache. Where's Opshinsky?"

"He's making a couple of trips in the DC-4 for the CIA. Seems they had a video of him tossing Pineiro."

"So they are blackmailing him, using his services in their operations."

"Yep."

"I thought he was smarter than to let something like that happen."

"He let his anger overcome reason."

"What was he so angry about?"

"Mistreatment of that woman lying dead in my field by her husband."

Adams scraped the toe of his snakeskin cowboy boot in the sandy soil. "You gave this story to the *Union Appeal* hoping it would go national. You thought that the more exposed the story, the less the terrorist would want to reveal themselves by coming after you. Not bad thinking. It just might work."

"I've got to try and find Hebrone. Let him know what's happened."

"Yeah. You know I've got to check all these facts. You got a telephone number for your CIA contact?"

"Inside. His cell phone. Names Aardwolf. Old guy that went to collage with John Madden. He'll verify everything."

He pointed to the south where the bodies lay. "Autopsies will be available soon. We'll know what killed the father and daughter."

"I'm pretty sure it was impact with the ground."

"Hell of a way to die."

"It was abrupt."

. . .

Sheriff Adams left the cottage as Rose English drove up.

"What in the world is going on down here?"

"Hello, Rose."

"Don't "hello" me. Tell me what's happening. Why are all those people out in that field? Is that an ambulance? Jay--?"

"Now, Rose, settle down. Shack found a couple of bodies this morning as he was starting to put out fertilizer."

She sat in a recliner in front of the fireplace. "This is getting to be a habit, finding bodies on your farm. Who are they?"

"A father and daughter, from South America."

"Does it have anything to do with that bomb caper thing? Oh, my goodness, did you kill them?"

"No, I did not kill them. It does have something to do with the flight to Venezuela, but I don't know what, yet."

"Do you know them?"

"Yes. They flew from Florida to South America with us. We left them in Valera. I have no idea how or why they ended up here."

"Seems pretty clear to me. Somebody is sending you a message. You made somebody mad. Every time you and Hebrone Opshinsky go off somewhere you come back with things all screwed up."

She surprised me with her intuition. However, I'm surprised a lot now days.

"Go away, Rose. I have to make some phone calls."

She stood up. "If you want some company, come to the house. You can eat supper with me."

"Thanks."
"Six o'clock."
"Okay."

At the door, she stopped, turned around, and pointed a finger at me, shaking it. She had a disturbing smile, as rigid as if it wasn't hers. It stayed on her face for a time, and then she went out the door, closing it behind her. I knew that she grew irritated at me because of how my life was affected by the traits deeply bred into my southern soul. My casual willingness to question authority, my sassy attitude in the face of regimentation, and my lack of reverence for received wisdom. There was little Rose could say, for she was exactly the same way.

Putting more wood on the fire, I went and looked up the number for Captain Tony's bar in Key West.

"Yeah?"
"Who's this?"
"Who you calling?"
"Looking for Skinner."
"Who you?"
"Jay Leicester."
"This me. How you doing, Mon?"
"Captain Tony's wife still hanging around the cash register?"
"She still hanging around. He ain't here."
"When's the last time you saw him?"
"Been awhile. His boat is off the ways and gone."
"It was there a week ago."
"Ain't now, Mon. I hear 'bout Smash. It my fault."
"How is it your fault?"
"Intro him to the candy lady."
"Don't blame yourself, Skinner. One can't control the weather."
"Control who you intro, dhough." He pronounced the "t" as a "d."
"We are going to do a memorial service, put up a headstone."
"Dat nice. Wish me could come. Smash would 'preciate it."
"If you see or hear from Hebrone, tell him to call me. Write my number down and let me know if you find out anything."
"Will do, and thanks."
"For what?"
"For saying it weren't my fault, even dhough it was."
"Say hello to Tony's wife for me."

We hung up, and I sat back in the chair staring at the fire, thinking about Skinner, Smash, and Hebrone. Skinner was a huge man, six foot six and over three hundred pounds with skin so black it seemed to shine. A true

"Conch", a name given to people who originally settled the Keys, Skinner was a tremendous athlete who played baseball. He was given a contract to play with the Pittsburgh Pirates, but a knee injury sidelined his career. Captain Tony took him under his wing, and he's been with him for over thirty years. When I was a young man flying the line, I spent a lot of time in Key West. Everyone who comes to the Keys sooner or later gravitates to Captain Tony's, which was the location of the original Sloppy Joe's, a bar made famous by the writer, Ernest Hemingway back in the twenties and thirties. It was here that he met his third wife, Martha Gellhorn, herself an accomplished writer. The bar was within walking distance from his home on Whitehead street.

There was a full-sized skeleton hanging beside the cash register purported to be that of Captain Tony's ex-wife. Whenever I'd had too much gin, I would start to flirt with her. Skinner would cut me off, call a cab, and send me to my hotel.

After Hebrone and Smash fled to Key West during hurricane Katrina, I'd called Skinner and told him about them. They'd become friends.

There was a knock on my door.

"Bill Graham. I've been expecting you. Come in."

He sat with me in front of the fire. He is a quiet, genteel man, with large sensitive eyes set in an oval face. Some thought he resembled a schoolteacher more than a managing editor of a newspaper. His expression was what could be described as saturnine, not gloomy or sad, but somber. He looked like a Quaker, old-stock American with bowed eyebrows supporting a righteous high forehead. Someone virtuous and shy.

There was a CD playing, an old one, by Jessie Coulter--*You did hang that moon, didn't you Waylon*. When the song stopped, Graham said, "You know, Jay, music is not so much an escape as it is a connection. A connection to the harmony underlying the universe, to the creative genius of the great composers, and to the people who feel comfortable bonding with more than words. I am awed, both in music and in writing, by the beauty of harmonies."

"It makes me want to drink Jack Daniel's whiskey and chase girls."

Graham smiled.

"How'd you find out, Bill?"

"About the bodies? We monitor police traffic and ambulance dispatches."

"Makes sense."

"This have anything to do with the CIA operation?"

"Seems so, but at the moment it's not clear exactly how."

"The sheriff's not talking. You want to fill me in?"

I told him all that I knew.

Graham sat in front of the fire, tapped his lips with a finger, thinking. "Why do we kill each other?"

"Man kills because he must be faithful to the fearful symmetry of his intelligent nature."

"Is that a quote from somewhere?"

"Probably."

"Like," *"The devil is come down unto you, having great wrath, because he knoweth that he hath but a short time."*

"That one I recognize. From the Bible, Revelation."

Graham laughed. "It is. So what happens next?"

"If I'm being sent a message, a warning, there may be no "Next." It could be they are merely letting me know my location is known to them. If not, I'm on the list for the slaughter. They'll get to Opshinsky after that." I turned and gave him a smile. "You might not want to get too close to me after today."

He stood. "We'll run this next week. Hopefully the autopsies will be back before then and we'll know for sure if they were dropped out of the plane alive. If there's anything we can do--?"

"Thanks." We shook hands and he left.

Chapter Twelve

Looking at the time, I saw that it was almost five o'clock. Placing a call to the Meridian Airport Tower, I said to the person answering the phone, "Is Paul Bradford available?"

"I'm sorry, he's gone for the day."

"Do you have his home number?"

"We can't give out that information."

"Is it listed?"

"I'm afraid not."

"Would you have him get in touch with Jay Leicester as soon as possible."

"Leicester--you the guy found the missing PA-18 last year. Paul talks about you often. Hang on a moment."

He gave me Bradford's home phone number.

"Hello Paul, Jay Leicester."

"I heard you flew an old DC-4 off a dirt road couple of weeks ago. I'll bet that was fun?"

"A barrel of monkeys. Listen, Paul, I need to tell you something in strict confidence, and I need your help."

"Anything."

"Somebody threw two people out of an aircraft within two hundred yards of my cottage near daylight this morning. Right now we don't know if it was fixed-wing or helicopter. I need you to go over everything from say midnight until seven a.m. See if any identifiable aircraft flew over this area."

"My goodness. I'll go back to the tower right now and view the radar tapes. You want me to notify the authorities if anything turns up?"

"No, get in touch with me. I'm sure law enforcement will contact you soon enough, but I need to know as quickly as possible. From the looks of the bodies, the craft they were tossed from had to be high enough for a radar hit. Don't count on having had any communication with them, though. I'm sure they slipped in under the scope and possibly flew out the same way."

"Kind of like the way you did with the DC-3 couple years back?" He laughed. "I'll be in touch."

"Thanks. I'm going to dinner, but will be back here by nine p.m. You can call my cell phone anytime." I gave him both numbers and we hung up. This was a long shot, but a necessary one.

Taking a quick shower, I dressed and headed to Rose's for dinner. This was one time that I truly needed her company. Turning into the drive, I saw Shack's truck was there. Good, I thought. We can discuss all the ramifications concerning terrorist threats against yours truly.

Shack was leaving as I entered the house. I asked him to stay for awhile; there were some things we needed to talk about. All three of us sat at the kitchen table.

"There is a possibility, however remote, that terrorist could come looking for me. I need for you two to be alert for any signs of strangers."

Rose put her elbows on the table. "Kind of like that Mongol motorcycle gang, or those MS-13 scum's of the earth Latinos that were supposed to come hunting for you a couple of years ago? Or Shack's buddy, Henderson, who tried to sneak into my house in the dark of night and do us bodily harm, but ended up getting hung from a tree in your backyard? Is that the kind of strangers you are referring to?"

"Rose, when you talk, I see flowers growing."

"I am a woman and a lady, not a flower."

"The term "woman" is a fact. Lady is a matter of opinion."

Shack laughed. "He's got you there, Rose."

She stood and walked to the sink. "We need to be serious for a moment. How real do you think this threat truly is?"

"Real enough that they threw two people out of an aircraft to their death beside my cottage. One of them being the wife of a man Hebrone killed in the same manner. That's a powerful message. I'm just not sure of its meaning."

Shack got up to leave. "So what do you want us to do?"

"The only thing you can--keep your eyes open for anything unusual."

"I'm off, then. If I see anyone that looks like they are from the sand box, I'll let you know."

"The article is coming out tomorrow in the *Union Appeal*, so I don't know what that'll bring. Hopefully not much. I won't be named, but reporters will be nosing around."

"I'll be sure and read the article," Shack said with a little pleasant sarcasm. "Goodnight."

Rose set the table for supper. "Alella is coming next week. Do you think I should tell her to delay for a while?"

"I don't see any danger toward you or her. There is no reason to spoil her homecoming. I'm the target."

"You want a glass of buttermilk with supper?"

"I do not."

It was a pleasant evening. I needed the company.

Returning to the cottage by nine o'clock, I shut off the engine and stood beside the truck. In this sylvan setting I live like a bear in a cave, and really feel more at home than ever before in my eventful life. When I am in these woods there is always a feeling of powerful purity at once childlike and profoundly stubborn. The stars seem to align to create a sense of inertia, or at least a weariness for further wandering. By ignoring certain social conventions, I have been able to create for myself an atmosphere conducive to relaxing, reading, and free from distraction. At least until now. I had a hunch this was going to turn out badly. Then I remembered that intuition is nothing but the outcome of earlier intellectual experience.

The phone was ringing as I walked inside. "Yes?"

"Jay, Paul Bradford."

"Hello, Paul. You got anything?"

"There was a radar hit at five a.m. Lasted less than thirty seconds. Right over the area of your farm. Then nothing. They must have run in at treetop level, popped up, opened the door and tossed out the people, then ducked back down and flat-hatted out of the area."

"Okay. Thanks, Paul."

"Sorry I couldn't be more helpful. Call me if you need anything else."

I fed B.W., double checked the locks on the doors and windows, put my trusty magnum on the table next to the bed and turned in. The alarm was set for six a.m. I wanted to be in town early to pick up a copy of the *Union Appeal.*

.   .   .

I woke before the alarm, afflicted, it seemed, with some kind of pathological laziness. Maybe it was depression. Maybe just bad character. It seemed one's worst characteristics remained when the good traits abandoned one. It was good to be alive, though. If I were much younger, it would be even better.

A quick shower and a short drive to town put me in front of the *Union Appeal* soon after it opened. Bill Graham was sitting in his office with feet propped up on his desk reading the edition hot off the press. He handed me a copy, motioned toward a chair, and pointed at his coffee cup. I nodded, and scanned the headlines:

NUCLEAR ATTACK ON U.S. SOIL BY RADICAL ISLAMIC TERRORIST THWARTED BY GOVERNMENT OFFICIALS

An unknown source, in an exclusive interview with the Union Appeal, revealed that the CIA had broken up a terrorist cell in south Florida who planned to assemble and detonate a nuclear device in a U.S. city--

It was a good, well written article with the byline shared by both Tannehill and Graham. Which shows the character of the publisher.

Bill handed me a cup of coffee. "The story went out over the wire service at midnight. Should be a fun day."

"Yeah, lots of fun."

The phone rang. Bill picked it up. "The Washington Post, you say. Not Woodward or Bernstein? Well, I'm disappointed." He looked at me, covered the receiver with a hand. "And so it starts."

Waving goodbye, I picked up several copies of the paper and left the office.

During the drive back to the cottage, I thought about the clean, concise journalistic writing put forth in the article by Jack Tannehill and Bill Graham. I have come to believe that language is capable of inhabiting the imagination far more intensely than any picture, however doctored. The same principle applies to the journalism in the *Union Appeal*. No film, made by the greatest directors and actors, can provide the experience of the words of Leo Tolstoy in *The Death of Ivan Ilych*. Descriptive language supplies deeper perception than any visual image.

Turning off the gravel road onto the terrace row that leads to the cottage, I spotted a dark-colored car parked next to the porch on the north side. Stopping at the tree line, I could see someone sitting in the cypress glider. Easing closer, the array of antennas on the car became visible. So many that one could probably operate two radio stations using them. Sheriff John Quincy Adams.

He was sprawled out in the glider, both arms stretched out and resting on the back railing. His Stetson hat was tilted rearward on his head, legs extended, feet crossed at the ankles. He seemed to be studying the tips of his expensive cowboy boots.

Walking upon the porch caused him to stop looking at the boots and turn a hard stare at me. His eyes squinted as if he was trying to read my thoughts. He was gray-headed and gray-eyebrowed, but there was no other indication of his age. His weathered face, which had known so many thousand criminals, was extraordinarily youthful, and his blue eyes sparkled merrily from behind spokes of sun wrinkles. His face was altogether an Italian caricature and he was inordinately proud of his ancestry.

"The High Sheriff. What brings you back out in the woods?"

"I see you been to town for the papers."

"Yes. Here, you want a copy?"

"I've already read it."

"But how--?"

"Never mind. The pathologist phoned with a prelim. No other injuries. Died from blunt force trauma."

"Falling from an aircraft will do it every time."

"You being funny, Leicester?"

"No, and what you so snippy about this morning?"

"Your Mr. Aardwolf didn't answer his phone. I called CIA Headquarters in Washington. They've never heard of him. There is no record of one Muhib Bahri being killed in the line of duty, or for that matter, ever having been employed by the agency. They have no knowledge of a terrorist cell operating in south Florida, nor any information of a nuclear threat on the United States. That's why I'm a little "snippy.""

I got a queasy feeling in the pit of my stomach. "John, I don't know what to--"

"There are two bodies found on your farm currently undergoing autopsies. You got any ideas, Leicester?"

"We flew to South America, brought people and bomb parts back. I don't see how--?"

"No record of any flight to Venezuela."

"Denial and misinformation is a trademark of the CIA. Give me some time to think."

"If I find any connection between you and Marina Pineiro, Jay, you can kiss it goodbye."

"You think I killed her? And her father? Come on, John."

"Your record with women is not the best."

"Any harm that's come to a woman by my hands has been justified, and you know it."

"That's what the record shows."

"John, you really don't believe I had anything to do with killing these two people?"

"Personally, no. Look at the facts, though. Nothing you say can be verified. Give me something, anything, that I can use to prove your story."

"Hebrone. If I can find him. Wait--the two pilots who flew me from Miami to Philadelphia. I hired them away from the CIA to fly for an Ad agency in Jackson. Come inside, we'll call them. They can at least testify they saw Aardwolf."

"Verinis Advertising Agency, this is Estelle. How may I direct your call?"

"Jim Verinis, please. Jay Leicester calling."

"I'm sorry, Mr. Leicester. Mr. Verinis is at this moment on his way to Vancouver, British Columbia. He'll be out of the office until next week."

"You have a contact number for him in Vancouver?"

"No, but he's due to call in today. Can I give him a message?"

"Have him call me immediately. It's vital that I speak to him or one of his pilots today."

"I'll give him the message."

Hanging up the phone, I thought, "Get a man an airplane and he wants to fly all over the country." Looking at Adams, I said, "You think if I were guilty of murder that I would've given that interview to Tannehill and Graham?"

"Be good cover."

"If I was going to kill a woman, or anybody for that matter, do you really think I'd do it so overtly, leaving the bodies out in the open field on my place? Not to mention killing her father for no reason."

"All good cover to fool the old country bumpkin of a county sheriff. Give me something I can bite into."

"For God's sake, John."

"Look, Jay. I don't think you did this. Hell, I know you didn't. Find Hebrone, get me a statement from the pilots, and locate Alec Aardwolf. We'll get the facts corroborated and put this to bed. I have a friend who's the sheriff near where you say this clandestine landing field is located in south Florida. I'll have him check it out. It will also take some time for the blood work to come back from the pathologist. In the meantime, don't leave the county."

"Good day, John."

At the door, he turned and looked at me, "By the way, the Pineiro woman was three months pregnant."

"Ah, God--"

The first thing I did when the sheriff left was dial the number for Alec Aardwolf. It rang for five full minutes with no answer.

Out of frustration, I called Skinner at Captain Tony's Bar in Key West. No news from Hebrone or his boat. Slumping down in a chair, I read through the article again in the *Union Appeal*. It was good journalism. There were some concerns I had about next week's edition and coverage of the two bodies. Tying them to the terrorist article would expose me too easily. Any good investigative reporter could put two and two together and figure out the "anonymous source." There was plenty of time to talk with Tannehill and Graham before they went to press, though. At the moment there were more pressing matters. Such as why Alec Aardwolf abruptly disappeared from the scene, why the CIA denied the terrorist nuclear threat, and the where-a-bouts of Hebrone Opshinsky.

    I suddenly felt alone in a room full of shadows. Maybe my conscience was bothering me. Conscience is the detective that watches the direction of our steps and decries our transgression. It is a vigilant eye before which each imagination, thought and act is held up for either censure or approval. I think there is no greater argument for the existence of God in the world today than conscience. A medical doctor by the name of Romano, once wrote, *"The smaller the understanding of the situation, the more pretentious the form of expression."* This seemed to be my case at the moment. I went for a walk in the cold.

Chapter Thirteen

There is a place to which I go when the mind overloads with fear. A southern country that exists in the air. A host of sirens surrounded by cowboys and Bluecoats. The Jesus of the cross, and pilots killed in crashes, and wild men of the mighty river. I wander this country of inherited song, singing its lines of rhyme. Here is the Holy Virgin, spinning gold with black-eyed Susans. Cotton-Eye Joe strumming a guitar, his face grave as headstones. John the Baptist in the Jordan.

A borderless country, this damp swamp, where prophets holler Judas to the rope. Soldiers are trumpeters. Its constitution a spreadsheet. Its war cry *Lorena*. Its flag is Joseph's Coat. Its language is Arcadian Cajun. The rambling boys of pleasure and the ladies of easy leisure are dancing the dos-a-dos. The bold Emmett Till, the sweetheart of the Mississippi River, waves regally down from the House of Blues. Singing "Don't You Longs for Freedom Time?" with two hoochie-choochies and a banjo on his knee.

Blackface Napoleon. St. Peter on the trombone. The Savior moans on Calvary. The pregnant woman falls from the sky. None of the people are real, which I don't really know. They must have been once to be tombed in a song? The poor man's mausoleum. No one in this country will hurt me, or kill me, or force me to speak when I don't want to. They all understand I have nothing to say. I do not wish to talk, but to listen.

No father will beat me. No mother will leave me. My body does not weary. There is the hope of love. The pipes are calling from glen to glen. Recruiting-sergeants are tricked by cattle herders. I see myself in Gulf Water land, the circle around its sun. I know its dependable geography. The Mighty Miss is a lament, the cow pond a murmorous creek. The city on the hill is

Jerusalem, Mississippi. Cowgirls yodel the Twenty-Third Psalm. The black angel spreads her wings and falls into the grotto where her mother calls. And there, in the deer hollow, Abe Lincoln is hanging from a Black Oak tree. In Dixie Land we make our stand. To live and die in Dixie.

I meander the topographies like an off-course pilot, knowing everything I seek is somewhere in the piney woods if only I could be pointed the way. But now I'm tramping to Zion on High. In the outworld, everyone leaves in the end. But people in the songs always stay. Long after I have gone, they will still be there. Forever, in fact. They are choiceless.

I wake with a start. All of the dream seemed real, equal, which is one definition of madness. The world had lost proportion. The past is not over and the future has happened many times.

After a hot shower, I made coffee, and at eight a.m., called Verinis Advertising Agency. Estelle said she'd given Mr. Verinis my message and that he would call me sometime today. I hung up and dialed the number for Alec Aardwolf. Still no answer.

The temperature had turned off cold. It was a gray day with high, thick clouds fat with moisture. A north wind blew in gusts. I built a fire and poured another cup of coffee, turned on the radio and sat in front of the warmth-producing flames. A song played that I hadn't heard in forty years: "Mule Skinner Blues"

> *Well, good morning, Captain*
> *Well, good morning to you, sir*
> *Do you need another mule skinner*
> *Down on your new mud run*
>
> *Well, I'm an old mule skinner*
> *From down Kentucky way*
> *And I can make any mule listen*
> *Or I won't accept your pay*
>
> *Little water boy, come here boy*
> *Bring that water bucket around*
> *If you don't like your job*
> *Water boy, put that bucket down*

Being a mule skinner would be a wonderful life.
The phone rang. "Leicester."

"This Citation is the best thing that's ever happened to me. I love this airplane. The pilots, these ladies are true professionals. You did good on both counts. What can I do for you, Jay?"

"You opening a branch office in Vancouver?"

"No, it's a national convention. Making some contacts. Never hurts to meet new people in the industry."

"I need to talk to one of the pilots."

"Why?"

"Somebody says I did something bad. I need them to vouch for me. Identify a colleague of theirs in the CIA and confirm they flew me from Miami to Mississippi."

"Lord, I do not want to know the details. One of them will call you this afternoon."

"Thanks, Jim."

As soon as we hung up, the phone rang again. "Yes."

"The wolf welcomes you."

"Where are you?"

"In the gulf, south of Cedar Key. I just downloaded the USA TODAY by satellite. Reading about our adventures is a little discomforting, even though we are unnamed."

"We've got a problem. They killed Marina Pineiro and her father."

"That's too bad, but why is that a problem for us?"

"Someone dropped them, alive, out of an aircraft into the field south of the cottage."

"I'll put into Cedar Key. Pick me up early in the morning."

"It's too cold for the Stearman. I'll see if Earl Sanders will furnish a plane."

"I'll be waiting."

Hanging up the phone, I was relieved. It would be good having him here.

. . .

Earl Sanders answered the phone at his flying service. "Well, Jay Leicester. Annie and I were just talking about you. We read something in the newspaper this morning about an extremist terrorist group in Florida and an unnamed source from Union. She said that it sounded like a caper you'd be involved with."

Annie and Earl Sanders are longtime friends who have been associated with aviation their entire adult lives. They own and operate the only Fixed Base Operation on the Meridian Airport, offering fuel, maintenance, flight training, and charter flights anywhere in the continental United States. They erected a huge building that can hangar thirty aircraft, up to and including large corporate jets.

"Earl, I need to pick up Hebrone Opshinsky down at Cedar Key in the morning. What you got sitting around on the ramp that's not too expensive?"

He thought for a moment. "Everything we've got for charter is flying tomorrow. There is a Cherokee Six fresh out of engine overhaul that's available. You fly it and pay for the fuel and it's yours at no charge."

"Deal. What time you open in the morning?"

"Somebody will be here by six a.m."

"Have the Cherokee Six fueled and ready to go. I'll be there by then. Thanks, Earl."

"Not a problem. Jay, I've got to ask, is that you and Hebrone they are talking about in the newspaper article?"

"Earl--"

"Yes?"

"Tell Annie I love her."

"Have a good flight, and be careful."

We hung up. The less he knew the better for everyone.

It was noon and I was hungry. Cereal sweetened with Tupelo honey, bananas, and low fat milk filled the bill. Just as I finished, the phone rang, again.

"Mr. Verinis said you wanted to talk with us."

The pilots said that both of them would confirm flying me from Miami to Philadelphia, but had no knowledge of Alec Aardwolf and did not remember seeing him when I boarded the Westwind. At least it was something.

Retrieving my flight case, I pulled out aeronautical charts and planned the trip to Cedar Key. On a direct course, it would be about three hundred miles and with the speed of the Cherokee Six at around one hundred and fifty miles per hour, I figured two hours of flight time. With a fuel burn of sixteen gallons per hour and a four-hour round trip with eighty-four gallons on board, we'd have over an hour reserve on landing back in Meridian. This was good because the George T. Lewis Airport at Cedar Key had no fuel services available. The runway, though paved, was short, only 2,355 feet in length. It was ideally suited for the Cherokee Six, which needed only one thousand feet for landing and fifteen hundred feet for takeoff.

With the flight plan done, I checked the forecast weather. It looked to be good all the way down and back. I put the flight bag away, built a fire, and sat quietly for a moment thinking about Andrew "Smash" Bullard. I was going to miss him.

The newly overhauled three hundred horsepower Lycoming engine fired instantly to life when I engaged the starter. The entire airplane shook momentarily like a big metal can filled with rocks until the engine settled into a smooth running idle. While the oil pressure, oil temperature, and cylinder head temperature warmed into the green arcs on the gauges, I familiarized myself with the Cherokee Six cockpit. Along with the Cessna 206, the Cherokee Six is one of the finest single-engine airplanes ever built. With its thirty-two foot nine inch wingspan, twenty-seven foot nine-inch length, and a wing loading of nineteen and half pounds per square inch, it will haul anything you can cram into the cabin. This was a 1977 model with updated radios. It had a GPS (global positioning system) which I programmed for the Cedar Key Airport. The flight path was almost exactly the one we followed in the DC-4 to the landing strip in south Florida.

One hour and fifty minutes after takeoff, I spotted the small landing strip at Cedar Key. The single runway was oriented northeast/southwest or 5/23, 50 degrees and 230 degrees magnetic. Passing overhead, I noted the wind favored runway 5. Announcing my intentions over the CTAF (common traffic advisory frequency) of 122.9, I lined up on final approach.

Shutting the engine down on the ramp, I saw that the airport was deserted. No people, no planes, and no Hebrone Opshinsky. There was a payphone on a post adjacent to a small parking lot. A loud-sounding motorcycle pulled into the lot with two people aboard. A male and female. The bike was an old chopped down Harley, but even from where I stood, it appeared in immaculate condition. The couple was not what one would expect to see riding that type of bike. They were young, clean cut, tanned, with wind-blown hair. They walked to where I stood beside the wing.

"We saw you land. What kind of plane is that?"

"It's a Piper."

"Can we look inside?" the young man asked.

"Sure, help yourself."

The young woman wore a pair of ragged, cut-off jeans that revealed much more of the female anatomy than an old man like me needed to see. It was safe to say she wore no underwear, nor favored the close shaved look. I concentrated my gaze around the airport looking for Hebrone.

Emerging from the airplane, the man, who I guessed to be in his early twenties said, "I've been thinking about taking flying lessons. It looks like it would be a lot of fun."

"Anyone who can ride a bike like that one would make a good pilot."

"Thanks, I rebuilt it myself. We're in school at Florida State. My dad has a house here on Cedar Key."

"You didn't happen to see a man about my age, gray hair, walking toward the airport, did you?"

"No, we didn't see anyone."

It had been almost an hour now and I was beginning to worry. Hebrone was not a man to be late for anything. There were many reasons he could be delayed. He could have had engine problems, limped into another anchorage, be lying ahull-waiting rescue. The boat could have sunk, or he could have accidentally fallen overboard. A lot of boats have been boarded and taken over by drug runners in this area. Hundreds of reasons--

"You two want to take a ride in the Piper?"

The two looked at each other. "You bet."

"I need to fly out over the entrance to the harbor, look for a boat. You two could be of some help."

We looked for forty-five minutes, but saw nothing of Hebrone or his beloved Wheeler sportfisherman.

Back on the ground the young woman said, "Thanks for the ride. If we see anything of your guy, we'll tell him you're waiting." With that, she climbed aboard the Harley, revealing even more of that intriguing female anatomy.

I waited another hour, then called the Coast Guard from the payphone.

. . .

I landed back in Meridian with dry fuel tanks. Earl Sanders and I stood by the Cherokee Six while the lineman filled them with gasoline.

"Eighty-one gallons. You cut that pretty close considering there are two gallons of unusable fuel in the tanks."

"Yeah." There were other things on my mind.

"So, Hebrone never showed."

"I don't understand it, Earl. The man's always on time."

"If he called from his boat, he must have used a cell phone. Why don't you get the authorities to triangulate the signal? Would give you his exact position at the time of the call."

"Sometimes, Earl Sanders, you come up with a good idea."

"Glad to be of service. You owe me for eighty-one gallons of fuel."

During the drive back to the cottage, I thought about Hebrone. First Smash is dead, now he's missing. What if he's dead? It wouldn't be--Then only fools and little children--.

Arriving back at the farm, the first order of business was to inform the Coast Guard about the cell phone call. The person who took the information promised to pass Hebrone's number along to his superiors with my request. He'd call me with any news on the boat.

As I hung up, Rose drove up.

"Where's Hebrone?"

"He didn't make the rendezvous. Probably had engine trouble." I did not want to alarm her, but Rose is no fool.

She whirled around, her eyes narrowing like a cat's when it sees a stranger enter the room. "You're lying to me. Something's happened to him. I can feel it."

"He called me from the boat, said he'd read the article that ran in the newspapers. I told him about the two bodies dropped from the aircraft. He asked me to pick him up at Cedar Key. He didn't show. The Coast Guard is looking for the boat. We're triangulating the cell phone call to get an exact position."

She sat down hard in front of the fireplace. She was a woman of passion, of courage and ardor. But as is often the case with such deep-feeling people, her vulnerabilities were many. She was handsome--in the way a flower, encountered in an old book, is not young anymore, but is handsome. When she was young, she was a belle in a town of beauties.

"Everything is arranged for Andrew's memorial. The stone company is holding off. They need the words you want inscribed. I guess we need to delay until we know about Hebrone."

"Yes, let's wait."

Chapter Fourteen

After Rose left, I built a fire and sat in silence, remembering dead pilots. So many crashes, so many maimed and burned and broken. So many bright futures consigned to the ashes of the past.

There was one that hit me especially hard. He was a Captain, a mentor, and a man who had that rare quality of leadership. He possessed a combination of bravery, ability, integrity, dignity, straightforwardness, and compassion. He would single out a fledgling for something good, and not berate him for an error that could cause disaster, but use it to teach. He was in a category by himself. I felt that he was not a man born of woman, but that God had issued him to Southern Airways. He taught me much, but fate stepped in and dealt him a fatal blow.

There were others who were very bright and affable, but all too often failed to question cogently or listen carefully or observe keenly. They would not think deeply enough about their airplanes and problems. Something was profoundly wrong with the way they learned to solve weather and system failures. There are three basic types of uncertainty dealing with aviation. The first results from incomplete or imperfect mastery of the aircraft. The second depends on limitations in current aviation knowledge. There are areas to which no pilot, however well trained, can provide answers. A third source of uncertainty is derived from the first two: this is the difficulty in distinguishing between personal ignorance or ineptitude and the limitations of present aeronautical knowledge. I have observed pilots struggling with uncertainty and their numerous psychological mechanisms to cope with it. They use black humor, making bets about who would crash and who would survive, and engaging in some degree of magical thinking to maintain their poise and an aura of competence in front of their passengers while flying through uncertain emergencies. All of us instinctively latch on to certainty when faced with uncertainty. Igor Sikorsky, a true pioneer in aviation, once said of the early days of flying, "We were ignorant, and we were ignorant of the fact that we were ignorant. This is ignorance squared, and it often led to disaster." Things have improved over the years.

Looking at my watch, I saw that it was already three o'clock. A drink was in order. Early, yes, but still in order. Pouring a snifter of Martell Cordon Bleu cognac and retrieving an El Credito cigar, I sat in front of the fire and tasted the thick, harsh, brown liquid. It exploded on my tongue like the vowels of a new language. I lit the cigar. Alcohol and tobacco are both bad things, but then we all die from the things we love.

An hour later the fire had burned low, the cognac snifter was empty, the cigar ready to be put in the ashtray to die a natural death, as any good cigar should, and my mind was relaxed.

On the outside chance that it would prove fruitful, I dialed Alec Aardwolf's number. To my astonishment, he answered on the first ring.

"It's about time you called."

For some reason it didn't sound like Aardwolf. I didn't know what to say. I had to quickly collect my thoughts. "Who is this?"

"I've had a cold. My throat's a little hoarse."

"So what do you think about your draft pick this year?"

"Draft pick? Oh, okay. With the fourth place pick in the first round, we took Darren McFadden, running back from Arkansas. Personally I thought we should've taken Leobis McKelvin, the cornerback from Troy State. Not only is he a good cover guy, but a fantastic return man. Al Davis usually does what he wants, though."

"Have you heard anything from Hebrone?"

"He's sitting right here with me."

"But how could that be? Where are you?"

"The debriefing building. You remember the place."

"Yes, I recall. Put him on the phone."

There was a short pause. Then, "The wolf welcomes you."

"You lied to me."

"We had to know if you were being followed. Aardwolf needed to know if the terrorist group was making a threat they intended to carry out, or if it was a bluff. It was the only way."

"And?"

"You were not tailed."

"How nice to know."

"The CIA, by whatever means, has determined that the terrorist group gave up on the nuclear device and is now concentrating on a dirty bomb. Something along the lines of what they did in London and Spain. I'm going to stay and work with them for a while."

"You're going to miss the memorial for Smash."

"I know, but this is important."

"Where is your boat? Skinner said it was off the ways."

"I took it to a friend's dock up on North Island."

"The Coast Guard is searching for it, and they are triangulating the call you made to me."

"Aardwolf has taken care of the Coast Guard. Forget about them."

"Okay."

"Did you enjoy the cutoff jeans?"

"They were agents?"

"She said that you were a gentleman, didn't stare too much. I'm proud of you."

"Screw you, Opshinsky."

"Keep alert. We're still not sure what these people's intentions are toward you."

"Tell Aardwolf to call your "in-country" buddy, Sheriff John Quincy Adams and get him off my back. Clear me of killing the Pineiro woman and her father."

"I'll pass that along. Be careful."

"You too."

Opening the back door, I walked out to the edge of the yard and stared into the woods. A reconnection with wildness always awakens strong emotions. I remained there until cold shivers racked my body. Inside, I fought the urge for more cognac, deciding instead to turn in early. Lying awake for a long time, I thought about the exact words for Smash's headstone. There were to be only a few changes from Captain Call's epitaph for Deets.

Over a cup of coffee early the next morning, I printed the words on a sheet of paper, folded it, put it in my pocket, and headed for Rose's house.

Walking out the door, I glanced at the field south of the porch. The sun was rising above the trees, casting a flame across the dead grass where the two bodies, one three months pregnant, were dropped. The fire seemed a cremation of the spirit.

"Hebrone is fine, Rose. The trip to Cedar Key was all a scheme to see what the terrorist were plotting."

"Men and their stupid little games. All with little thought to the anguish they put us through." Late in life, she had come to the reluctant conclusion that men were more trouble than they were worth. Lately, she seemed to have little use for anything male. "All the men around here, you included, are the worst of a bad lot. I'm tired of worrying about men and their needs."

"You seem to think a lot of Shack."

"He's different. He's a cattleman."

"Standing knee deep in cow shit makes him better than the rest of us?"

"He deals with the struggle of life everyday. Understands how the world works. You don't."

There is a time, if one is smart enough, to know when not to push the argument. "When do you want to do the memorial for Smash?"

"It will take a week to get the monument inscribed, delivered, and set in place. I want to do it at the cemetery."

"Hebrone will not be able to make it. He's continuing to work with the CIA on new threats from the radical Islamic group."

"Maybe I should go ahead and order two more headstones, one for each of you. Those people still gonna explode an atomic bomb?"

"No. They are working on a dirty bomb."

"What does that mean?"

"One that will spray deadly chemicals across a wide area of heavy population. Like Saddam Hussein did with the Kurds in northern Iraq. Kills everything it comes in contact with; Men, women, children, and animals."

"Why? Why would any human do that to others?"

"I don't know, Rose. I'm sure there's a lot of Jewish people who would like to ask Hitler that same question."

"Well, they will have to travel to hell, for that's where he is, sitting around having a hot time with Lucifer."

"You need anything from town? I'm on my way to talk with the folks at the *Union Appeal* about next weeks article on the bodies found in my field."

"What's there to talk about?"

"It would be nice if the location could remain obscure, with no names mentioned."

"I don't understand. The people who want to harm you already know where you live. They dropped the bodies from the sky into your field."

"True, but the more press this gets, the more the crazies come out of the woodwork."

"There's nothing I need from town. I'll call the headstone folks with the inscription."

.   .   .

It was clear and cold and the drive to town was pleasant. Two bodies dropped from the sky. An airplane buried in the ground along with the dead pilot. A man hung from an oak tree at my back door. A woman committing suicide by diving her airplane into the ground just south of my front door. I wondered that when the bizarre becomes commonplace, is there hidden cost to the self?

Bill Graham listened to my concerns about the story he was writing on the deaths of Marina Pineiro and her father, and how it tied in with his "anonymous" source and the nuclear threat from the radical Islamic terrorists group. He understood and promised to keep me and my farm as obscure as possible. He also pointed out that there were as many as twenty people at the site of the deaths and that there was no way to silence them. A good point, but fending off gawkers, weirdoes, and outside Press was my main concern. I told him I wasn't too worried about retaliation from Pineiro's people.

"Ah, "*Qui male agit odit lucem,*" Bill said. "He who acts badly hates the light."

"Yeah, let us hope."

I would have liked to read a proof of the article before it went to press, but that is an absolute no-no for a journalist, besides, I knew he could be trusted.

Arriving back at the cottage shortly after noon, I found Sheriff J.Q. Adams waiting. This was getting to be a habit.

We shook hands. "High Sheriff. What brings you out to the woods, again?"

"Blood work's back on the bodies. Nothing unusual." There seemed a perfervid aura in the mannerisms and movements of the man. "Here's something else you need to see."

He handed me a poor photocopy of a letter. It was clear enough that I could make out an incredible accusation against me. I understood the sheriff's demeanor now. It stated that I was the father of Marina Cicogna Pineiro's unborn baby.

"I only met the woman once. That was in south Florida at the clandestine airport the day before we departed for Venezuela. This is beyond preposterous."

"Sounds like someone is wanting to make life miserable for you. I got no choice. We gotta do the DNA test."

I said nothing, hoping that the dignity of silence would destroy the mystery of evil. It didn't work.

Adams scrubbed some mud off his boot. "The sooner you do this, the quicker we can put it to rest. The clinic in Decatur, the new one just south of town, is expecting you this afternoon."

"Why don't you and I ride down there right now, at taxpayer's expense."

"Good idea, but I'm on the way to Jackson."

"Where was this letter postmarked?"

"It was faxed to my office from a Florida number."

Walking inside, I took an empty pill bottle, picked out a Q-tip, swabbed the inside of my mouth for several seconds, then sealed it inside the bottle. On the porch, I handed it to Adams. "Here, tell your daughter there's enough of my DNA there to work with. If she needs anything else, let me know." His daughter ran the forensics lab for the state.

He laughed, tossed the bottle in the air and caught it at the apex, and headed for his cruiser. Opening the door, he stopped and looked at me. "You're okay, Leicester. I see why Hebrone Opshinsky likes you."

After lunch, I found myself with nothing to do. The weather had warmed enough that there was no need for a fire. Walking out on the porch, I stood looking to the north, into the hollow where the big deer bed at night. It is so quiet. One can almost hear the pulse of the silence. It is like the beating of an angel's heart.

Going back inside, I built a fire, anyway. It's comforting to look at the flickering flames, hear the crackle of the wood, smell the smoke, and feel the warmth of the heat. Settling into my favorite recliner, I picked up a book from the side table and opened it to where I'd left off. I was about two hundred pages into Michael Ondaatje's awesome narrative titled, *Divisadero*. It takes place in the 1970s in northern California and is about a father and his two teenage daughters who work their farm near what was the old gold rush country. An incident of violence--of both hand and heart--sets fire to the rest of their lives. So far, it is a multilayered novel about passion, loss, and discordant demands of family, with unforgettable characters. I was anxious to see how it would end, but did not want to rush it. Good writing, like fine wine, should be savored.

An hour later, I closed *Divisadero* and placed it on the table. The temperature had cooled, so I added more wood to the fire and it felt good. I thought about what would be the five most important books I'd read and why. *Moby Dick*--A masterpiece about our need to conquer nature even as we worship it. *Huckleberry Finn*--It makes art out of vernacular English. *A Movable Feast*--It makes the reader feel young again. *The Old Man and the Sea*--Teaches that "man can be destroyed but not defeated." Finally, I would include Walter Isaacson's bio of *Einstein, His Life and Times*--One of the great learning experiences of my short life.

My phone rang.

"There's a woman at my door. She's looking for you. Says her name is Carmen Cicogna. What do you want me to tell her?"

"That I'll be there in five minutes."

Chapter Fifteen

The late afternoon temperature was turning colder. Darkness would be swift and, with no cloud cover and the air crisp and clean, the stars should put on a magnificent display. Milky ways, constellations, far away galaxies, and Einstein's theory of time and space warping the fabric of the universe, was not what concerned me at the moment. A woman with the last name of Cicogna was at my friend's house looking for me. That was what was on my mind. It also frightened me. This could be an elaborate trap, with Rose caught in the middle. A mile from her house, I dialed Shack's number.

"Yeah?"

"If I don't call you back in exactly fifteen minutes, come to Rose's armed to the teeth."

"Understood."

Ah, friends like Shack.

A dark-colored limousine was parked in the drive. A man sat behind the wheel, slumped down in the seat. I tapped on his window with the barrel of my magnum.

He let the window down. "Jesus, Mister. Is that thing real?"

"Who are you?"

"Willie Whitten. I'm the driver for the limo service."

"From where?"

"Jackson. Lady flew in to the airport, I picked her up and we drove all the way out in these woods. She's looking for a man. Long way to come to find a man, if you ask me, although she didn't--ask me, I mean."

"You got some I.D.?"

He handed me a commercial driver's license and the state-required permit to operate a limousine service. He matched the photo I.D. on the driver's license and I was familiar with USAVE Limousine Service.

"Stay in the car. Do not get out."

"I ain't moving. Is something wrong?"

"Not yet."

Knocking on Rose's door, I entered the living room without waiting for her to answer. Sitting on the couch holding a cup of coffee was someone who appeared to be an exact clone of Marina Cicogna Pineiro. The face was younger, no scars, and no hard lines caused by a hard existence. She stood, carefully placing the cup and saucer on the side table.

Extending a hand, she said, "You're Jay Leicester. I'd recognize you anywhere. My sister spoke often of you."

Shaking her hand, I found it warm, with a strong, firm grip. "Your sister?"

"Marina Pineiro. I've come to claim her and my father's bodies. Take them back to Florida for proper burial. My name is Carmen Cicogna."

I looked at Rose. She had an amused expression. Her meeting with this woman obviously had been pleasant and the statement about the dead woman speaking of me often seemed to interest her.

"Excuse me a moment, ladies."

In the kitchen, I used Rose's phone to call Shack. "Everything's under control, but stay where I can get you. I'll explain tomorrow."

"Yes, you will."

Back in the living room, I said, "Miss Cicogna, let us leave Miss English to her evening and go to my place. We can talk there."

"Fine. I'm sorry for the interruption, Miss English. Thank you for your help."

"Oh, I'm always happy to help when it concerns Mr. Leicester. He needs a lot of help."

We walked outside.

"Get in my truck. I'll have your driver follow us."

She stood beside the door waiting for me to open it for her. I did, and was suddenly aware that she had a peculiar odor, an intimate, nearly forgotten scent of a strong and healthy woman.

I instructed the driver to follow us.

Pulling up beside the cottage, I watched the limo inch slowly along the terrace row and into the tree line. The driver parked behind my truck and shut off the engine and lights. This was the first time a limousine had been to the cottage and probably the only time the driver had used a terrace row as a driveway.

Carmen Cicogna walked over to the limo, said something to the driver, and came back to where I stood. We went inside. I turned on the lights, threw logs on the fire, while she made herself comfortable on the couch. B.W., my cat, did not come out from his hiding place to investigate a stranger's arrival. This was unusual, though with that animal most things he does never surprises me.

"Miss Cicogna, you might see a large cat emerge from the back. Do not be alarmed. He has not eaten a guest in a long time."

"Please call me Carmen. I love cats, though my German Shepherd does not tolerate them."

The fire blazed and the flames made her face appear rather evil, witch-like. I was able to observe her closely. Her hair was ebony-colored, silky-smooth and shoulder length. Her nose was a little crooked, the eyes almost black with a hint of purple that made them the exact shade of blue berries. Her stare was cold and merciless. There was a deathliness in her expression, of cruelty seen and done, but it was not the eyes that such terrors live, it was somehow in the bones of the face.

I guessed her age around thirty-five--give or take. Not a tall woman, five feet five, but well built, and weight around one hundred and ten pounds. She appeared in good shape, but it was hard to tell. She wore black slacks and a dark blue sweater. A silver cross hung around her neck and there were no rings on her fingers.

"Would you like a drink?"

"No, thank you."

"You lied a while ago. Your sister never talked about me. We met only once, the day we flew to Venezuela with a load of food for earthquake victims."

She reached into a pocket and handed me a folded sheet of paper. "I wanted to see your reaction to what I said, especially in lieu this." She pointed at the paper.

Looking at the page, I saw that it was an exact copy of the accusation sent to Sheriff Adams. "I've seen this. In fact DNA is being compared as we speak to prove I'm not the father of your sister's baby."

"My sister and our father were staying with me in Florida before they went back to Venezuela. I know who the father of her baby was, Mr. Leicester. I know why they returned to South America. I know what happened to my sister's husband, and I know what he did to Muhib Bahri." Her deep-set eyes had a haunting intensity, her face an enticing touch of melancholy.

She had my attention. "Then you know who killed your sister and father?"

"Yes, and I know why. It is all your fault and that of your copilot, Opshinsky."

"Miss Cicogna, Carmen, I'm sorry for the loss of your father and sister. I'm saddened they died on my farm, but Hebrone Opshinsky and I had nothing to do with their deaths. Your sister's husband shot a man in the head on board an airplane we were hired to fly. As a consequence of his action, he himself was killed. If someone blamed that death on us, then they are simply wrong. Why your sister and father returned to Venezuela was never discussed. The complexity of the cargo and the people involved was not something we were aware of. We were hired to fly an airplane. Simple as that."

She shifted position on the couch, stared at the fire. "My sister's husband was a terrible man. He treated her like dirt. Beat her, berated her, and used her as a servant. Ordered that she keep her body covered, wear a veil, and keep her mouth shut. He deserved to be tossed out of an airplane. I hope he relived his entire sinful life all the way to impact with the water."

"What was his nationality?"

She turned her head toward me. The long, shiny black hair followed slowly along like a snake coiling. "He was born and raised in Venezuela, but was deeply involved with Saddam Hussein's regime in Iraq. Big pals with Saddam's two sons, Uday and Qusay. Later, he worked closely with the insurgents, developed close ties with al-Qa'ida and the Iranians supplying weapons in Iraq."

"Your sister fled from him and came to live with you?"

"Yes, and he couldn't allow that to happen. He would lose face. When this deal for enriched uranium and the plot for an attack on the US came together, my sister was part of the deal. She would be returned to him."

"Part of what deal? How could she become part of something between a terrorist cell operating in Florida buying nuclear bomb parts from Iran, which if I understand correctly, came from Iraq originally?"

She moved a strand of hair from in front of her eyes. "This involved the identity of the father of her unborn child."

"Why are you here, Miss Cicogna? Why did you come to me?"

"If your copilot had not killed my sister's husband, she might be alive today. They killed her and my father in retaliation for your deeds."

"Who is "they?"

"His friends in Venezuela. The one's involved with buying and selling weapons."

"Not the terrorist or al Qa'ida?"

"No. Look, I know this is not your fault, but you need to know they will come after you. Maybe not today, but they will come."

"Do you know specifically who these people are?"

"I do. You want to strike first? If you do, I will help."

"I am not a killer. I'm an aviation consultant."

"But your friend, Opshinsky?"

"Listen--Carmen--I don't understand how you know so much about us, or the operation we were involved with. But I do know there is a lot you are not telling me. Unless you start at the beginning and let me in on everything, then it's best you leave."

"I'll take that drink, now."

Pouring two snifters of cognac, I handed one to her, added more wood to the fire and sat down.

Carmen Cicogna crossed her legs, swirled the dark liquid in the glass and smelled long and hard, then took a sip. "Ah, Cordon Bleu. Nice."

I was impressed.

She smiled for the first time. "I saw the bottle when you poured."

"I'm waiting."

"My business is diamonds. I work for DeBeers. Any stones sold east of the Mississippi River comes through me."

"You furnished the diamonds Muhib Bahri used as payment for the nuclear bomb components."

"Very good, Mr. Leicester. Everyone said you were an intelligent man."

"Go on."

"Muhib Bahri did acquire those stones from my company." She paused, as if collecting her thoughts, wondering how much to tell me. "He was also the father of my sister's baby."

This stunned me. "He let her return to Venezuela and Pineiro? Let him slap her around on the airplane when we landed in Valera?"

"He had no choice. There was a plan to get both Marina and Father returned to us, but Pineiro found out Bahri was seeing my sister. That's why he killed him, not because he tried to prevent assembly of the nuclear device."

Taking a long drink of the cognac, I let this information settle in my mind. Looking hard at Carmen Cicogna, I thought that she was smart, serious, small, delicate, and ebony-haired, and if it wasn't for the slightly crooked nose, could be described as pluperfect. There was a brooding depth, and a beguiling aura about her. "I have to ask--are you CIA?"

"I am not. My business is diamonds." She looked at me, waiting for the questions she knew would come.

Shrugging, I turned up both palms, said nothing.

"How do I know so much about the CIA operation?" She was intuitive. "I was engaged to a fighter pilot. He was killed in the first gulf war. Shot down north of Kuwait City. His A-10 plane was found, but his body was never recovered."

"I'm sorry, but how--?"

"His father was Alec Aardwolf."

Now it was clear.

We watched the fire, the flames settling into an orange, crackling warmth, and sipped the cognac, savored the silence that should have been awkward, but wasn't.

"How did your sister end up with Pineiro?"

"He was the kind of man people fell in love with because of what he looked like rather then who he was. If you knew him, you wouldn't buy fertilizer from him."

"You are from Venezuela?"

"Caracas. My father owned a string of bakeries. It was a successful business. Enough to send me to Miami for my education. My sister stayed and worked in the business. That's where she met Pineiro. It's a long story, but as you know, it ended badly."

"Where are you staying tonight?"

"Some hotel in the capital. I plan to meet with the authorities tomorrow. See about getting the bodies released and then make arrangements for them to be flown back to Florida."

"Why don't you send your driver back to the capital and stay here. In the morning I'll take you to see the Sheriff. We can talk more about the threats to Opshinsky and me."

The look on her face questioned my motives.

"It will save you from having to drive back from Jackson in the morning. There's a spare bedroom with a lock on the door. The sheriff is a friend. I can help expedite the release of the remains."

She agreed. I walked out to the limo and told the driver he was free to return to Jackson. The lady would remain here. He seemed perplexed, but drove away, retracing his drive along the terrace row.

Back inside, I found B.W., my cat, sitting in Carmen Cicogna's lap. They both looked at me as if I was some intruder.

Chapter Sixteen

I woke to the sound of running water. Carmen Cicogna was in the shower. Going into the kitchen, I made coffee. Walking back to my bedroom, I saw the door open to the bath. She stood by the sink away from the door-- not a cute little college girl--no, this was a woman with full breasts that were plain to see in the flimsy bra and white, low-cut panties, her navel centered in a little pot belly. She looked as if she would take a swing at me if I entered the bathroom.

"Sorry, the door was open."

"I'm sure you've seen a woman's body before. The steam was stifling, I opened the door. Now, do you mind if I finish my toilet?"

All I could think of to say was, "Coffee is ready."

"Fine." She closed the door.

At eight o'clock, I dialed Sheriff John Quincy Adams' office. His secretary put me through. "John, I have Marina Pineiro's sister here. She's come to claim the bodies. Is there any problem with releasing them today?"

"None that I can think of. Bring her to my office. There are some questions I need to ask."

"What kind of questions?"

"Leicester--"

"We'll be there in an hour."

She sipped at the coffee, looking at me with a strange expression. "Any problems?"

"No, but the sheriff wants to meet you. He has some questions."

"What kind of questions?"

"He wouldn't tell me."

"I thought you two were friends?"

"I told him we'd be there within the hour. You want some breakfast?"

"No, this is fine." She raised the coffee cup.

"I'll go get a quick shower and dress."

"Can I watch? It's only fair." She laughed. It was a friendly, casual sound. It let me know it was all in fun.

As I dressed, the thought struck me that Carmen Cicogna seemed a little too--happy for a person about to be claiming the bodies of her father and sister. But then we all respond differently in the face of death.

Carmen stuck her head in the bedroom as I was dressing. "There's a rough-looking man getting out of a truck and heading to the door."

Shack rang the doorbell.

"Come in. Thanks for standing by last night."

"What's going on--oh, I didn't know you had company."

"Shack Runnels, meet Carmen Cicogna."

"Pleasure, ma'am."

"Mr. Runnels."

"Shack. Everyone calls me Shack."

"Why? Do you live in a rundown house?" She smiled when she asked the question.

"Mr. Leicester gave me the nick-name. You'll have to ask him."

"Carmen, Shack is the one who discovered your father and sister in the field."

"Oh--"

"I'm sorry for interrupting your morning. We'll talk later, Jay."

"We're on the way to see Sheriff Adams. I'll get in touch when we get back."

"Good. Was nice to meet you, Miss Cicogna. I'm sorry about your folks."

"Same here, Shack. Thank you for your sentiments, and please call me Carmen."

After he left, Carmen asked about him.

"He and Rose English, the woman you met last night, own big cattle farms adjacent to each other. They welcomed me into this part of the country when I made the move from the capital. Kept me from making foolish mistakes with the locals. Taught me who to trust and who not to associate with."

"Seems like good neighbors to have."

"Yes. You ready to go?"

During the drive to Decatur, she was quiet. A silence seemed to hang around her. It seemed to follow her, like the eyes of an oil portrait, or pond water at night with a full moon. It was as if her presence made everything around her silent.

As we approached the city limits of Decatur, I asked, "Your thoughts?"

She looked at me as if returning from a long way away. "I'm sorry. I was remembering my sister and how strange life could be. How fleeting our existence."

We parked in front of the sheriff's office. For some reason, I had an ominous feeling about this meeting. There was a sense that John Quincy Adams was keeping something from me.

It turned out that I was wrong. Sheriff Adams and Carmen Cicogna were cordial with each other. The formalities and paperwork for release of the remains went smoothly and quickly. The questions he had for her were about her sister. Why she was in the states, how long had she been here? Carmen told him who the father of the unborn child was and who in Venezuela she thought was responsible for the deaths of her sister and father. Everything went too smooth. I kept waiting for the bomb to explode.

"Miss Cicogna, would you excuse Mr. Leicester and me for a few minutes. There are some things of a personal nature we need to discuss. We won't be long."

"Sure."

He paged his secretary. She appeared at the door. "Would you please take Miss Cicogna to the coffee room? We'll join you shortly."

After they left, Adams closed the office door, sat down behind the desk, laced his hands around the back of his head, and stared at me.

Here it comes, I thought.

"Leicester, this is the strangest case I've ever been involved with. My colleague in south Florida found your clandestine airstrip. It was deserted. No planes, no hangars full of electronics to track aircraft all over the world via satellite. There was no nearby motel, no building with debriefing facilities. Then, suddenly, he was warned off of looking further into it. Told it was a matter of national security, and highly classified government operations involving Homeland Security, the CIA, FBI, and the Pentagon. What do you know about this, and where is Hebrone Opshinsky?"

"It's like I told you the other day, John. Only now, the terrorists have refocused their efforts on making a dirty bomb. I know little about this, thank God. Hebrone's working with the CIA, doing what, I don't have a clue, and I really don't want to know. I'm only interested in who might come after me for Pineiro's death, which still doesn't make sense because he was going to die anyway with the detonation of the nuclear device."

"Like I said, it's a strange case."

"When can she get the bodies?"

"The lab will release them sometime today to the funeral home. I would guess by tomorrow they will be ready to transport. I'll give you the name of the mortuary. You can contact them for details."

"Did you run my DNA through the data base?"

"Why would I do that?"

"Because any good law enforcement officer would."

"Yes, we ran it through. There were no matches for you, no involvement in unsolved crimes. Did you expect something to turn up?"

"No, but if one can always see the road ahead, it's not worth the trip."

Adams stood, escorted me to the door. "If we are going to end this meeting with cliches, here's one: Don't interfere with the enemy when he's hurting himself."

I had no idea what that meant, but didn't ask.

When we left the sheriff's office, the secretary gave me the phone number of the funeral home that would prepare the bodies for the trip to Florida. The sky had grown overcast and the wind blew in strong gusts. A cold front was due in tonight with the threat of sleet and snow showers. This type of weather system is usually benign in the deep south, except when freezing rain covers everything with ice, causing trees to topple, power lines to snap, which results in widespread outages that last for days. Then nothing moves. I hoped this would not happen to trap Carmen Cicogna out in the woods, alone with me, in a small cottage. If it did, we had plenty of firewood, a generator to keep the freezers cold, and plenty of food. Plus, Rose and Shack would check on us.

Glancing over at Carmen, I saw that she was leaning against the door watching the winter scenery pass by. I wondered if she was thinking of her father and sister. A phrase came to mind: *Venari Lavari Ledere Ridere Hoc Est Vivere.* "To hunt, to bathe, to play, to laugh--that is to live." I thought: "To err, to fret, to grieve, to learn--that, too, is to live."

Arriving back at the cottage, we had to run for the cover of the porch as a cold rain pelted down in scattered deluges. Carmen laughed at getting wet.

Inside, she said, "Brrr, can we build a fire?"

"I'll have one going in a minute."

"Where is your cat?"

"He's out chasing coyotes. Don't worry, he hates the rain and wind. He'll show up momentarily."

"Aren't you afraid he could be injured or killed roaming around in the woods?" There was genuine concern on her face.

"This time of the year there's not much to worry about. The coyotes stay close to their dens, the bad snakes are in hibernation, and there are few stray dogs. A bobcat staking out territory could be a problem. Life is short, one must live it without fear."

"Yes, I'm aware."

"How about for lunch we have New England clam chowder and a bottle of good French Burgundy on this cold and rainy winter day?"

"That sounds wonderful."

Suddenly there was a loud noise at the window behind the couch where Carmen sat. B.W. had jumped upon the sill, rattling the whole cottage.

"There's your friend." I pointed at the big cat.

Opening the door, I let him in. He ran and jumped upon the counter, surveying the situation. Satisfied all was in order, he joined Carmen on the couch and let out a loud meow as if to say, "I can speak English when the occasion demands it, however today--"

Going to the wine cellar, a true underground cellar dug when the cottage was built, I looked for a good white wine to match the chowder.

A friend, who owns a wine store on Magazine Street in New Orleans, insisted I buy a case of white Burgundy that, he preached, was one of the finest vintages of the last decade. I was reluctant for two reasons; the price of French wines, and my taste is more for reds. He sold me the case at his cost. Having Carmen Cicogna for lunch was a good occasion to see how the wine was aging.

While the chowder warmed, I opened the 2005 Batard-Montrachet, produced by Pierre-Yves Colin-Moray, from the southern part of the Cote D'Or known as the Cote de Beaune. Another reason I shy away from French wines, especially Burgundy is the complexity of growers, producers, negociants, and appellations. Deciphering a Burgundy wine label can be intimidating. There is a commune name, or village of origin, followed by vineyard name, if any. Next, a controlled appellation, which includes grape variety and minimum and maximum alcohol content. Then a statement as to who or where the wine is fermented, matured, and bottled. A vintage, the year the grapes were harvested, and finally, the producer or negociants. One must be intimate with all of this information, for it is easy to buy something for a high price that is undrinkable. I much prefer to pick a bottle of wine with a label that reads, *Beauleau Vineyards, Napa Valley Cabernet Sauvignon, 2005.* Simple, easy and good.

Carmen picked up the bottle. "Ah, Batard-Montrachet. I've had the 2005 Meursault-Les Perries and the Puligny-Montrachet. It will be fun to see how this compares. I've heard some great things about it."

The lady knew her wines.

The Batard-Montrachet was an opulent, rich wine with balance and finesse. There was an elegance and harmony, which are hallmarks of a top wine. I watched Carmen as she tasted the golden liquid.

After two sips, she said, "This has great stature and sophistication, with clean lines, rich flavors and creamy textures. There is a classic Montrachet intensity and a range of butter, hazelnut, floras and lime flavors."

"It goes well up against the heavy cream of the chowder."

"Yes. Thank you for sharing this. I am surprised you are so knowledgeable, and to find this wine in the middle of the woods in rural Mississippi, is simply wonderful." She held up her glass in salute.

After lunch, we sat in front of the fire savoring the last of the burgundy. The wind was really howling. Enough that it was effecting the flames in the fireplace.

"Would you please call the funeral home and ask when we may expect to leave?"

"Sure. What airline would you like for them to notify?"

"Airline? Oh no, I will transport them home on my company plane. It's waiting at the International Airport in Jackson."

For some reason, I assumed she'd flown in on the airlines, but then the diamond business is big money. It should not have surprised me there was a corporate airplane at her disposal. "Two caskets will require a lot of baggage room."

"My plane is a Boeing Business Jet. There is plenty of cargo space."

The BBJ is a forty million-dollar airplane. The diamond business must be even better than I thought.

After talking with the funeral home, I wondered how Carmen Cicogna would take the news.

"The director of the mortuary says that it will be day after tomorrow before they can deliver the remains. He offered an explanation that made sense. There was no use arguing the point."

"Well, if there is nothing we can do--"

Putting more wood on the fire, I wondered what I was going to do to entertain this woman for two more nights. Company was not something I am used to.

"I like it here," she said dreamily, curling up on the couch, closing her eyes like a cat. "It's peaceful."

At two o'clock, I called Shack. He said he was on the way to put out hay, wanted to get through early, before the weather worsened. He'd come by after that.

"So tell me about the diamond business. How did you get involved with DeBeers?"

"Could I have a glass of water?"

"Sure."

She took the glass, smiled. "My involvement in the industry came quite by accident. I was studying Economics at the University of Florida and one of my classmates was the granddaughter of Gladys Oppenheimer, the matriarch of the family that controls DeBeers. Raquel and I became friends and took an apartment together off campus. She invited me to London for summer vacation. I met the whole family, and after we graduated from college, we went to Miami, entered Grad-school and got MBAs. She was going into the family business in London, and arranged a job for me in New York. I learned the business from the ground up, eventually taking over the East Coast."

"Does DeBeers really control the diamond world?"

"We very carefully regulate the distribution of our inventory."

"Seems an easy thing, with no competition. Or if competition pops up, you smack them down. Like the Arkansas mine."

"We erred with that decision. But the man would not do business with us. We had to protect our interest."

"You personally met with the man?"

"I only met him once, and the meeting was brief."

"Pontius Pilate only met Jesus once. A great deal of treachery can be accomplished in one brief meeting."

She set up on the couch, looked at the fire. "He could be a billionaire today if he'd listened to me. Instead, he chose to keep lying." She turned, stared at me. "I don't fear men for the lies they tell, but for the fact that they appear to believe them."

"So you shut him down."

"Yes."

"I'm sorry if I seem accusatory. The pilots that flew for that company lost their jobs when it went out of business. They were friends of mine."

"A lot of people get hurt because of stubbornness."

"It must be nice to know your company is so secure."

"Oh, but it isn't. We are scared to death of two things. The Russians have billions of diamonds stored away. If they were to release them all at once, it would destroy the entire industry. We cannot control the Russians." She sat back on the couch.

"The other threat?"

"Man-made stones. Technology has reached a point that one carat diamonds can be produced within forty-eight hours in small machines. Stones so perfect that even nature doesn't produce them in abundance. Since they are made the same way as those produced in the earth, they are undetectable. We cannot sit on our laurels."

Shack drove up with Rose in tow. It was a good thing, because I was not being nice to my guest.

Rose and Shack stood in front of the fire.

"I can't get my butt warm. Shack won't fix the heater in his old truck." She rubbed her rear end vigorously, unconcerned as to how it might look to others. Looking at Carmen, "How's he treating you? He can sometimes be a little abrupt."

"Mr. Leicester has been the perfect gentleman."

"Yeah, that's him, alright. Always the perfect gentleman." Looking at me. "Would the perfect gentleman make a pot of coffee for his guests?"

"Coming up." I was glad to have something to do.

Shack followed me into the kitchen. "Rose told me all I need to know. When's she leaving?"

"Looks like day after tomorrow. There was a delay at the funeral home getting the bodies ready for transport."

"How much danger you in? Is it a real threat?"

"It's real, but I have no way of knowing how it will come, or even if it will. We'll just have to stay alert."

"I hear that."

"Looks like we are in for some weather tonight," Rose said as she helped pour the coffee. "Weather channel says we might get some snow."

"Long as we don't get heavy ice." Shack said.

The wind and rain, mixed with sleet, started in earnest. Rose and Shack decided to leave before it got too messy.

"I'd invite you all to dinner, but it doesn't look like a good night to be out and about. We'll check on you tomorrow."

The weather did get worse. The temperature went below freezing and we lost the electricity an hour later.

Chapter Seventeen

Screams woke me. I grabbed my magnum from the nightstand, noticing the electricity was back on. The clock was flashing midnight. I had no idea what time it is, only that it is after daylight. Running to the other bedroom, I find the door open, but no one there. In the kitchen, Carmen is standing, looking out the windows.

"Sorry, I screamed with delight when I saw the snow. It must be six inches deep." Looking at me, she suddenly said, "Oh, my goodness, you don't have any clothes on, and you are holding a gun."

My hands shook as I dressed. How could someone react so childishly to a few inches of snow? It was a pleasant sight, though. The cold front was gone, the wind calm, and the woods pristine.

After breakfast, Carmen wanted to walk in the snow. I fished around in the closet until I found a pair of rubber boots that would fit her, and we started down to the pond on the west side of the cottage. We had to pass through a small scope of hardwood and pine and, I have to admit, the scenery was breathtaking. When one walks in this country, one approaches a comprehension of why description crumbles to cliché. Unspoiled snow-covered land is like music, for it resembles nothing but itself. To appropriately describe it is why we have poets.

It was colder than I realized. It needles its way into your pores. It is like a torturer finding out the secrets of your body. Carmen shivers, but does not complain. We see animal tracks in the snow around the edge of the pond, but the water is frozen and nothing drinks.

Back at the cottage, we built a fire. Carmen warms in front of the flames.

"That was wonderful. I haven't seen such beauty in my life. It was so quiet. No wonder you like living here. Snow in the city is simply a messy nuisance, but out here--I could get used to this."

"Yes, everything goes out of fashion very quickly, except living in God's country."

She looked at me rather oddly, and smiled.

"There is some paperwork I need to attend too, would you like something to read?"

"If there is something you recommend."

"I'm not familiar with your taste in literature, but for a cold winter day, I know just the book."

Going back to my small library, I retrieved a signed first edition of *The Shadow of the Wind*, by Carlos Ruiz Zafon. Handing it to her, I said, "Anyone who enjoys novels that are scary, erotic, touching, tragic, and thrilling will love this. It is set in Barcelona in 1945, and is about someone systematically destroying every copy of a book titled--what else--*The Shadow of the Wind*. I found it an epic story of murder, madness, and doomed love."

"I'm sold. Interrupt me only for lunch." She laughed, curled up on the couch and started to read.

Leaving her with the book, I went to my small office and proceeded with some billing long overdue. The sun was bright, and reflecting off the snow giving the inside of the room an ethereal glow, as if somehow everything was lighted from within. I could smell the pleasant aroma of wood smoke from the fire. She was right, this diamond broker, living here was something one could get used too.

The phone rang, breaking my rural Eden-like experience. "Jay Leicester."

"Would you like to fly a charter today?"

"Earl? I'm not listed on your certificate as a Part 135 Charter Pilot. What's going on?"

"Yes, Mr. Williams, that's correct, a local flight over northern Newton County. A man is here from South America who wants to survey some land. I thought maybe since you know the area so well you'd be the best for the job. He has a map with the area that he wants to look at circled."

"My farm is at the center?"

"That's correct, Mr. Williams."

"Is he alone?"

"Yes. You can use the Cherokee Six."

"I'll be there in forty-five minutes. How's the snow situation?"

"We are fully operational."

"Thanks, Earl."

"Yes, Mr. Williams. Your passenger is waiting."

Sitting back in my chair, I began to think this through. Very good of Earl to be so alert. Who was this person from South America? Was he making a recon of my farm for some evil purpose, or was he simply surveying timberland. There have been a lot of foreign companies buying tracts of timber in the south. I'd flown some of the surveys myself. I spent a month flying section lines for a chemical company out of Mexico that bought all the pine stumps over vast square miles of Mississippi, Alabama, and Florida land. They hauled them to a plant and made over a hundred products from them. But if this had something to do with the CIA operation, did the man know what I looked like? Why would he need to overfly my farm? They already dropped two people out of an aircraft into my field. They knew where it was. I guess the only way to find out was to fly him around.

"Carmen, I have to run down to Meridian. Something has come up that needs my attention. Would you like for me to take you to Rose's house, or call her to come and stay with you?"

She looked up from her book, thought for a moment. "If it's alright, I'd like to stay here and read. B.W. can keep me company and I know where the firewood is. I'll be fine."

"There's plenty of food in the fridge. The wine cellar is just off the kitchen. Feel free to select anything to your taste. I should be back before dark. If you need something, Rose's number is on the table beside the phone."

. . .

Walking into Sander's Flying Service, I spotted a small man with dark hair and a pencil-thin mustache sitting in a chair. Earl came out from the back and introduced us.

"This is Bill Williams, your pilot."

He stood, reached out and took my hand. It was like a steel vise had me in its grip. It was painful.

"Fermin Velazquez, Captain. You have kept me waiting for over an hour. Could we please go?"

"Sorry, Senor Velazquez, the snow slowed traffic. If you will show me the route you wish to take, I'll file a flight plan and we can be on our way. Mr. Sanders will bring the aircraft from the hangar."

The little man retrieved a briefcase almost as big as he was, and unfolded an old aeronautical chart that had a big red circle encompassing most of northern Newton county and the southern and western part of Neshoba county. "I want to cover as much of this area as we can. You are familiar with the country? Can we fly low, two hundred feet?"

"We can do that. What is it exactly that you are looking for?"

The small man looked at me with a sly, almost wicked grin. "I am seeking a rustic location to build a high-class whorehouse, Captain. What is it to you what is my business? You are hired to fly me over the area. That is your only concern."

"Well, Senior, if you were looking for whiskey stills, I'd fly a bit higher. If you are looking for cattle rustlers, no one steals cows with six inches of fresh snow on the ground. However, if you are truly looking to build a house of ill repute, I can tell you from experience that what I know of the ladies in this area, you will have to operate the business by hand for awhile."

The little man laughed out loud. "Ah, Captain. A man with a sense of humor. I like that. Let us fly. I will tell you of my true reason for the survey."

After a thorough, though quick preflight due to the cold, we sat in the Cherokee while the engine warmed. Fermin Velazquez showed me his chart again and explained that he was working for an oil company surveying land where they had recently acquired the mineral rights. With the price of a barrel of oil over one hundred and forty dollars, old leases were being revisited. The circled area on the map was land where they wished to buy new leases, sections where owners to the mineral rights could not be located, and he wanted to see if any wells were being drilled.

"I thought the county kept records of landowners?"

"True, but people die and heirs live elsewhere. Some have sold the mineral rights to other companies. It gets complicated."

"How much you paying an acre?"

"We are prepared to offer five hundred per acre for a ten year lease."

"Why do you think there is oil in these parts? I thought the Little Creek Oil Field, centered around McComb," I pointed to the small town on the map, "Was as far north as it went."

"We have geology reports that this area, one we call Stag Horn Field, is full of oil. The problem has been that it is deep, well over thirteen thousand feet. Technology has been developed to drill to that depth, but it is extremely expensive. However with the price of oil what it is today, it is now profitable to drill to that depth."

"Five hundred and acre, huh? Not bad."

"Do you know someone in the area with land, Captain?"

Doing some quick calculations, I figured my two hundred acres would bring ten grand. I wondered if I owned the mineral rights?

An hour and a half later we landed back at the Meridian Airport. Senior Fermin Velazquez did not shoot me, throw me out of the airplane, nor was he involved with Pineiro's gang in Venezuela, nor with al Qa'ida, Iran or Iraq, or terrorism. He worked for an oil company looking for oil leases. A card he gave me listed a local phone number where he could be contacted if I knew anyone who wished to lease their mineral rights.

I thanked Earl Sanders for his alertness, and promised to send him a bill for the pilot service. He laughed, waved me away and said that the check would be in the mail. Heading back to the cottage in the woods, I suddenly had a queasy thought. What if Carmen Cicogna was not who she said she was, had swapped identities with her sister. I had a case like this a few years ago. I had been fooled then, but not again.

Turning off the gravel road onto the terrace row that led to the cottage, I started to think about the best way to determine the true identity of Carmen Cicogna, and why it was that I was suspicious she'd swapped identities with her sister, Marina. No, now I was confusing myself. Why would Marina have become Carmen? Maybe to save her own life. She knew she would be killed and sacrificed her sister instead. But she would have had to hate her a lot. Maybe Carmen became pregnant with Muhib Bahri's baby and Marina was jealous. The identity switch would have to have occurred before we flew the DC-4 to Valera, but the father was along. He would have known his own daughters apart. This line of thinking was illogical. Maybe I'm becoming paranoid in my old age. However, if Marina was working with the terrorist and had decided to become a martyr then she could have been sent to kill me. Women are strapping explosives to themselves and killing innocent men, women, and children everyday in Iraq. But then why didn't she do it last night? Ah, this is too insane.

Parking beside the cottage, I walked upon the porch. Through the window, I could see Carmen sitting on the couch, but she was slumped over to one side. She looked as if she were dead. I could see the fireplace. The fire was out. Lunging through the door, B.W. raised up on the couch and looked at me as if I had gone mad. Carmen opened her eyes, sat up, the book she was reading, The Shadow of the Wind, fell from her lap to the floor.

"Oh, you're back. I seem to have fallen asleep."

"Who are you?"

"What?"

"Are you Carmen Cicogna or your sister, Marina? Tell me the truth."

"I don't understand. What are you--Oh, you think we may have swapped identities for some evil purpose. You are intelligent, Jay. But one must not let imagination overwhelm logic. Hand me that bag." She pointed to a large handbag beside a chair.

Handing it to her, I put my hand inside the pocket of my jacket and fingered the magnum. If there were explosives in the bag, then it wouldn't matter, I thought foolishly, a little too late. Well, it had been a confusing day.

She took out a photo of her and Marina, a close up clearly showing their different features. Then she handed me a Florida driver's license with her photo on it. The difference was obvious.

"Satisfied?"

"Yes, I'm sorry. It pays to be careful, though."

She bent down and picked up the book. "This is an amazing read. I'm over half way through and can't wait to finish it. There can be few more enticing-sounding places than the *"cemetery of forgotten books."*

Rebuilding the fire gave me some time to collect my thoughts. Waking to screams, Earl Sanders calling about a South American wanting to overfly my farm, and memories of sisters, one who was truly evil and swapping identities with the good one, almost costing me my life. All this had my brain in tilt mode.

From the couch, Carmen closed the book, picked up B.W. and sat him in her lap. "Do not worry, Jay. I will not berate you for thinking I was Marina. I do not berate people, I berate ideas. A lot of good people have bad ideas."

"How kind of you," I said with more sarcasm than intended.

For the rest of the afternoon both Carmen and my cat treated me with the hushed deference usually reserved for convalescents or lunatics. Turning on the stereo, I put in a CD from the seventies titled, The Outlaws. It had Willie Nelson, Jesse Colter, Waylon Jennings, and Tompall Glaser belting out country and western songs that made the listener want to dance, drink, or fight. Turning the volume up, the loud music gave life to the cottage, the sound passing through in anguished, ragged waves. B.W. went and hid under the bed.

At five o'clock the funeral home called and said they could bring the two coffins to the airport at noon tomorrow.

By the time dark enveloped this country like black ink, my disposition had improved and I began to wonder what to feed my houseguest. She finished the book, gently closed it, and stared at the fire.

After a time, she looked at me, and as if quoting from memory, said, "The last sentence in that book is so poignant about life. *"Like figures made of steam, father and son disappear into the crowd--their steps lost forever in the shadow of the wind."* It makes me want to cry. Thank you for sharing this with me. I will remember it forever."

"Zafon writes like Gabriel Garcia Marquez meets Umberto Eco meets Jorge Luis Borges for a sprawling magic show."

Carmen laughed, clapped her hands together. "Yes, yes. That's it exactly. I'm surprised you read so many Latino/Spanish writers."

"Good writing is easy to read. It makes little difference to me the country of origin. Besides, there is little to do in these woods in the winter."

"You don't have a girlfriend?"

"Not at the moment. The last one ran off to Seattle with a banker."

"That is hard to believe."

"She wanted more than I could give. I'm not good at long term commitment."

Carmen looked hard at me. "I'm getting hungry. Do you have anything to eat? Maybe a good bottle of wine?"

"Do you like lamb?"

"I do."

"There are some two inch chops that have been marinating for a couple of days. We can oven-grill them and find a good Pinot Noir to accompany."

"Wonderful. Can I see your cellar?"

She spent almost an hour looking over the small, eclectic wine collection. She knew a great deal about wine. Maybe more than me, but then I'm no expert.

An appreciative client sent me a case of Burgundy for recovering an aircraft he'd sold to a building contractor who went belly up, but kept flying the plane without paying for it. We had to steal it one dark and stormy night from a hangar in San Diego. It was a fun night. The wine was a 2005 Bonnes-Mares Grand Cru from Domaine G. Roumier. I had not tried it, though most wine writers lauded it, both for the vintage and the Domaine.

The lamb was wonderful and the Burgundy excellent. It was dense with ripe black fruit--plum, blackberry, and black currant--along with mineral and spice.

Carmen looked at the wine through candle light, swirled it in the glass, smelled the aroma, and tasted the brilliant ruby-colored liquid. "This starts out lush and silky. The tannins are there, but discreet and supportive, letting the fruit take center stage. It shows great freshness and length as the complex fruit washes over the palate."

"Goes good with the lamb, too."

She sat her glass carefully on the table. Her deep, penetrating eyes glaring at me. "You are a strange man sometimes, Mr. Leicester. You have a flair for the understatement. It can be annoying at times."

"Maybe I'm simply trying to keep life real."

"Yes, maybe. But I wonder--"

After dinner, I poured glasses of a vintage Graham Port and served some Stilton cheese that needed eating. We sat in front of the fire. It was an awkward time, as we didn't have much to talk about. We knew this was the last night we'd be in each other's company.

Taking one of my Charlemagne cigars from the humidor, I asked if she minded if I smoked.

"Please, I love the smell of a good cigar."

"These are made in Miami." That wasn't true, now, but it was at one time. The factory moved to the Caribbean.

More awkward silence.

"Could we go look at the stars?"

"It's cold out."

"We won't stay long."

Standing on the south side of the porch, we had an unobstructed view of the sky.

Pointing to the constellation Orion, she said, "That's the only one I recognize."

"Yes, it is obvious." Our breaths formed little clouds of vapor that quickly disappeared like ghosts.

"You a religious man?"

"Jesus is the way, the truth and the life."

"The Bible tells us how to go to heaven, but not how the heavens go."

I didn't say anything, flicked the ashes off the cigar.

"We used to go out in the company's boat on calm nights from Miami. We would shut the engines off and let the Gulf Stream carry us along for hours. The speed of the current seemed to match that of the rotation of the stars, giving us the illusion that we were suspended in the sky watching the earth turn."

I tried to imagine what she was describing, but had trouble wrapping my mind around the concept.

"Can we go inside? I'm getting cold."

"Sure," I said, putting my arm around her shoulder.

We both stood in front of the fire warming. Carmen looked up at me, placed both hands on my shoulders. The dark, blueberry-colored eyes glistened in the flickering flames.

"I am tired, Jay Leicester. I will retire, now. We will have breakfast in the morning, then you can drive me to the capital city and the airport."

"Sleep well, Carmen Cicogna."

She kissed me lightly on the cheek and disappeared into the spare bedroom. I heard the door lock click shut.

·   ·   ·

The snow was almost gone, melting fast in the sun as the temperature climbed into the fifties. The drive to the Jackson International Airport was messy. Though the highway was clear of snow, it was slushy, wet, and slick.

We buzzed our way through the gate and drove directly out to the Boeing Business Jet. The auxiliary power unit was running, the crew standing by. An attendant met the car, informed Carmen that the cargo was loaded, and that they were ready for departure.

She turned to me. "Would you like to come aboard, look around?"

"No thank you. I'm familiar with the BBJ, have flown a number of them."

"I guess this is good-bye, then." She hugged me. "Thank you for hosting me. If you ever find that 'right' woman and want to give her a diamond, I know where you can get a good deal on a perfect blue-white."

She turned, climbed aboard without looking back.

I moved the car outside the security fence and watched them taxi away from the ramp. I did not stay to watch the takeoff. Instead, I headed for the silence of the woods.

Chapter Eighteen

Leaving the airport, I decided to drive over to Banner Hall, a tall, four-story building located in north Jackson across Interstate Highway fifty-five from Highland Village shopping center, an upscale mall that has been in operation for forty years. Banner Hall houses one of the top four independent bookstores in the United States, *Lemuria Books*. It is owned by John Evans, a friend who has guided my literary education since 1974. He has taught me much, introduced me to such literary giants from the last century such as Faulkner, Steinbeck, Fitzgerald, and Hemingway, and important writers of today, Jim Harrison, Cormac McCarthy, Tom Franklin, Charles Frazier, and Richard Russo, to name just a few. There was a new book by Randy Wayne White out titled *Black Widow*, and I wanted to pick up a copy.

To my disappointment, Evans was in Chicago attending the American Book Association convention. I bought a book titled, *Redemption Falls* by Joseph O'Conner that John was holding for me, along with a few others. On my way out of Banner Hall, I stopped by the Broad Street Bakery and bought a dozen loaves of assorted fresh-baked bread. The loaves freeze well and would last six months or more.

The drive back to my farm was pleasant, even though the roads were still messy, especially once off the interstate. At the cottage, I wrapped the bread, put it in the freezer, and settled down to look through the new books.

My cell phone made its ugly-sounding noise.

"She's here, she's here," the excited voice proclaimed in my ear.

"I didn't think she was coming so soon?"

"Well, she's here, now."

"I'll be there in half an hour."

Alella had arrived from Spain. Rose was beside herself. The nurturing instinct was a strong part of her personality. I had learned the hard way not to be negative in any way toward anything or anybody that she was caring for. It would be good to see Alella, and I was anxious to meet this young doctor with whom she had fallen in love.

Taking a quick shower, I dressed and headed for Rose's, thinking that an attack on my life as retribution for the death of the terrorist, Pineiro, by his loyal friends, could put a lot of innocent people at risk. It wasn't me who threw him out of the airplane, though I probably would have done what Hebrone did had the roles been reversed. It also dawned on me that the *Union Appeal*'s article on the two deaths in my field was due out tomorrow.

Alella met me at the door, barefoot, and looking even more beautiful than the last time I saw her. She threw her arms around my neck and hugged me tight. I held her away from me to look at her. She still wore her hair shoulder length, but it was no longer streaked with white. She was tanned, and her black eyes were large, round, and unsurprised. They were like looking at polished ebony and depthless as a toy animal. She still had that unexplained puffiness beneath them that was so alluring. She wore a sensualized intelligent look, her mouth provocative, the lips long and full.

"Senor Jay, I have missed you so much."

"Same here, kiddo. Welcome home. We must spend some time together, fly the Stearman down to the coast and enjoy the sun and sand."

"It is so cold, no? It is not so cold in Madrid."

"We'll pick a warm day."

Suddenly appearing behind Alella like an apparition was one of the most stunning creatures I've ever seen. Tall and gaunt, with silky black hair cropped short, she wore shiny, skin-tight leather pants. Her legs were long and slim and she, too, was barefoot. A white, loose, short-sleeve blouse covered square shoulders, and slim, muscled arms ended with hands that were wide with long delicate-looking fingers. The nails were clipped short and painted black. She stared at me with dark eyes that glistened with intelligence. Looking at her made me think that the intimate union between the beautiful, the true, and the real had once again been proved.

Alella turned. "Oh, Senor Jay, may I present Alicia Atienza. She came with me from Spain."

We shook hands, then she kissed me on both cheeks, a custom I despise in any nationality, however the perfume she wore made my legs tremble.

"Ah, so this is the famous Jay Leicester, the one responsible for my little Alella's rescue from the evil uncle. She speaks of you often with fondness. It is a pleasure to make your acquaintance, Senor." She spoke perfect English with no accent. Her bearing oozed a calm self-confidence, but there was no arrogance about her.

I studied the face; sharp, etched, perfect bone structure and precisely symmetrical. I once read that the most famous supermodels, actresses, and magazine cover girls have a face that if divided in half and the two placed together would match perfectly. So it was with this woman.

"It is my honor, Miss Atienza. Is this your first trip to America?"

"Yes. However I spent a few years in England. That is where I learned English. I am from Andalusia."

"Then you are familiar with Maribel Tomas?"

She looked at me in surprise. "My great grandmother on my father's side. How amusing that you know of her. You must be an aficionado of the corrida de toros?"

"I think that in the bullfight the Spaniard has found the most perfect expression for defining the human quality."

She laughed a deep-harsh chuckle. "Spain is the only country where death is the national spectacle."

It was my turn to laugh.

Looking at Alella, but talking to me, she said, "Then you also know of Cochita Citron?"

"I am familiar with her."

"She was my great aunt on my mother's side, God rest her soul. If you understand Andalusian culture, Senor Leicester, you would know the great accomplishments of those two women who fought the bulls."

"We must have that conversation. Please, call me Jay."

"Okay--Jay. I look forward to many conversations with you."

Alella had been standing off to the side with an expression that seemed a little anxious.

"You arrived sooner than I expected?"

"We had a month break over the holidays. There were some important decisions to be made and I needed to talk about them to Rose."

"You're not pregnant?"

Alicia laughed.

"No, I am not."

"Well, it's wonderful to have you here. Where is Rose?"

"She is in the kitchen."

I found her elbow-deep in flour, preparing to fry chicken.

"Jay, I'm glad you're here. You will stay for supper?"

"Sure. If you've got enough?"

She looked at me as if that was the dumbest thing I ever said. "Did you see Alella? Doesn't she look wonderful? Spain and college must be good for her."

"She said she's not pregnant." Rose turned and looked at me. "She is lovely as ever. I met her roommate, Alicia."

"Roommate? That's not her roommate. That's Doctor Alicia Atienza."

"You mean--but I thought? Oh, my, my."

"Now, Jay. I don't want you reacting in some stupid homophobic way."

"Just a minute, Rose English. I don't give a rat's ass about what her sexual preference may be. I was simply amused to learn our little Alella was batting for the other team. With everything she went through with the uncle, it doesn't surprise me."

"It doesn't have anything to do with the uncle or anything that happened to her in Mexico. She was born with her sexuality, had no control over it."

"You've discussed this with her?"

"I am her mother."

"That's why you were so upset about the letter she sent from Madrid. You thought Alicia Atienza was a man."

"But it all worked out, didn't it?"

"Seems so. Did she say why they came early?"

"Not yet, but I think it has to do with Doctor Atienza and her residency. Alella probably wants to move with her to whatever city the hospital is located in. It would mean transferring from the University of Madrid. I'm sure she'll get around to the discussion when she's ready."

"What are you going to tell her?"

"She's a grown woman, Jay. She can make her own decisions. I will advise her to finish her education, get a degree. It's important for her future. That's all I can do."

"If you need me to talk to her, let me know."

"Thanks. I can always count on you."

"Have you two finished discussing my love life and my future?" Alella stood in the kitchen door, arms crossed under her breasts.

Rose washed her hands, dried them on a towel, and went and hugged her neck. "We love you so much. We only want what is best for you. And know this, Alella, whatever your choices in life, we support you and love you. Never forget that and never doubt it."

"Senor, Jay. You feel the same?"

I went and took both of her hands in mine. "There are no absolutes in this world, Kiddo, but I absolutely feel exactly as Rose. As far as your young doctor, I am impressed and look forward to getting to know her much better."

"You both make me so happy. I will go tell Alicia all is well with my family." She went back into the living room.

Going up behind Rose, I put my arms around her waist. "It almost feels like we're married."

She pulled away. "Get away from me. There are two things that you will learn in life that are, as you say, absolutes. One of them is that you and I being married will never happen."

"What's the other?" I asked, smiling.

"None of your business."

During dinner, Alella confirmed what Rose suspected. Doctor Atienza's residency was at the Hospital Ramon y Cajal in San Sebastian. There was a good university there and Alella would continue with her education.

"Ah, Donostia. (The Spanish word for San Sebastian.) I know the city well. Spent two weeks there in the Nineties working with a corporate flight department that was transitioning from Spain to America. The Barrio of the *Old Quarter* was my favorite. The Basilica church of Santa Maria and the Municipal museum of San Telmo, along with the church of San Vicente are places that survived the devastating fire of 1813 that wiped out the rest of the city. These are magnificent buildings and worth the effort to visit. I remember the Gros district was where the finest restaurants and Tapas bars were located. Some of the best food in all the world can be found there, not to mention the ocean views and beaches. You will love San Sebastian."

Alicia looked at me with a strange, enigmatic smile. "Yes, San Sebastian has the best surgical residency program in all of Spain. I am very lucky to have been accepted from over two hundred applicants."

"Well, you have the hands for it."

She looked at her hands as if seeing them for the first time. She opened and closed the long delicate fingers as if milking one of Rose's cows. "Yes-- were that it was only the hands."

We adjourned to the living room. Alicia and I sat beside each other on the couch. I could feel the warmth each time we touched and each time I felt her pull away. Her presence intoxicated me. She was the forbidden fruit and I felt guilty--this was Alella's companion. But, my god, she was beautiful, smart, and mysterious.

Going to the kitchen on the pretense of getting a drink of water, I returned and sat in another chair. For some reason, I felt it necessary to tell both of them about the recent events that had occurred. I went over the trip to Venezuela, the deaths of Marina Cicogna and her father, the possible threat on my life, and the *Union Appeal* article due out tomorrow. I wanted them to be informed in case something happened or they saw someone or something out of the ordinary.

"Senor Bullard--he was involved in this? Is that why he is dead?"

"No, Alella. Smash was not working with us on this case. His death was an act of nature." Looking at Rose. "You told her?"

"In a letter. They were friends and he was, after all, a part of this family."

"It's not a problem. I just didn't know. When are we going to do the memorial?"

"Day after tomorrow. Is that okay?"

"Sounds right."

We talked more about Alella and Alicia moving to San Sebastian and its location on the Bay of Biscay and its closeness to the border with France. Rose, having never traveled to that part of the world was the most interested.

At nine p.m., everyone seemed tired. The girls having traveled for two days were ready for some rest. I bid them goodnight and drove back to the cottage. After feeding B.W., who was sulking because I went to Rose's and left him alone, I turned on CNN to catch the late news before going to bed. Anderson Cooper, a news pundit, interrupted his usual coverage of Mama and Obama's fight for the Democratic nomination for the run for the White House, with breaking news about a corporate jetliner exploding over the Gulf of Mexico killing all aboard. The latest information was that a Boeing Business Jet belonging to the DeBeers Corporation had departed Jackson, Mississippi, enroute back to its headquarters in Miami and had just reached cruising altitude when the explosion occurred.

Grabbing my phone, I called a friend who worked as an air traffic controller at Memphis Center. He was home. "Jay Leicester. It's been a long time."

"The BBJ that blew up in the gulf, I need all the details. Can you help me?"

"I just saw the news flash on the t.v. What's your interest in the crash?"

"One of the people on board had been staying with me. I drove her to the airport to board the plane."

"God, Jay. I'm sorry. Let me make some calls. Memphis would hand the flight off to Jacksonville pretty quick, but maybe I can get you some altitudes and speeds, and if the crew reported any anomalies. Give me half an hour."

"Thanks. I'll be waiting."

Hanging up after giving him my phone number, I sat back in the chair. Boeing jets do not blow up, even with a rapid decompression or catastrophic engine failure. I had a queasy feeling in the pit of my stomach. The airplane should have been at cruising altitude long before reaching the gulf. There was no use speculating. I could only wait for the phone to ring.

It was hard not to think about why Carmen Cicogna's airplane blew up. If it happened out over the gulf, how did they know it was an explosion? Would the terrorists have known she was visiting me? She'd flown in to retrieve the bodies of her father and sister. Was she followed to my place? Did they-- the terrorist--think we met for some reason related to their failed nuclear plot? Or was this involved with their dirty bomb somehow? She'd stopped by Rose's house first looking for me. Would they think she's part of this?

I picked the phone up on the first ring.

"Leicester, here's what I was able to find out. There were handed off to Jacksonville Center before they crossed the coastline. Memphis had stopped their climb at flight level 290 due to crossing traffic. Jacksonville issued the climb to a cruising altitude of flight level 410. The last return showed them out of 350. Two boats witnessed the fireball and watched debris rain down. They called it in to the Coast Guard. There was no mention by the flight crew of any problem. I'm sorry, Jay."

"Thanks. You've been a lot of help."

Hanging up the phone, I thought of what could have caused this accident. Failing a wing falling off or a tail separating from the plane--the rudder problems with the Boeing 737 model had been resolved--there was only one other explanation. An explosive device with a pressure detonator. It was probably set to go off when the airplane reached thirty-five thousand feet. That meant the bomb was placed in an unpressurised area of the plane, or sophisticated enough to be placed in the cabin and blow when the cabin pressure reached maximum differential, which would be about 35 thousand feet. That way, it could have been brought aboard with catering, or a carryon bag, or placed in a casket. Either way, the results would be the same--a lot of innocent lives lost.

I called Rose.

Chapter Nineteen

Rising early, I made coffee and took a cup out to the front porch to check the temperature and weather. A copy of the *Union Appeal* was leaning against the door. I had no idea who delivered it. The sky was clear, the temperature in the forties. It was going to be a pleasant day.

True to their word, the *Union Appeal* ran an in-depth article describing the deaths of Marina Pineiro and her father. The manner from which they died was accurate, but the location well disguised, as was the person who discovered the bodies. The article went on to describe details of the on-going investigation by the Newton County and State authorities.

Picking up the phone, I called the paper. Bill Graham answered. "Good job. Thanks for keeping me anonymous. Runnels probably appreciates it, also."

"Word will leak out, Leicester. Count on it."

"Did you drop off a copy at my place this morning?"

"No. Your friend, Runnels was by early, picked up a few copies. Said he'd deliver one to you and Ms. English."

"Yeah, must have been Shack."

"News said something about a corporate airliner blowing up south of Pascagoula yesterday. Left Jackson bound for Miami. Knowing you're in the business, I wondered if you had any info on the event? Maybe knew somebody on board or the pilots?"

Did Bill Graham already have information that I didn't know about? Knew Carmen Cicogna stayed with me, and wanted to see if I'd offer up the story? Probably not. If he had, he'd just come out and tell me.

"Bill--"

"Yes?"

"You better come out and see me."

"Oh, my goodness. This has something to do with the threat on your life and the two deaths."

"Noon be alright?"

"I'll be there."

As soon as we hung up, the phone rang.

"You want me to come?"

"How'd you hear?"

"It's all over the news in Florida. Aardwolf is upset. He was close to the woman."

"Yeah. She was almost his daughter-in-law. She spent three days here. Seemed like a nice person. Did you know she supplied Bahri with the diamonds?"

"Aardwolf told me."

"You and him getting to be friends?"

"I don't get close to people."

"What about me?"

"What about you?"

"You're close to me."

"You're like my child, Leicester. You need taking care of. That's our job."

"Our?"

"Me, Rose and Shack."

"Any ideas on who and why they blew up the Boeing?"

"Who--the same ones that are coming after you. Why--I'm not sure. Give us some time."

"You better stay where you are. I'll be okay."

"If anything shows up down here, I'll let you know."

"Alella's home."

"Why now? Anything wrong?"

"Everything's fine. She's transferring to a university in San Sebastian to be with her new friend, Doctor Atienza, who starts a three year surgical residency at a hospital there."

"Is Rose in favor of the move?"

"If it's what Alella wants, Rose is for it. We're doing Smash's memorial tomorrow."

"Sorry I can't be there."

"Yeah, me too."

"Try not to get killed, Leicester. The wolf would miss you."

"Goodbye, Hebrone."

. . .

Bill Graham showed on time. I admire punctuality in a person. Shows intelligence, the antithesis of intellectual arrogance. He listened intently, making notes in a tiny notebook that folded over the top. He wrote with a maroon-colored Mont-Blanc fountain pen that cost more than a week's salary. I hope it was a gift. He asked the right questions and I was able to admire the clarity of his intellect, the breadth of his information, and the profundity of his knowledge, all which would bode him well in his chosen profession of journalism.

"How will they be able to tell it was a bomb rather than mechanical failure?"

"They will look for the black boxes first. Then it will depend on how widespread the wreckage and if any remains are recovered. You can bet that Boeing and General Electric, the engine manufacture, will do everything they can to determine why that plane went down."

"Tell me about the black boxes?"

"There are two. A Cockpit Voice Recorder that will let them hear the last thirty minutes of conversation between the flightdeck crew. If the pilots were experiencing a problem they can hear it and understand what action was taken, if any. The other box is the Flight Data Recorder. It shows thousands of flight parameter's concerning aircraft movement. The old FDR used only twelve parameters. The new digital boxes are amazing. Using the data, they can now create a computer simulator model showing the exact flight path and engine thrust settings of the last few minutes of flight. They are not black, by the way, but painted day-glow orange. You can ask me why they are called 'black boxes,' but I honestly do not know."

Graham looked at me with a wry grin, but said nothing. He capped his Mont-Blanc, sat back in the chair.

"We are doing a memorial tomorrow at the cemetery out on the blacktop. I'd like for the *Union Appeal* to be there. Maybe write a few words. He was a good friend."

"You talking about Andrew "Smash" Bullard?"

"Rose English."

"Yeah. She called Jack about covering it. One of us will be there. You were friends for a long time?"

"Ten years. A lawyer friend of mine introduced us. Smash was headed for big trouble, had an uncontrollable temper. Would go into black rages and no one could handle him."

"But you could?"

"We'd both played in the NFL, same position. I was older then Smash, and he respected that I didn't patronize him or treat him like scum."

"Was he on medication?"

"No. He was big, tough, mean, and he had a temper. He simply needed some direction, needed to be told no, you can't do that without serious consequences. Smash was smart, much more than I, in some areas. He needed to keep himself out of bars and beer joints where drunks wanted to challenge him. That's where he got into trouble. Beat a man to death in a bar on the coast. The local DA wanted to make a name for himself by sending Smash to prison. Thank God for security cameras. The video clearly showed who was the aggressor. Smash got probation. That's when we met."

"You had no problems with him?"

"None. We became friends. He worked well with me."

"What about Hebrone Opshinsky? How'd he get on with him?"

"The two men respected each other. I guarantee you each would have died for the other, without hesitation."

"Opshinsky coming to the memorial?"

"He's in Florida. Busy with something he can't turn loose."

"You mean the CIA?"

"Let it go, Bill."

"You know I can't run this story on the airplane crash the way you told it, especially with the Cicogna woman staying with you while she was here to retrieve the bodies of her sister and father found dead in your field. It would expose you and everything would be wide open."

"I know. You'll protect me as far as you can."

"We'll do our best. Maybe run the background story like we did this week, add in the unfortunate crash of the airplane with the sister come to retrieve the bodies of her kin. Should be a great human-interest thing. Keep our anonymous source secret."

"I wouldn't want Rose or Shack exposed to any danger."

"See you tomorrow at the memorial."

After Bill left, I thought about Marina Cicogna, her sister, father, about Muhib Bahri and Pineiro, and about Smash. We all die separately together. This seemed like a war. I heard Billy Graham--not the journalist, the renowned evangelist, say, "War does not increase the rate of death. It only accelerates it. The rate is always the same: 100%. We all die." I also remember reading about an English general who said, "Death is the enemy of life, at any age, with pain or without."

This was depressing. I grabbed a heavy coat and started out for a walk in the woods. Just as I hit the front porch, Shack drove up. "Where you headed?"

"For a walk, clear my head."

"It's winter, Leicester. Ain't nothing to see in the woods but dead grass. Come ride with me, we'll go look at some fine cattle."

"Then we'll be going to look at Rose's herd. Them scrawny things wandering around on your place certainly ain't nothing to look at."

It must have been providence, because this is just what I needed.

Shack drove his ratty old pickup slowly along the gravel road. Rose was right, the heater didn't work and the bare springs of the seat stuck you in the ass, but the motor purred like a Singer Sewing Machine. Shack was not into aesthetics. We turned off at the bottom of a steep hill, just before reaching a railroad spur that ran to town, into a two-rut lane leading into a field spotted with oak and sweetgum and shallow, spring-fed creeks with running water that was crystal clear. Even in the cold of December, it made one want to swim in it. Across the second creek, we pulled in among a hundred head of cattle that paid no attention to us. It was a fine looking herd. There was pride in Shack's voice when he talked about them.

We stopped in the field and he turned off the engine. The first thing to hit me was the smell. The winter air was crisp and clean, then you caught a whiff of the herd, a strong, pleasant odor, kind of like a horse that had been run hard and put up wet. It was a familiar aroma from my childhood on a diary farm. At least now I didn't have to break the ice on a water bucket to get a rag wet enough to wash the teats on a hundred and fifty head of milk cows at four-thirty in the morning. It was a hard life, but one I cherish and wouldn't trade for anything in the world.

"I was sorry to hear about the Cicogna woman."

"I should never have flown that DC-4 to South America."

"You start blaming yourself, I'm gonna think less of you."

"It's true."

"Yeah, and if you hadn't taught Smash how to sail, he wouldn't have drowned in the Atlantic Ocean during a storm."

"I appreciate what you're trying to do, Shack, but it's more complicated than that."

"You see that bull over there?" He pointed to a huge animal that had been eyeing us and seemed undecided what to do about it. "That bull is going to breed with one of those cows, and in the spring that cow is gonna calf. If all goes well the calf will fatten and I'll sell it and make a dollar. But if that cow dies giving birth through no fault of anything but God, who's to blame? The Bull? Me for bringing them together? We're all simply part of one big cattle operation. When shit happens and it does, no one's to blame."

"Like when you hung that Henderson fella from my oak tree and was going to put a 9mm bullet in his brain and Rose stopped you. That the kind of "big cattle operation" you talking about?"

"Sometimes you are a hardheaded s.o.b."

"I've been hanging around you and Rose English too long."

He laughed. Then he rubbed a stubble of beard on his hardened face and changed expression. "Are we gonna be in danger? Those friends of Pineiro coming after you? I read the two articles in the paper. It won't take a rocket scientist to work out a hit on your sorry ass. They already know where you live."

"Hebrone's looking into it from Florida. It's still a little puzzling why Pineiro's people are so sore about him dying. He was dead anyway, had his plan succeeded."

"Maybe he had another plan, or the original plan changed and his people didn't know about the dive-bomb into Walt's little playground."

"Interesting theory."

"All my theories are interesting. Just ask that old bull standing there." The bull stuck his tongue into this nose, turned and walked over to a group of cows.

We sat in silence, watching the cows, listening to the soft noise of the winter field. My depression seemed to disappear with the herd as they ambled toward the various feeders set strategically across the farm.

"You know why I like winter, Leicester?"

"There are a couple of risqué ideas running through my mind."

"No snakes."

"They are here, they're just denned up."

"I treat snakes like mosquitoes, dispose of them with one stroke of whatever weapon I got in hand."

"A man who knocked out a Brahma bull with his fist is bothered by a small thing like a snake. You know, some snakes do good."

"What good can a snake do except tempt Eve to screw up paradise?"

"They keep rats and rabbits in check."

"A good cat can do that."

"Snakes are smart."

"I guess you've measured their intelligence?"

"I've experienced it."

"Leicester, you can't spell snake, much less measure their ability to rationalize thought."

"At least I know how many poisonous species live in these woods."

"I reckon you gonna tell me there are more than the rattlesnake and the water moccasin?"

"There are four."

Shack looked out the window of the pickup like there might be a snake crawling on the ground. "Only ones I ever seen was a rattlesnake and water moccasin. What others you think there might be?"

"The Eastern Diamondback rattlesnake, the copperhead moccasin, the water moccasin, better known as the cottonmouth, and the coral snake."

"Both them moccasins are the same."

"No, they are not. True, they both have venom that is hemotoxic, but their temperament is a lot different."

"Their temperament? God, Leicester, snakes are snakes. They don't have mood swings."

"It's true. A cottonmouth will do everything in its power not to strike. I've nudged them with my boot, lightly stepped on their back, only to have them crawl away or lie perfectly still. When they do strike, especially if it's a defensive one, it may be a dry bite. They want to save their venom for prey, not waste it unnecessarily."

"Why in the world would any sane person nudge a water moccasin with their boot? Hebrone said you were a little nuts, now I believe him."

"I saw a herpetologist do it on t.v. I tried it, it worked. Now don't attempt that with a copperhead. They are mean and irritable creatures, and do not make dry bites."

"I guess you've experimented with copperheads, too?"

"No, but I did have an interesting encounter with one at the pond on the west side of the cottage one summer."

"I can't wait to hear this."

"It was in June, about noon, and hot. I was riding around the pond in my truck, looking at the water through binoculars, counting the turtle population, and seeing how thick they were getting. If the count were over fifty, I'd set a trap and relocate some to the creeks on the back eighty. A big copperhead eased off the dam into the water, working the edge of the pond. He was between five and six feet in length and thick as both my thumbs together. All I could see after he entered the water was his head and the wake he left. Loading my .22 cal rifle, I fired three shots at the head, which was no larger than a half-dollar. The snake disappeared. Glassing the edge again, I saw him surface twenty yards further along the bank. I fired three more times. He disappeared again, only to reemerge further around the pond. We repeated this until the copperhead made it all the way round."

"I believe you need some target practice. How many times did you shoot?"

"Twenty-seven."

Shack laughed.

"Then I got out and walked to the water's edge. Fifteen minutes later the snake stuck his head up on the far side and I shot at him again. He worked his way around and I continued to shoot. Suddenly he submerged and all was quiet for ten minutes. The water was glassy-smooth, the wind calm. I thought maybe I'd finally hit him."

"That's one hell-of-a story, but what does it have to do with snake intelligence? It seems to me like nothing but bad shooting."

"Well, I happened to look down and five yards out in the water from where I stood, that copperhead was raised up four inches out of the water sitting there staring at me. Before I could raise the rifle to fire, he submerged. A short time later, I saw him come out of the water, cross the dam, and disappear into the woods on the other side."

"So you're telling me that snake knew it was you shooting at him? Well, that's just an amazing tale of Leicester and the intelligent snake."

"That's not the end of this story."

Shack closed his eyes, leaned back on the headrest. "Ah, God. There's more."

There was more. I went on to tell how at the same time the next day, the copperhead and I had a repeat performance. My accuracy was like before, only this time the snake came quickly to where I stood and came out of the water towards me at tremendous speed. Something had told me to bring my 12-gauge shotgun. The Browning dispatched the copperhead, but the event convinced me that there was an innate intelligence in that animal.

Shack just shook his head at the tale. "What about the other one?"

"What other one?"

"You said there were four poisonous creatures."

"The coral snake. They are rare, but they are here, and they have a look-a-like, a king snake also crawling about. You do not want to confuse the two. The true coral has no fangs, and they are not aggressive, but they have a neurotoxic venom that is nasty."

"How would one tell the non-poisonous from the bad guy?"

"The color bands. Red next to yellow is the coral. There are some mnemonics if you wish to learn them. The most important: Red on yellow kill a fella."

"God, you're just full of intelligence. I may have to nickname you the "Snake."

"Nah, Kenny Stabler has that moniker."

Shack reached to turn the ignition on the truck, but stopped, and looked at me. "What scares you, Leicester? You have to be afraid of something. Spiders, are you frightened by spiders?"

"I like spiders. We only have two that are poison--"

"God--not another lecture. I just want to know what wakes you in the dark of night in a cold sweat?"

"Anybody taller than me. I'm intimidated by anyone I have to look up at to see their eyes."

"Ain't many people taller than you. Why would height have anything to do with it?"

"No clue."

"What makes you happy? Besides making love to all those women coming and going from that little cottage you live in."

"Flying. The joy of flight is a refuge from painful personal emotions. As I gain more experience, I do not think more of myself but less of others. Pilots, even so-called great pilots are wonderfully weak and timid. Flying is simple, direct, and learned. It takes a simple, direct, and learned person to command an airplane and crew."

Shack shook his head, started the engine. "I had to ask."

We drove back to my place and I got out.

"See you at the memorial in the morning, Leicester."

It wasn't until he turned onto the gravel road and headed to his cattle farm that I realized what he had done. He'd gotten me out of my depression. I'd bet Rose had something to do with this.

Chapter Twenty

It was a flyer's day, clear, cool, winds calm. Smash would have liked a day like this. I thought it important to conduct the memorial, though they are really less about death than the odd shapes life takes, the patterns that death allows us to see.

I picked up Rose, Alella, and Alicia in my car and we drove to the cemetery. Rose was dressed in a dark suit, the girls in identical black pantsuits with black, flat shoes. I wondered why they would have such clothes with them traveling all the way from Spain. But then women have always left me in a state of confusion when it comes to wardrobes.

There were more people at the cemetery than I expected. Shack and his wife were there. Both Jack Tannehill and Bill Graham from the *Union Appeal* stood off to the side. Many people from Rose's church, and a woman I recognized as the secretary to the Mayor were there. As we parked, she rushed the car to inform us that the Mayor was out of town and that she was there to represent him. Her name was Missy Applegate. She was a drab woman, middle-aged, hardworking, deliberate, and calculating. Her southern blood gave her the perfect temperament for dealing with obfuscatory Mississippi rednecks. She had never married, and was not known to date. I had only seen her from afar, but up close, she was a muscular, compact woman with wide shoulders, and an inordinately small waist. She knew how to dress to favor her figure. She also had that southern quality of doing the absolute best one can in order to rise to any occasion.

While Rose introduced the Mayor's secretary to Alella and Alicia, I walked over to look at the stone marker. It was cut from dark marble, the face shiny black with gold etchings outlining the shape in two parallel lines.

Smash's name, date of birth and death were in white letters with the following inscription:

> *For some we loved*
> *The loveliest and the best*
> *That from his vintage rolling time hath prest*
> *Have drunk their cup around or two before*
> *And one by one, crept silently to rest.*

This was familiar to me, however at the moment, I could not remember the author. Smash would have liked the inscription.

"You did good with the stone marker. I like the inscription," I said to Rose as she walked over to where I stood. "Smash would laugh at the lines, but he'd appreciate them."

"From the *Rubaiyat* of Omar Khayyam."

"Ah, now I remember. Much better than the one that I wrote."

"Gather everybody around, Jay. You have to say a few words."

"What? I haven't prepared anything. I thought we'd have a prayer. Where's your preacher?"

"He's conducting a funeral in town. Get on with it. Say something nice, and thank the folks for coming."

"People, would you gather around."

Rose, the girls, Missy Applegate, and Shack and his wife stood together. The rest moved in close.

"We'd like to thank all of you for coming out. Andrew "Smash" Bullard was a personal friend of mine. We worked together for ten years. Now, he has slipped the surly bonds of earth and dances the skies on laughter silvered wings. He has departed from this strange world a little ahead of us. That means nothing. For us old comrades, the distinction between past, present and future is only a stubborn illusion. Smash died doing what he wanted--"

There was a sudden screech of tires, the roar of vehicles with no mufflers, and the loud, boom box blare of country music. Two pickup trucks slid to a stop and four men got out and slammed the doors. All eyes turned and looked, aghast, at the interruption.

The four young men, two from each truck, approached our group, walking across other graves. One of them, the driver of the lead truck, was a huge man dressed in overalls, and a lined Levi jacket with no sleeves. He wore worn, dirty boots. He had long, thick curly black hair that hadn't been washed in a week, a large head, a flat pug nose, a thick neck, big scarred hands, and a grimy beard. His eyes were sunk deep, and dirt was ground into sun-blackened skin which shown like grease. The other three were smaller versions of him. It was still well before noon and all four were drinking Budweiser beer.

The big man, who appeared to be around thirty years old, took a big gulp of his beer, squashed the can and tossed it back over his shoulder toward his truck. It bounced off the hood. "We hear y'all are burying some Yankee nigger. Don't cater too much to planting niggers in our cemetery." He leaned back, placed both thumbs in the straps of his overalls in a defiant manner.

His companions echoed his sentiments. "Yeah, we don't want no nigger buried here."

We were all stunned. No one moved, or said a word. Then I heard the click of a camera shutter. Bill Graham was calmly taking pictures of them.

"Y'all hear what we said? Cat got y'all's tongue. Maybe y'all just a scared bunch of nigger lovers."

The first one of us to react was Missy Applegate. She walked straight up to the big man. "Will Hegewood, you shut your filthy mouth. Your mama raised you better than that. I know she did. You got no call coming around here saying things like this. For your information, we aren't burying anybody. We are having a memorial for a brave man who drowned. But you and your hooligans here wouldn't know the difference. It doesn't matter though, a man's got a right to be buried where ever he pleases. Now you pick up that beer can, get in them trucks and git out of here. And don't be stepping on those graves when you leave."

I heard Alicia Atienza shout, "Ole!"

None of the men said a word. They got back in the trucks and left, tires squealing. I looked at Shack and pointed toward my car.

"Let it go, Jay. Ain't none of them boys got birth certificates. They was shit from a cow's ass. Their presence sickens livestock."

A hundred yards away, near a tree line at the north west corner of the cemetery, stood a lone figure. He appeared to nod, then turn and walk away behind the church. I heard a car start and drive away. I would have sworn it was Hebrone Opshinsky. But it couldn't be.

Missy Applegate apologized to everyone for the actions of the men and promised to inform the Mayor who would see that they were punished.

I began to think about the four drunks at the cemetery. Thoughts and ideas often start as feelings without logic. I made a vow to meet them again. Somewhere, sometime.

Shack put a hand on my shoulder. "Ole Smash would have loved to be here today. He would have enjoyed it."

"Maybe he was here. Yes, maybe he was. Did you see that man standing across the cemetery?"

"Yeah, but he was too far away for me to recognize. You know who it was?"

"No, I just wondered if you saw him?"

I went over and spoke to Jack and Bill. Thanked them for coming and asked if I could have a copy of the photos they took today. Graham promised to e-mail me a set.

We drove back to Rose's house. Shack and his wife stopped by. Rose made coffee while Alella and Alicia changed into jeans and sweaters. I could not help but look at the gazelle-like legs of Alicia. She had a magnificent body honed, no doubt, by a strict exercise routine. I wondered if she was bi-sexual. Admonishing myself for the second time about carnal thoughts toward her, I again remembered she was Alella's partner.

Coffee was poured and all gathered in the living room.

"If you want honey, you know where it is."

"Yes, mother."

"I am not your mother."

"My mother would have brought me the honey."

Alicia laughed.

Going into the kitchen, I added a dollop of the brown viscous sweetener to the coffee and wondered why honey did not spoil. I think it has something to do with it being anhydrous. It's a research project for a cold winter day.

Back in the living room, Shack was rather quiet. I have noticed this is true when he is around his wife. My suspicion is that she is the true genius of the family and that he learns much from her. I have always found her to be a pleasant woman with a vast literary knowledge. She, like her husband, does not suffer fools gladly. The two seem a perfect union. How lucky, I thought, to have neighbors like them.

"Did you see the way the Mayor's secretary confronted the drunks?" Alella said. "All the men stood around, but she was not afraid."

It was a true statement, and I was suddenly ashamed.

"Yes, Missy Applegate is not an appeaser." Shack's wife said.

"What is an "appeaser?" Alella asked.

"An appeaser is someone who feeds the lions, hoping they will eat her last." Shack's wife answered.

Alicia clapped her hands and laughed. "That is a true statement. The lady would have made a good fighter of the bulls."

Shack looked up at the mention of bulls.

"Doctor Atienza's great grandmother and great aunt were bullfighters in Spain. Females in the ring are very rare in that country." I said.

Shack looked hard at Alicia. "You ever do that? Fight bulls?"

"I have trained with the cape, but my true interest is with medicine."

Alella stood. "Alicia and I are going for a run."

"How long?" Rose asked.

"Maybe an hour. We will run the swamp road all the way to the end. I want to show Alicia the back country."

"Take my cell phone. One of you may fall or hurt an ankle."

"She's a surgeon, Mama Rose. We will be fine."

"Take the phone."

Alicia stood, shook hands with Shack and his wife. "It was nice to meet you, Mr. and Mrs. Runnels. I hope to see you again while I'm in America."

Alella took the phone and the two left out the front door. The swamp road, as the locals called it, is a county road named the, *Ray Richardson Road*. It was two miles of true rough terrain, but is kept up fairly well by the county road crews. Alicia would get a good idea of rural Mississippi.

Shack and his wife left soon after. Rose and I sat at the kitchen table.

"I like Missy Applegate. She handled that situation with the boys rather well."

"She's a fine woman. Grew up with Hegewood's mama, as I did. He turned out to be a thug. I want you to let it go. You and Shack don't go doing nothing stupid like with that Henderson fella."

"Okay. But if I happen to run across them…"

"Go home. Worry about terrorist shooting at you. Leave those sorry rednecks alone. They'll get what's coming to them soon enough."

"It was a good thing, the monument and memorial to Smash. I thank you."

"We do not want to forget. Ever. Now go."

. . .

An hour after I got home, the phone rang.

"They have not returned and there is no answer to the cell phone. I'm worried."

"I'll pick you up in five minutes."

Grabbing my jacket, I checked that the magnum was there, and ran for my truck. The thoughts running through my mind were fast, furious, and frightening.

"They were going through the swamp road," I said to Rose. "Maybe they decided to continue around to the north, out to the blacktop, then around by Shack's place. That would be about five miles and would take a little longer. We'll make the drive and look."

"Why is Alella not answering the cell?"

"I haven't a clue, but try not to worry."

Worry--how could we not worry. Terrorist had already killed two people on my farm, and threatened to kill me. Somebody blew up a Boeing Business Jet, the people on board connected to me. The four drunken rednecks from the funeral this morning could be a threat to two young women running along a desolate backcountry gravel road.

We turned onto the *Ray Richardson Road*. It was narrow, crooked, and ran downhill through the swamp bottom, across a railroad track, then up a hill with switchbacks, passing through cattle fields, and finally dead ended into another gravel road. If they had turned north they would run into Road 210, a paved county road that ran east and west. A mile and a half west, they would have turned south on a gravel road that lead past Shack's place and on to Rose's house. That was the route I hoped they traveled.

There was no sign of them on the swamp road. At the dead end, I turned north. Rose hollered to stop. She jumped from the truck. Her cell phone was lying beside the road. Before I could tell her not touch it, she had it in her hand.

"It's turned off, Jay."

"I have an idea. Call Shack and see if he saw them pass his house."

"You do it, I'm too upset."

Dialing the number, I thought that Rose had never come unglued before. But she was close at the moment and, again, it was my fault.

"Shack, Alella and Alicia have not returned from their run. Did you see them pass by your place?"

"Okay, thanks."

"They are at Shack's house having coffee."

We sat in a truck in the middle of a gravel road and hugged each other in relief. Tears rolled down both our faces.

We picked up the girls and drove them home.

"I am sorry, the phone must have fallen from my back pocket while we were running and I did not notice it."

"Not a problem, Alella. The important thing is that you are safe."

"It is dangerous country we were running through, Senora?" Alicia asked.

"It can be. When you were late, we became concerned."

"We have dangerous roads in Spain. Only there it is the Basque people blowing up things. They want to have independence from the mother country."

"Yes, well we have a different kind of danger here."

Rose was right, I thought, a different kind of danger. A neighbor, a newcomer to this idealic country, who brought unwanted complications, the kind that could get them killed.

Chapter Twenty-one

Another dream: I slide under the murky pond water, but there is a ribbon of light. My fingers feel the muddy silt on the bottom. It is strange and cold. Water muffles everything, except my own breathing. I hear the screams. I have heard many people die. It gives me no pleasure, never did. These screams seem to be coming from high up and they are the agonal sounds of women.

I wake to wind blowing strong. Then the rain came down heavy and with the hard wind it seemed even heavier. It was going to be a nasty day.

After a shower, I made coffee, built a fire, and fed B.W. Sitting in front of the flickering flames, I turned on my laptop computer to check the e-mail. There was a dozen photos from Graham, all depicting the memorial service. There were good close-ups of the four drunks. Meeting Mr. Hegewood and his running mates again was going to be a real pleasure. There was also a photo of Missy Applegate, a shot from behind as she was admonishing the drunks. She had a nice body. There was a time in my life when I would have thought that admiring the rear end of a fifty or sixty year old woman was exploiting the elderly. I have not entertained that conceit in some years, but if I had, Missy Appelgate's ass would have ended it.

As soon as I shut the computer off, the phone rang. It was Hebrone.

"Please tell me you were not at the memorial service yesterday."

"Okay. I was not there. I have some information on the BBJ explosion."

"I'm listening."

"Aardwolf and his people have uncovered an odd organization operating in the Tampa area that calls itself *The Brethren Club*. It is run by a man named Donald Tarrants. We're not sure if that's his real name, but we know him by no other."

"What does this "odd" organization do, supply clowns for children's birthday parties?"

"You want to hear this?"

"I'm sorry, it's raining here."

"It is a brokerage for terrorism."

"What does that mean, exactly?"

"They put people together. You need an assassin; they'll arrange the meet. You need a bomb maker, they know one. If you want to build a portable nuclear device, they know someone to teach you."

"How big is this organization?"

"Not possible to know who's a member or who's temporary, being that they're a brokerage."

"You got information from *The Brethren Club* how?"

"We had a talk with Tarrants."

"He just volunteered information?"

"It was a special kind of interrogation."

"Ah, one that was not video taped."

"Pineiro's people wanted to be put in touch with someone who could get a device on board DeBeer's Boeing. Tarrants arranged the meet. That's as far as his involvement went. We think you need to look at the funeral home."

"Is that a guess or you know something?"

"It makes sense. Catering would be delivered to the aircraft, not placed on board. The flight attendant or a crewmember would have handled it and notice an unusual device. That only leaves the cargo."

"Thanks. You sure you weren't at the memorial?"

The line went dead.

Pouring more coffee, I sat back down in front of the fire. B.W. sat on the stone hearth off to the side, his yellow eyes staring at me, the tail switching like an angry snake.

"Hebrone says we need to look at the funeral home for blowing up the Boeing Business Jet."

B.W. raised his head, licked a paw.

"The owner of the funeral home or one of his employees could have been bought off to allow an explosive device to be placed in one of the coffins."

B.W. had been with me almost four years now. It was hard to remember when he replaced Savage, my German Shepherd.

"If the weather clears by tomorrow, I may ride over to the capital city and have a talk with the people at the mortuary."

My cup was empty. I got up and poured another.

"That Spaniard, Alicia, is one good-looking woman. Don't you think?"

B.W. pulled his head back and licked his chest. I wondered if I could do that?

"Alella is lucky to have found her."

I drank more coffee.

"Maybe we should ride up and visit them when the rain lets up."

B.W. didn't care one way or the other.

I got up, took the laptop into the back to run off copies of the photos from the memorial. I printed out copies of Hegewood and his clones so I could familiarize myself with their faces. Missy Applegate's rear profile I did not print out. Some things are better left alone. Stacking the photos in a folder, I put them in a drawer and called Sheriff John Quincy Adams.

"Did you hear about the Boeing Business Jet blowing up over the Gulf of Mexico this week?"

"I did. The woman who came to claim the bodies of her father and sister. How tragic."

"It was not an accident. Hebrone has uncovered some information that points to sabotage."

"Opshinsky. I might have known."

"Information points to the funeral home. The explosives could have been planted in one of the coffins. You know anything about the people who run the mortuary?"

"No, but I know someone who does. A Highway Patrolman who's stationed in Meridian worked as a mortician for that funeral home before going to the academy. You want me to call him?"

"If you don't mind. Owner turns up clean, it could be an employee, maybe a new hire. I'm planning a visit to the business tomorrow. Shake'em up a little, see what falls out."

"Under what authority?"

"Maybe I'll be an accident investigator for the NTSB or the FAA. Or an insurance investigator. I'll make something up."

"Couldn't that get you in trouble? Sooner or later, those government agencies will approach the funeral home with the same questions."

"That could be weeks before that happens."

"Good luck. I'll call as soon as I talk with the roadman. Oh, sorry I missed Bullard's memorial, had a bank robbery that morning. The "Billy Goat Bandit" struck again. Citizens branch. No one hurt."

"I understand. You need to catch that guy. He's gonna hurt someone sooner or later."

"We'll get him. He'll make a mistake. I heard about Hegewood's appearance at the graveyard. Wish there was some law he broke. I'd love to lock him up."

"Forget about him and his henchmen. They'll get what's coming to them."

"They're not worth doing time for, Jay."

"Understood. I'll be waiting for your call."

It was almost noon. Outside the kitchen window the sky was dark, the clouds low and heavy. The wind blew short occasional bursts of rain against the panes of glass. This low pressure could hang around for days. Even when it moved through, it could stall in the gulf and move back up as a warm front with even more rain.

I called Rose. "You fixing lunch?"

"Everyday for fifty years. You want to come and ogle the young doctor? Charge your battery, or is it because it's forbidden fruit?"

"What are you talking about?"

"I know men, and don't forget--I know you better than you know yourself. Come on, I will see that you do not make an ass of yourself or embarrass Alella. Bring B.W., he needs some feline company."

"What I really wanted was to talk about Missy Applegate. What's her story?"

"You're a liar. But come on, we're having lamb stew with my homemade rolls."

B.W. sat beside me in the truck. The wipers moved slowly. It embodied most of what I wanted in life, alone with my cat, going someplace, protected from the rain and cold.

Just as I parked in Rose's driveway, my cell phone rang.

"The Highway Patrolman said the owner is as clean as a whistle. The business has been in the same family for seventy years. I'd look at an employee."

"Thanks, John. We'll talk after I interview them. Get caught up on all this other stuff."

"Good. Be careful."

"Thanks."

Inside Rose's house, the girls had music playing, but since I think Willie and Waylon are still the cutting edge of new music, I didn't hear much that I enjoyed. However, the lamb stew was delicious, and the fresh rolls would make you hurt yourself.

Alicia wore a pair of jeans that seemed painted on. She had on a long-sleeved leotard garment that clung tightly to a slim, well-shaped torso. She had small, perfect breasts and wore no bra, nor was such support needed. Her short black hair glistened and the dark eyes held steady when she looked at you. She and Alella were both barefoot.

Alicia smiled at me, which was a luminous sight. I tried to imagine her working a young bull with the cape, her slim body moving close to the horns, steady, calm, unafraid and with a coordinated gracefulness to match any torero. Then I saw her making a midline incision and running a gut with those long delicate fingers looking for necrotic tissue causing a blockage.

"Senor Jay, you wish some more tea?"

"What? Oh, yes. Thanks, Alella."

Alicia looked at me. "You seem to be in deep thought. Care to share?"

Rose eyed me. She knew exactly what I was thinking. I don't know how, but she knew. "Yes, Jay. Tell us what you were thinking?"

"I was wondering about your surgical residency. You plan to specialize or do general surgery?"

"My decision is not made. There is so much to learn, so many techniques to master."

"What about neurosurgery? That would be my choice. The brain controls everything. That's where it's all centered. The heart is a pump. The lungs, the kidneys, the other organs have their specific functions, but the brain controls them all."

"You are familiar with the workings of the brain, Senor Jay?"

"I've read several books by and about Harvey Cushing, the father of neurosurgery in the United States. If I was in medicine, I would lean toward that part of it."

She ran a hand though her short hair and latched those black eyes on mine. "What would be your second choice?"

"A family practitioner in a small community. I can think of no better personal satisfaction than tending to the health of a group of people who depend upon you. That would be idealic."

"And your third choice?"

"Pathology. I love a mystery."

Alicia laughed, pinched off a tiny bit of roll and ate it.

"Are we going to continue throughout the anatomy until we run out of body parts to specialize in?"

"I wanted to see how your brain works."

"My brain works just fine."

"Sometimes self-delusion is a close companion of errant judgment."

"You think I'm delusional?"

"Family medicine, pathology, neurosurgery. You are all over the spectrum." She laughed, tossed a roll at me.

I threw it back--hard--and she caught it.

She got up and took her plate to the kitchen. I liked watching her. She had lightning reflexes and soft hands. She also filled out the jeans in a memorable fashion, and her short black hair hung loose and free.

"Senor Jay, you and Alicia are arguing?"

"No, Alella. We are getting to know one another. I like her."

"That is good, no?"

Rose patted her arm. "Yes, daughter. That is good."

Later Rose cornered me in the kitchen, alone.

"So, how do things stand with the threats?"

"Nothing's changed. I wait. Nothing happens," I shrugged. "Nothing happens."

"What about the plane crash?"

"Hebrone called, said maybe a bomb was placed on board."

"How would he know that?"

"He's working with the CIA. They know a lot of things."

"Why don't they know if those terrorist are coming after you?"

"They're working on it."

"Who put the bomb on board that woman's plane?"

"Someone from the mortuary. Maybe in a coffin."

"How awful."

"I'm going over and talk with the funeral home tomorrow."

"After you talk to them, what are you going to do?"

"What I usually do, plod along, try not to bump into things, see what develops."

"What if nothing happens?"

"I nudge it a little."

"Yes, you usually do."

"It's personal. They killed Bahri, Marina and her father, then the sister and an innocent flight crew. They threaten to kill me. I take that seriously. Things need to be evened off a little bit. The identity of Pineiro's group will be found out, and then we will do what has to be done."

Rose turned on the dishwasher, came and sat at the kitchen table. B.W. jumped in her lap.

"Graham, from the *Union Appeal*, sent me some good photos of Hegewood and his goons. A nice one of Missy Applegate's ass, too."

"I don't want those boys to get away with how they acted at Andrew's memorial, but I don't want you and Shack doing anything to get you in trouble."

"Don't worry. One day, at the right time, Hegewood and I will have a talk."

"Stay away from Missy."

"Why? She looks like she might enjoy some company."

"For once, just take my advice and stay away." Her expression was sincere.

"It's a promise."

"Good. Now go in there and be nice to Alicia."

"I'm always nice."

I sat on the couch. Alicia and I were alone. She came and straddled my knee, facing me. I could feel the warmth of her through the fabric that separated us. It was an erotic heat.

"We are going to be friends, are we not?" She whispered, her face close to mine.

"You will be going back to Spain in a month. We will probably never see each other again. Why do you care if we are friends?"

"Alella thinks of you as a father. I care for her very much. That is why I want us to be friends."

"Even though I'm delusional?"

She laughed, and brushed a hand across my cheek. "I think you are very intelligent and I like you. I want us to be one big happy family." She reached down and put both hands on my thigh and pushed off my knee. "So what do you think?"

"I think the medical profession in Spain is in good hands and Alella is a lucky woman."

Gathering up B.W., I bid the ladies goodbye and drove home, planning to spend the rest of the afternoon preparing for the visit to the funeral home in the capital. Developing a good cover, asking the right questions, and garnering a little luck was important.

After stoking the fire, making a pot of coffee, and turning on the radio to a country station, I started thinking of what information we already had. The Highway Patrolman vouched for the owner. I would take him at his word, but that was the person to start with. At least get his reaction. After that, I'd just wing it.

After a while, I got up and paced in front of the fire. Something was bothering me, but I couldn't put my finger on it. Looking out the back door, I saw that the rain had eased into a steady drizzle and the wind had abated to five or ten knots. Tomorrow would probably not see much improvement. The trip to the mortuary was still on, though.

Moving my laptop out of the way, I picked up a book that I was about halfway through reading. The laptop was a highly technical device. My definition of technology is anything invented after I was born. I looked at the book titled, *Coal Black Horse*, by Robert Olmstead, about a fourteen year old boy sent to find his father on a Civil War battlefield. Now here, I thought rubbing the spine of the book, was a whiz-bang technological creation that is superbly designed, wickedly functional, infinitely useful and beloved more passionately than any electronic gadget. The book is a more reliable storage devise than a hard drive. It sports a killer user interface and no instruction manual is needed. It is instant-on and requires no batteries. It is just an incredible device.

    I read until finishing Olmstead's story of a young boy's struggle with the brutal carnage of a senselessness of war, closed the book and went to bed thinking of the final words of the novel.

It was a sleeper's world frosted, silent, dark and starkly beautiful, and he remembered the tranquillity. He remembered the days in the valley riding the coal black horse. The horse rising to the bit, its hot breath blowing back at him, the shedding sweat from its sleek black neck, flecks of foam from its quivering nostrils. He remembered his father. He remembered the dead. He remembered nothing moving in the darkness of those nights---Sleep, he remembered thinking, sleep a little longer.

Chapter Twenty-two

"Name's Leicester," I said to the woman who sat at the small desk inside the front entrance to the castle-like building that served as Haverstein's Mortuary. A three level structure, it sported four turrets with sharp points, and was constructed with dark stone. I would not have been surprised if it had had a moat surrounding it.

"How can we be of service, Mr. Leicester?" She was middle-aged, hair up in a bun, dressed in a black suit with white blouse and wore no makeup. She looked over half-lensed glasses at me while peering at a computer screen. She was a stereotypical receptionist for a funeral home.

"I'm with the National Transportation Safety Board. I'd like to talk with the owner."

"May I ask what this is in regard too?"

"I'd rather discuss it with the owner."

She seemed undisturbed by the rebuff. "Just a moment. I'll see if Mr. Haverstein is available."

A tall dignified man returned with her. He extended a hand. "I'm Carl Haverstein. What can I do for you?"

"You have some place we can talk in private?"

I handed him an ID case that contained my Airline Transport license and my Flight Instructor's license. Both carried the blue and white seal of the federal government and looked officious to the uninitiated.

He scanned the ID, handed it back, and said, "Please follow me."

His office was plush, not garish, but old moneyed. Deep, expensive leather chairs and dark paneling with polished well-made desk and credenza. The office had probably been his father's and his father's father.

"Have a seat, Mr. Leicester. Would you like coffee?"

His mustache was neatly trimmed. His nose was strong. His dark eyes were deep-set. His brown hair was curly and short with touches of gray. He wore an expensive, tailor-made dark suit with a white shirt and red striped tie. I figured him to be my age or a little older.

"Coffee would be fine."

He went over to a side table and poured two cups.

"You with the NTSB?"

"I'm sure you've heard about the unfortunate accident of the DeBeers business jet. We understand you prepared the remains for shipment that was aboard the plane. We are following up leads."

Haverstein got up, walked to a window behind his desk that reached from floor to ceiling, at least ten feet tall and looked out. He put both arms behind his back and clasped his hands together. He remained in that position for several moments. Then without turning, he said. "I looked at your credentials, Mr. Leicester. Now why don't you tell me who you really are and what it is that you want?"

He turned and faced me. There was no anger in his expression, although his eyes showed that he was not a man to be fooled easily.

"You employed a man who is now a State Highway Patrolman. He has vouched for your truth and veracity. I am sorry for the deception, but it was necessary until we could meet and be alone."

He returned to his desk, sat up straight in the chair, placed both hands flat on the leather top. "Go on."

He listened carefully and intently as I told him the whole story. At times he leaned forward placed his elbows on the desk. When I finished, he got up again and assumed the same position in front of the window. It must be his place to go and think deeply about things, I thought.

Finally, he turned and faced me. I was stunned to see tears rolling down his cheeks.

"Mr. Leicester, I have a daughter who is thirty years old. She spends a great deal of time on the island of Aruba. We have a home there. A year ago, she met a man from Caracas. He is here often with my daughter. She is a licensed mortician and he expressed an interest in the business." He paused, looked at me. "I want to be kept informed, please."

"It's a promise, Mr. Haverstein. I will put the word out to all the agencies. You will be kept in the loop. For now, do not mention this to your daughter or the boyfriend. Where are they at the moment?"

"In Aruba. They left day before yesterday."

We shook hands.
"Don't think the worst. Let it play out."
"Sure."

. . .

During the drive back home, I watched the wipers lose the battle with road grime and thought about Aruba. A nasty little island. Teenage girls are drugged, raped, and disappear forever on that little sandpit. Law enforcement there is atrocious.

Haverstein furnished the name of his daughter and the Venezuelan boyfriend, and the address on Aruba. This was a job for Aardwolf. I pondered jumping on an airliner and going there myself, but quickly decided against it. If I was a target, being in familiar territory had its advantages. Besides, I could be sure the girls were safe.

It was one p.m. when I turned off the gravel road onto the terrace row that led to the cottage. A car was parked behind mine. John Quincy Adams sat behind the wheel. The rain was heavy.

"You spending way too much time out here in the woods. Come on inside and we both can stay dry."

He sat on the couch. "Someone beat Will Hegewood damn near to death in the Post Office parking lot at ten a.m. this morning. Talk to me."

"John, I swear, I know nothing about it. Carl Haverstein can vouch that I was in his office in Jackson this morning."

"How'd that go?"

"Sad. His daughter may be involved, along with a boyfriend."

"Did you or Shack arrange this beating?"

"No. That would be pretty stupid, don't you think?"

"You two--boys--never been known for your smarts." He grinned.

"What about witnesses?"

"Nobody saw a thing."

"Ten a.m., downtown Union, Post Office parking lot, and no eyeballs?"

"People don't want to get involved."

"Good for people."

"What's next with the funeral home thing?"

"Hebrone and his new pals can handle it. They'll notify the agencies with the need to know. The father wants to be kept in the loop."

"Can't blame him for that."

"You might want to inform your Highway Patrol buddy. He could offer some support to his ex-boss."

"I hope I don't find out you had anything to do with Hegewood's beating. Though you would have my admiration."

"Stay close, John. The bad guys may still be after me."

"I'm always close. Don't ever forget that."

John Quincy Adams drove off into a rain that was getting harder by the minute. He was a good cop, and we were becoming friends.

I fixed some lunch and dialed Alec Aardwolf's cell phone number. To my surprise, he answered. I told him what Haverstein related to me. He was familiar with the boyfriend's name.

"He's a member of Pineiro's old group. Do you think the daughter's involved or was this guy using her?"

"How would I know, Aardwolf? It seems a stretch to me that he'd been seeing the woman for a year, planning to gain access to coffins to plant bombs in order to blow up a plane carrying the sister of the deceased. How could anyone know what funeral home would be used? Who would know two people would be killed at my farm? All of this makes no sense."

Aardwolf chuckled. "Welcome to my world. You have no idea of the complexities of some operations, of the inanity and minutia that threads through them."

"Where's Hebrone?"

"Off tending to some personal stuff."

"How long you people gonna keep using him?"

"Mr. Opshinsky was free to leave some time ago. He chose to stay of his own volition. He thinks he can keep you from being killed if he continues to work with us."

"What do you think?"

"I think you're in grave danger, Mr. Leicester. Be very careful."

"Why? Why am I the target?"

"We've been over this. They have to save face. You're the easiest, and time is running out for them."

"Tell Hebrone to call me."

The rest of the afternoon, I spent as restless as a bear in a cage. Unable to read, I paced, added wood to the fire, kept a roaring blaze. I watched the rain, loved the rain, cursed the rain. Wanted it to stop, wanted it to rain forever. I sat a fifth of Jack Daniel's Black Label whiskey on the countertop, looked hard at it. Like an alcoholic, I savored what effects the dark liquid would have, how it would calm me. How it would solve all my problems, answer my questions. Why did she run off to Seattle with the banker? Why is somebody trying to kill me? Who beat up Will Hegewood? Suddenly laughing at myself, I put the Tennessee sour mash back in the cabinet, realizing the hangover I'd have tomorrow and, instead, made a pot of coffee. B.W. covered his face with his paws, moved further away from the fire.

Total darkness came hard and fast, and when I looked out the kitchen window all I could see was my own reflection. I didn't look old, maybe a little weathered. Like a man who's flown too many airplanes. Heard too many lies. Seen too many bodies. Lost too many friends.

My doorbell rang. Who would be out in this rainstorm at night? Where is my magnum? However, someone coming to do me bodily harm wouldn't announce they were here by ringing the bell. I retrieved the magnum anyway.

Flicking on the porch light, I observed a lanky, blond-headed man with a ponytail. He raised up a hand to block the light. He had on a light windbreaker over a T-shirt even though the temperature was in the forties. Blue jeans and cheap tennis shoes finished off his attire.

"State your business."

"You Leicester?"

"I am."

"Hebrone sent me."

Holding the magnum in my right hand, I opened the door. "Who are you?"

He stood rocking on the balls of his feet like a well-trained athlete. His arms were long and hung loosely at his sides. "Name's Josie Saunders. Everybody calls me Conch."

"Because you like to eat snails, or you are a true conch?"

"England, America, Bahamas, the Keys. Fourteenth generation."

"Hebrone sent you why?"

"Thought you needed some outside help. Some local boys needed to be taught a lesson, and then some big guns coming after you."

Josie "Conch" Saunders. That name was familiar, but I couldn't put it together yet.

"It was you worked over Will Hegewood at the Post Office in Union this morning?"

"That was me."

"Stick out your hands."

He complied. There was not a cut, scrape, or swelling. A pro. Then it hit me. I remembered Josie Saunders. But only by reputation. If you compare him to Hebrone Opshinsky, he's ten times more deadly, a better shooter, handles a knife with much more expertise, more intelligent, and has absolutely no conscience. I sensed his veneer of formality was no more than a flimsy firewall against violence. I had met similar characters, though not quiet so talented as Conch.

"I drove up from Key West, eighteen hours, straight though. Arrived in time to intercept your local yokel at the Post Office."

"How long you been out here on my porch?"

"Long enough."

"Where's your car?"

"Out at the tree line."

"Why aren't you wet? It's raining cats and dogs."

He almost grinned. "Dodged the drops. Keeps me in shape doing that."

I almost believed him.

"Come on in. I have some questions."

"Nice gun." He pointed at the magnum. "Good for up close. Need four and a half inch barrel for accuracy, though."

"It's always worked for me."

Inside, B.W. looked at the man, snarled, and ran in the back to his Querencia.

Conch took off his windbreaker. The long arms were muscle and sinew. Under the T-shirt, a six pack rippled with each movement. The man was in good physical shape. Then I saw the eyes. Black, cold, there was no soul. A true killer.

"How did you know what Hegewood looked like? How to find him?"

"Hebrone sent him some kind of special registered letter that he had to pick up and sign for. I waited around till he showed. His description was accurate."

"How did Hebrone know what he looked like?"

"Saw him at the graveyard."

So he was there. Why didn't he at least say hello?

"Did you know Smash?"

"Skinner introduced us. Good man."

"Hebrone?"

"Long time. We did a few things together. Owe each other."

I did not want to know.

"This isn't your fight, Conch."

"Ain't yours either. It was Smash they disrespected and I reckon he can't do anything about it."

"That's right. So I guess that makes it our fight."

"Any fight will do."

"Hegewood give you any trouble?"

"He was not much to me," Conch said.

"He's big and strong, but he doesn't know how."

"Most people don't know how," Conch said. "Guy's his size don't often need to."

"Except when they run into somebody that do."

He didn't smile, but his eyes almost did.

"We'll take care of the other three one at time."

"Sheriff said nobody made you at the Post Office."

"I am more stealthy than the F-117 fighter, the B-2 bomber or the Aurora."

I wondered how he knew about the Aurora project. It was still in the "*Black Watch*" program. I didn't ask.

"Hebrone said you'd fill me in on these Venezuelans who want some kind of revenge for the killing of their leader."

"Hebrone threw him out of the airplane, but it's me they're coming after."

"Yeah, you two working together. They know about Hebrone. Don't want to deal with him. He's too dangerous. You a easy target."

"Maybe I'm not that easy."

Conch did smile, and it was a nice smile. "Don't worry. We gonna make it hard on'em."

I felt better already.

He was clean-shaven, relaxed, and looked as if nothing exciting had ever happened in his life. He stared at the fire and I thought he might go to sleep.

"You were born in Key West?"

"No. Born on a sponge boat off Grand Bahama Island."

"Sponge boat?"

"Yeah. You know what that is?"

"As a matter of fact, I do. Had a friend, Norman Sawin, ran one of the last sponge boats, the *Langosta*, a two masted schooner built by Joe Albury on Man-O-War cay. He taught me how to use a hooking pole, looking through a water-glass, a wooden glass-bottomed bucket. How to tell good sponges from a rotten or inferior variety. Sheep's wool was the best, then "Checker-boards," so called because reef sediment sifted over them like flour. Next in value was the "Velvet." Least desirable was the coarse grass sponges. I remember another that was not attached to the sea bottom. There were called "Rollers."

Conch looked at me. "The largest sponge ever taken out of the Atlantic was found in the Bahamas. It was a roller. Weighed ninety pounds, but only twelve after it was cleaned and dried. It was six feet in circumference. You know the season ran from October to May. My Ma was the cook on the Lily S. When the dinghies left the mother-ship the cook was the only one left aboard. Not only did she have to prepare a vast amount of food, she also had to tend the boat and keep it close to the dinghies. She did all this and gave birth to me."

"Too bad a world-wide blight wiped them out. By the time they were growing again, synthetic sponges were much cheaper."

"That's why my folks ended up in Key West. My Pa tried shrimping, but hated it. Got a job with the city. I grew up on the Island."

He didn't say anything for a while. Went, again, into that trance-like state, staring at the crackling flame. Then: "What happened to that cat?"

"He went in the back and hid."

"Yeah, cats hate me. Never understood why? I've always liked cats. We lived behind a fella that had some six-toed ones. They would growl and bow up at me."

"Cats are a good judge of character."

He looked at me with cold, bottomless, black eyes. It sent a chill through me. He held the stare for what seemed like hours.

"I never did anything to a cat."

"Who had the six-toes ones?" I already knew the answer, but wanted to see if he did.

"Some writer. He left, moved to Cuba before I was old enough to know who he was. They turned the house into some kind of museum. The cats stayed."

"Tennessee Williams, the playwright?"

"Nah, this guy wrote books. Won some kind of prize for his work. My Pa was a friend with a man who worked for the writer. Built a brick fence around the property. Bruce, I think. Yeah, Toby Bruce. Nice old man, let us swim in the pool when no one was there."

"I'll drive you out to get your car. You can stay here."

"Nope. I'm at a motel, down at the interstate. A place near the town of Newton. Need to stay where I'm not operating." He stood. "Been up for thirty-six hours. Tired. I'll come in the morning. We'll talk about the rest of your life."

"At least let me drive you to your car."

"I'll just dodge the rain drops. Be good exercise."

As soon as he left, I tried to call Hebrone. There was no answer. Aardwolf's cell phone went unanswered, also.

B.W. came out of hiding. I guess he could sense Conch was gone. He jumped up on the hearth and stared at the place on the couch where he'd sat. I thought that unlike Hebrone, at least the man talked. Those far off trance-like stares bothered me, but even in motionless repose, there was something electric about him, a sense of barely contained kinesis.

Buttoning up the cottage, I turned in early, hoping to dream about Spanish ladies, or sixty-year-old Mississippi women.

Chapter Twenty-three

The rain eased during the night. By morning, it was down to a steady drizzle. Sleep had been fitful and I was tired. Plugging in the coffeepot, I noticed Josie "Conch" Saunders emerge from an old Chevrolet four door sedan, a 1957 that had seen too much salt air. I was surprised the vehicle made it all the way from Key West. Maybe he thought like Shack concerning machines, not much for aesthetics, but mechanically perfect.

Opening the front door, I waved him inside.

"How long you been parked in my drive?"

"Couple of hours."

"I didn't hear you drive up."

"Coasted in from the tree line. You're careless and you sleep late."

"Thanks for the critique. I'm gonna get a quick shower. Coffee will be ready in a few." I pointed toward the kitchen.

Letting the hot water work its magic over my body, I thought about the conch people, which is a slang term for native Bahamians of European descent. After the American Revolution, many loyalists migrated to the Bahamas. Being more affluent and educated, the Loyalists came to look down on the early settlers, and called them conchs because that shellfish was a prominent part of their diet. By extension, the term "Conch" has also been applied to the descendants of Bahamian immigrants in Florida. Bahamians began visiting the Florida Keys in the Eighteenth Century to catch turtles, cut timber and salvage wrecks. Soon, most of the permanent residents in the Florida Keys were Bahamian in origin. A "Salt Water Conch" is a native to the Keys and a "Fresh Water Conch" is a non-native. Some of the best people I've known in my life were "Salt Water Conchs."

"Paid a visit to that little hospital on the way home last night. Looked in on Mr. Hegewood. Was kind of hoping his three friends would be there. Thought maybe we could talk some things over. But he was alone and sleeping."

"You were going to take them on by yourself?"

"Ain't but three of 'em."

His face was deadpan and serious. It was as if he was talking about swatting mosquitoes. No wonder my cat hid when he was around. There was some sort of evil aura surrounding the man. I don't think I've ever been in the presence of someone quite like him. However, if Hebrone trusted him, so would I.

What could have happened to a boy growing up on an island like Key West to cause him to evolve into a hardened soulless killer? A tenet of biology is that trauma is a catalyst for change. It's true on a cellular level and an emotional level. Something traumatic happened to Josie "Conch" Saunders as a youth. At the moment, I was thankful he was on our side.

We sipped the hot coffee. He took his black. He was silent, stared into the cup. It was as if he was alone in the room.

"So, Conch, what's your philosophy of life?" I asked, looking for some insight into what made the man tick.

He blew on the coffee, looked at me with eyes empty of emotion. "Expect an early death. It will keep you busier."

"Way I see things, we want to teach Hegewood and his boys some manners. You did well with him, but I'm not sure he understood why he took the beating. It's important that he and the others know it's not polite to disrespect the dead. We have to be careful. The county sheriff expects me and a local man, a cattle farmer and friend who lives up the road, to take action. In fact, he's already paid me a visit about the beating you issued out. The next time, my friend and I can establish alibis and you can teach the lesson. No one knows about you and that's the way we'll keep it. It's also important nobody dies or has lingering injuries. You good enough for that?"

"I'm a lot better than good."

"We'll ride into town, show you the layout and all the roads with access to my place. I want you to be familiar if we have to deal with the Venezuelans."

"Oh, they coming. Hebrone said it would be soon."

"There are some people I want you to meet. Some we have to protect at all costs."

"Understood."

The phone rang.

"We killed two last night. A third is on the way to see you. He's traveling alone and he's dangerous."

"How do you know this information?"

"One of these old boys died a little slower than the other. Talked a lot at the end."

"In other words, you tortured him until he told you what you wanted to hear?"

"Does it matter? You're in this mess because I threw Pineiro out of the airplane. I'm only trying to help."

"You certainly sent someone who seems qualified to be of assistance."

"He's been trained by some of the best. He's a little out on the edge, seen and done some bad things. He's reliable, though, and can be trusted. He's also as loyal as Smash."

"Tell me about the one that's coming."

"He was part of a highly-trained three-man team. Two are dead. The one headed your way is smart, was probably the team leader. He doesn't mind dying, so act accordingly."

"How'd you let him get away?"

"I told you, he's good. Use Conch, you'll need him."

"You can't come? I'd feel better if you were here."

"There's a mess to clean up. It will take a while."

"You're in trouble. What the hell did you do, Hebrone?"

"Forget about me. Take care of yourself."

The line went dead.

Conch looked at me. "Hebrone?"

"Yeah."

He shook his head.

"What do you know that you're not telling me?"

"Hebrone's a lone wolf. What he did, he did on his own. No one else was involved. You understand?"

"Yes." I had a real sickening feeling in the pit of my stomach. I knew exactly what he'd done. I only wish he'd gotten the third one.

Unplugging the coffeepot, and putting my cup in the sink, I turned to the man with the ponytail, the "Salt Water Conch," who'd better be as good as his reputation. "Come on, let's ride into town."

The rain had finally stopped. The thick clouds were beginning to break up, blue sky showed in fleeting spots. The road was covered in tree shadow and I smelled air of asphalt-scented rain. Winter always brought its metrical interplay of ice and cold, rain and shine, and sudden warmth. December is a fun month in the south.

By the time we crossed the railroad tracks, the sun was shining bright. Downtown was busy. There had always been a magisterial real town dignity about Union. It was still dignified and it was busy with real southern people.

They appeared sincere and sufficient, though most of them seemed tired. It was ten a.m. and there was only one parking slot left at the Post Office. We pulled into it, shut off the engine of my truck, and watched people go in and out of the building.

"Not a soul saw you work Hegewood over in this busy parking lot?"

"Oh, there was some saw it. There was one man who grinned and nodded. It was like, "Yeah, that SOB deserves the beating.""

We left the Post Office and drove out to the hospital east of town. Leaving Conch in the car, I went inside. The room Hegewood occupied was at the end of a long corridor next to an interior entrance to the cafeteria. Sheriff John Quincy Adams and a woman were standing outside the door. Turning and walking back the way I came proved futile. The sheriff had already spotted me. He waved me over to them.

"Mr. Leicester, this is Will Hegewood's mother."

"Ma'am. Sorry about your son."

"Thank you." She was a big blond woman who looked as if she might have grown up on a diary farm.

"Mr. Leicester was the one conducting the memorial for his friend."

She put out a hand and touched my arm. "I'm so sorry."

"Mrs. Hegewood has talked her son out of pressing charges against whoever did this to him."

"Missy Applegate told me what happened at the graveyard. I am ashamed. Will was not raised that way."

"My mother used those exact same words to describe my actions on several occasions, Mrs. Hegewood."

She seemed unnerved by uncomplicated kindness, having encountered it so rarely.

"The doctors say Will can go home this afternoon."

"I'll be in touch, Mrs. Hegewood," the sheriff said. "Come, Mr. Leicester, I'll walk you back to your car."

"Nice to have met you, Ma'am."

She bowed her head and entered her son's room.

As we exited the hospital, John said, "What are you doing here?"

"Wanted to see how the man was getting along. I had a genuine concern for his well-being."

"Cut the crap, Leicester."

"Okay. I was hoping his three running mates would be around. They need a lecture on good manners."

"You've elected yourself to be their teacher."

"Maybe."

"Do you want to go to jail?"

"No, John. What I want is for Smash to rest in peace. He can't do that without me meeting with those boys."

"Smash is at the bottom of the Atlantic Ocean, not in the cemetery out on Highway 492."

We arrived at my truck.

"Who's that?"

"A friend from Florida."

"So, he's the one beat up Hegewood."

Conch saw me with the sheriff and got out.

"Sheriff Adams, Josie Saunders. You both have a common friend. Hebrone Opshinsky."

"I might have known," John said. "Hebrone sent you to work over Will Hegewood so Leicester, here, wouldn't have to be involved."

Conch stood loosely on the balls of his feet, his arms hung by his sides. "Who's Will Hegewood?"

"The man you beat up at the Post Office."

"No, John. He's here because a hired assassin is on the way to seek revenge on me for the death of the man we talked about, Pineiro."

The two men stared at each other. Their expressions were not of anger or threat, but curiosity and admiration for the other.

"We'll talk about Pineiro later. I've got to get back to the office in Decatur. Call me at four o'clock this afternoon."

Conch said, "Can I see it?"

John looked at him. "See what?"

"The eye."

"How do you know about that? Hebrone--"

"He said you're never without it."

John reached in his pocket and pulled out a key chain. Attached to one end was a glass eye. He handed it to Conch, who rubbed it, looked intently at the eye as if it were some rare jewel and handed it back with a simple nod of his head. He got back in the truck without saying a word.

"Four o'clock, Leicester. We'll talk about this threat. I'll be waiting for your call."

Driving out of the hospital parking lot, I thought that the story behind the glass eye had escaped me and I was curious. "So, tell me about Sheriff Adams and the glass eye."

"Thought you two were friends. How come you don't know?"

"The subject never came up."

"Hebrone told me. Some notorious criminal was running amok in the south. Evil man. Killed people for no good reason. Was rumored he slept with his good eye open. Last man he killed, he straddled his chest all night.

Promised to shoot him at sunup. Kept his promise. Your sheriff cornered him and shot him through his good eye. Took the glass one for a keepsake."

"Why? What was so precious about that glass eye?"

"Hebrone said the man he killed, the one he sat straddle of all night, was the sheriff's brother."

This was all news to me. I can't imagine having never heard that story. But then there are a lot of things I don't know. One of the most important was how this Venezuelan assassin was gonna come after me.

"I thought we were going to keep my presence unknown? Yet you go telling the sheriff who I am."

"Don't worry about Adams. He's on our side. He understands how the game is played. But if it's blatant, or you violate the law where it's obvious to the public, then he has no choice."

We headed south on Highway 15, following the sheriff toward Decatur. I wanted to see where Conch was staying. There were reasons that I might have a need to know.

The small motel was outside the town of Newton, adjacent to Interstate 20. Parking in front of the room, we went inside. I needed to use the bathroom. The room was generic motel chain, generic furniture, and carpet. I've been in a lot of rooms like this. They worked fine. They housed you, kept you warm or cool--depending on the season. Let you bath and sleep and eat. They don't do much for the soul, but their mission had nothing to do with the soul.

Leaving there, we headed back north. At Union, we turned west on Highway 492. Three miles out of town, we took Road 210, a crooked, paved, state-maintained road that would lead around to the north of all our farms. A gravel road turned off Highway 210 and lead straight to the cottage. The same gravel road Alella and Alicia used on their run a couple of days ago. I wanted Conch to be aware of the approach and two or three other access roads where bad guys could come and go. It's important to know the lay of the land. Familiarity may bring contempt with human relationships, but being aware of your surroundings can save your life when someone is trying to kill you.

We passed by Shack's cattle farm, but he was nowhere to be seen. Rose and the girls were also gone. Probably off on a shopping trip to Philadelphia. Pointing out her place, I explained how she and Alella and Alicia could be in danger and why it was important that we protect them at all costs.

At the cottage, Conch said he wanted to drive the country roads by himself. Teach his mind the routes. He would return this afternoon.

"Make it five o'clock. After I talk to Sheriff Adams, we'll make some plans on how to deal with this bad boy coming up from Florida."

Fifteen minutes after Conch drove away in his rusted out old Chevrolet a beat up pickup truck with no muffler came roaring up and slid to a stop within feet of my front porch. Three men were seated in the cab. The driver shut the engine off, but no one got out. They just sat there.

Grabbing my magnum, I walked out on the porch, recognizing the three clones of Will Hegewood. This could get ugly really quick, I thought.

The driver opened the door of the truck with a loud squeak of unoiled metal. He stuck his head out and asked. "You Leicester?"

"State your business."

"We come to talk."

"Then start talking."

"We want to apologize for how we acted at the cemetery the other day. Can we get out? Won't be no shooting, will they?"

"Only if you start it."

"We ain't got no guns."

All three of the young men exited the cab and walked up to within feet of me. There were six rounds in the magnum. I was pretty sure that would be enough.

The driver inched forward. He was going to be the spokesman. The other two looked at their boots. All three were dressed alike. Wool shirts, overalls and muddy cowboy boots. I wondered if they were brothers.

"We was listening to Will and we was drunk. We are sorry. We didn't know who you was."

"Who am I?"

"You that pilot fella. Friends with that man killed all them people in that war. We didn't know."

"Who told you that?"

"Well, mostly Sheriff Adams. He said what happened to Will, him getting beat up, was just the start. Said our family members would start to disappear and turn up in pieces, in garbage bags. Then we'd start to disappear. We heard about them two bodies found in your field. Someone said they had crossed you somehow. One of them was a woman. Said you threw them out of an airplane while they was alive."

"So you're really not sorry you acted like an ass at the cemetery. You're scared you might die a slow agonizing death. You figured coming out here would stop that from happening."

"We was hoping."

"What if things are in motion and can't be called off?"

"Please, Mister. We are sorry and nothing like that won't ever happen again. We promise."

I thought he was going to cry.

"You boys get out of here. Put a muffler on that truck."

"Yes, sir. You'll call off them killers?"

"I'll see what I can do."

They got back in the truck and drove away. God, I'd loved to have heard what John Quincy Adams told them boys. I must remember to thank him.

Chapter Twenty-four

At four o'clock, I called John Quincy Adams. "How come you never told me about your brother getting killed and the glass eye?"

"When we first met, I didn't think you'd understand. Later, it didn't seem to matter. I figured Hebrone would have told you."

"I understand. Hegewood's posse paid me a visit this afternoon."

"Oh, God. Do I need to come and count the bodies?"

"Your little talk had them apologizing. Members of their family disappearing and body parts turning up in garbage bags--Good one, John."

"Boy's easily frightened. That's the trouble with young men like them following someone like Will Hegewood. They don't love who they are fighting for. Don't hate who they are fighting against. Except for a Saturday night fist-fight at some local bar, they've never seen the evil part of life."

"I hope all this is over now. There are more important things we have to deal with."

"Don't forget about Hegewood. He may not be satisfied."

"Hebrone called. A three-man squad was dispatched from Venezuela to deal with us. Two are dead, the third is on the way to pay me a visit. He's trained and, according to Hebrone, not afraid to die."

"Any other description?"

"None."

"This is not good news. Word from south Florida on Josie Saunders is he's capable of some bad stuff. I'm glad he's here to help you. Let me know the second anything happens. I'll pull all my deputies in to assist. The Highway Patrol will respond, also."

"Thanks. Care to divulge how you came by the info on Saunders?"

"No. It's not important. If we had some more information on this Venezuelan, we could set up roadblocks, put out a BOLO (be on the lookout) on him and the car. He could be coming by plane though, like they did with the father and daughter."

"Well, we don't have a clue. I'll inform you as quick as I know anything."

As soon as we hung up, the phone rang. It was Alec Aardwolf.

"We've interrogated Haverstein's daughter and her boyfriend. She wasn't involved. He, however, admitted putting the explosive in the coffin. It was a pressure detonator set to go off at thirty-five thousand feet."

"I don't understand. Why kill Carmen Cicogna?"

"Seems the diamonds she and Bahri delivered to pay for the bomb components were fake--cubic zirconium. It made them angry enough to retaliate. Had nothing to do with you, but they have not forgotten about Pineiro."

"Thanks Aardwolf. I heard what Hebrone did. How much trouble is he in?"

"No idea what you are talking about, Mr. Leicester. Be very careful." He hung up.

For whatever reason, he couldn't or wouldn't discuss Hebrone. Maybe the phone wasn't secure. Or maybe he hadn't heard that Hebrone had killed two members of a three-man squad sent to retaliate for Pineiro's death.

Looking out the front window, I saw Shack drive up.

Opening the front door for him, I said, "We have some new developments. You need to be brought up to speed."

Shack sat on the couch, crossed his legs. "I was coming by to tell you that I'm gonna drive through the fields to see if they've dried enough to finish with the fertilizing. If so, we'll probably start at daylight tomorrow."

"Sounds like a plan. Hebrone sent someone up from Key West in case we needed help."

"Are things starting to get that serious?"

"Yes. One of Pineiro's gang is on the way here. It started out as a three-man hit squad. They decided to take a crack at Hebrone first. Bad idea. Two are dead."

Shack uncrossed his legs. "Good."

"The one coming here is a real pro. A dangerous, smart assassin. We have to be careful."

"All of this for revenge?"

"Yes."

"What about this Key West guy?"

"He's turning onto the terrace row now. I'll introduce you."

"Do we need to be concerned about Hegewood and his thugs? See that they're taught some manners?"

"You haven't heard about Hegewood?"

"What about him?"

"The man we saw at the cemetery, the one standing on the far side, was Hebrone."

"Well, why--?"

Holding up my hand, I said, "I have no idea. But he sent this guy," I pointed out the window. "to avenge the insult, and to help me with the Venezuelan thing. Hegewood is in the hospital. John Quincy Adams scared the others with a tale of madness and mayhem. They came by today and apologized. As for their leader--we may have to deal with him later."

Shack looked down at his boots, shook his head.

Conch stopped out at the tree line, sizing up the situation with Shack's truck parked in the drive. Walking out on the porch, I waved him on in.

"Shack Runnels, Josie Saunders. His friends call him Conch."

The two shook hands, eyeing each other like two middleweight fighters before the bell.

"Shack's the cattleman. I pointed out his farm to you."

He nodded, looked Shack hard in the eyes. "Hebrone had good things to say about you. Said you were a man who came to the fight not to see who could win. You came to the fight to win."

That seemed to break the ice between them and they both relaxed.

"Jay just told me about your little fisty-cuff at the Post Office. You have any trouble with that Hegewood character?"

Conch looked at me. "He's just now finding out?"

"The man stays in the field with his cattle a lot."

Shack laughed. "Leicester doesn't communicate unless he needs help."

"Did he inform you of the man coming to kill him?"

"Again, just now. All I need to know is how can I be of help?"

"We can stay alert," I said. "We don't know how this man will come at me. He may take a few days to scout out my activities, figure the best way to catch me off guard, or he may simply come with guns blazing."

Conch looked at me. "He's too well-trained for that. He's sure you're expecting him, so he'll be careful."

"Okay. Then we wait until he makes his move."

Shack got up to leave. "Any other concerns we should have?"

"No. The Venezuelan knows only about me. Hegewood will be healing for a few more days. Being the coward he is, without his young thugs around, we probably won't hear from him. Just stay alert for anything unusual. And don't spray chicken shit all over my cottage tomorrow."

He left laughing.

Conch watched him drive out to the terrace row, sat back down. "Seems solid enough. Probably wouldn't run when things heated up."

"I have known brave men. I have wished to be one of them. But my conscious makes me a coward. I once saw Shack subdue a man twice his size, a lifelong friend. He hung him by the neck from an oak tree in my back yard and beat him with a trace chain to get information concerning a threat to one of his neighbors. So I think that when the fight starts, and when it ends, the cattleman will still be there."

Conch nodded his head. "That's what Hebrone said about both of you. It's why I didn't mind coming to this inland country setting. I don't like to get too far from salt water. He also said your sheriff was okay for a lawman."

"Both were Vietnam, in-country. Did a lot of the same things. Mutual respect."

Conch nodded went into one of his far-off trance-like stares, then suddenly: "What's this about spraying chicken shit?"

I explained the process.

He shook his head. "Farmers--"

"Come on, there are some people I want you to meet."

.   .   .

Alicia answered the door holding a small battery operated hair dryer. She waved us in and continued to dry her hair, then gave her head a shake, creating a loose, short, black veil that framed her face. She wore only a long white tee-shirt that hid very little of the lithe athletic body.

"Rose is in the kitchen. Alella is in the shower. Who is this?" She pointed the hair dryer at Conch.

"A friend from south Florida. Josie Saunders, meet Senorita Alicia Atienza, a medical doctor from Spain."

He nodded, but said nothing.

Alicia stopped, looked at him for a moment, then walked away, her bare feet padding across the wooden floor like a panther, the tee shirt revealing that she wore no other garments.

Alella appeared in the doorway of the living room dressed only in a towel, her hair wet and dripping. "Oh, Alicia did not say we had company." She turned and disappeared into the bedroom.

Conch looked at me. "What kind of place is this?" It seemed that I was not the only one mesmerized by the customs of our Spanish ladies.

Rose walked in. "Jay, I wasn't expecting you. Who's the ponytail?"

"Rose English, Josie Saunders. Hebrone sent him up from Key West. He's agreed to help with my problem."

"Why couldn't Hebrone come?"

"He's still tied up with some business."

"Mr. Saunders, welcome. Please have a seat."

"Conch. Everybody calls me Conch."

She looked at me, then back at him. "Okay--Conch. Sit, coffee will be served soon."

The girls came out dressed in sweaters and jeans, but with bare feet.

Conch sat beside Rose on the couch. It was hard to tell what interested him, but he always seemed to pay attention.

"You married, Mr.--Conch?"

"Married?" He said it as if the word was some foreign language. "No, I'm not married."

"I've tried to get Jay married a couple of times. He just keeps pushing the women away. Can't seem to fall in love."

I sat my coffee cup on the table beside the chair. "The medieval courtly tradition of romance holds that love is impossible in marriage because it is coerced."

Alicia laughed, sipped her coffee, and looked at me over the rim of the cup. To be looked at by her with those black eyes, even over a cup of coffee would sustain one for the rest of the day.

"Maybe he just likes to be alone," Alella said to Rose.

I'm always alone, I thought. No matter who I'm with I'm always alone in my thick head.

Rose gathered up the coffee cups. "The only difference in his love life and a sky diver is that there is no ambulance waiting at the landing zone."

Even Saunders laughed at that.

It was time for us to leave.

At the door, out of earshot of the girls, I told Rose about the Venezuelan.

"Can't you offer those people something to end this? Money? Get the CIA to release some of their captives. Anything?"

"Negotiating with a hired assassin would be like asking a cannibal to change the entrée."

She looked at Conch. "You protect him. You do like Hebrone would. Keep him safe."

He nodded, went to the truck.

"That man's okay, Jay. He reminds me of Hebrone, a man who can withstand circumstance. That's why I like buzzards."

At least Rose was not like a zoologist I once was involved with who, though she was wise and obsessive, claimed only a professional affection for the world around her. She married an ornithologist. They deserved each other.

"The one you call Rose--I like her. Tough old woman. Reminds me of my ma."

"Yes. She's quite a character. One of my closest friends. What about the young Spanish doctor?"

"Not hard on the eyes, but if I had my pick, it would be the other one, the one you call Alella."

"That's why they make vanilla ice cream, chocolate ice cream, strawberry-_"

"Hebrone said you had a cache of weapons. I want to look at them."

In the rear of the cottage, inside a walk-in closet, I opened the gun safe. It held a life-long collection of weapons and ammo. Saunders spent a half-hour carefully looking over each piece, finally selecting two, an AR-15 rifle and a 40-caliber Glock handgun.

"You got a plan?"

"Yes." He packed ammo into a small ditty bag and, almost as an after thought, picked up a K-bar knife. It was a Marine Corp issue and still in its original scabbard. Hebrone had given it to me years ago. "I'm going to disappear now. I will become a ghost. You will not see me, but know that I am never far away."

"I don't understand?"

"Locate a trap and, sooner or later, the trapper will appear."

It began to make sense to me.

"How do we communicate?"

"No need."

"You're sure about this?"

"An enemy loses more than a battle if he finds you waiting at his ambush point."

In the living room, he meticulously went over the two weapons, inspecting them with an attention to detail a Drill Instructor would have appreciated. He pulled the K-bar out and ran the edge over a fingernail, nodded, and returned it to the scabbard.

An image of a snail crawling across the blade of a knife, and making it, came to mind. It was a line from the movie *Apocalypse Now*. I think Marlon Brando said the words.

Saunders stood. "If the Venezuelan shows, I will kill him."

"I'm uneasy about this plan."

"You'll have to trust me. I know how this man operates. All will be well."

Closing the door behind him, Josie "Conch" Saunders vanished into the cold December night.

Securing the cottage, I turned in, thinking that there was one Venezuelan hit man that should be very concerned about a land-locked Salt Water Conch.

Chapter Twenty-five

The dream vanished instantly, the loud knocking and chimes of the doorbell did not. My bedside clock glowed six-thirty a.m.

Grabbing a robe and my magnum, I headed to the door.

The loud voice vibrated into the living room.

"Jay, it's Shack. Get up. Let me in!"

Quickly opening the door, I saw a man clearly on the edge. He was ashen. The eyes told the story. Something terrible had happened.

"What's wrong? Is it your family?"

He shook his head. Looking down at his hand, he held up three fingers. Tears filled his eyes.

"Three what, Shack. Get a hold of yourself. Three what?"

"It's Alella." He half turned, looked toward the east field. "Ah, god, Jay. They're dead."

"Alella's dead? Who else? Is Rose dead?"

"Please come with me."

I pulled the robe around me, tightened the belt. We got in the fertilizer truck and drove through the wet grass. I did not notice the aroma.

They were in a crumpled heap at almost the exact same spot Marina Pineiro and her father lay on another cold December morning.

Alella was the first that I recognized. Her throat, ugly, gaping. Lying under her, I saw the short, black hair of the young Spanish doctor; her eyes open in a vacant stare.

Moving Alicia Atienza gently aside as if I could somehow harm her, I looked desperately for the identity of the third person.

Josie "Conch" Saunders, lay on his back, the K-bar buried deep into his chest, thrust through a yellow sheet of paper with visible handwriting on it.

I forced myself to look at Alella and Alicia. They were dressed in running clothes and tennis shoes. So young, so vibrant a few hours ago. Looking up at Shack. I saw the tears, the hurt. He stood silent, shaking his head.

I knelt in the dew-soaked grass in this open field, this field of blood, for a long time, not moving, not feeling. The world had ceased to exist. Had no purpose. I had no purpose, except one, to punish whoever did this heinous thing. With every fiber of my being, with every ounce of strength, with every resource within my power to muster, I pledged to avenge these deaths.

I looked up in the sky to where I knew God was watching and begged for his understanding and forgiveness. Even if I must sacrifice my soul, my place in eternity walking those streets paved with gold, I swore this act would be paid for by my hands.

Shack brought me back from the brink of madness.

"Jay, what do we do?"

I realized then, that we had to be men. There were things to do, people to notify. Rose--oh, my god, Rose. Was she still alive?

"We have to get to Rose's."

"I know. What about them?" He pointed to the bodies.

Reaching over, I closed Alicia's eyes with my fingers, and it dawned on me that I did not know why they stayed shut.

"That piece of paper, Jay. What does it say?"

The K-bar had been inserted between ribs. It slid out with little effort. Saunders had been garroted, the wire still around his neck. The note, written in black ink made no sense. A foreign language, Spanish, I thought, but I couldn't focus enough to translate it. Folding the paper, I handed it to Shack. There were no pockets on the robe.

"Let's go back to the cottage. I'll dress, then we'll take my truck to Rose's house. We'll call Sheriff Adams from there."

While I dressed, Shack paced, his face still pale, eyes filled with tears. The muscles in his jaw twitched in angry spasms. I knew exactly what he was thinking. My thoughts were filled with more guilt than his were.

"You think Will Hegewood would do this?"

I looked at him, but didn't answer. Hegewood had already crossed my mind. He certainly had reason to retaliate against Saunders. But would he go so far as to kill two innocent girls? Two young people who'd never done anything to him. No, this was more sinister than some redneck like Hegewood.

At the moment, my mind was too cloudy to think things through clearly. I was too concerned about Rose, and too stunned at the morning's event for rational thought.

Throwing Shack a Glock pistol, I fingered my magnum.

"Let's go."

·   ·   ·

We burst through the front door. Rose appeared from the bedroom clad only in bra and panties, with a startled look on her face.

"Jay--"

"They're dead, Rose. Alella is dead. Alicia is dead. The man from Key West is dead."

She sat suddenly in a chair. It was as if her legs failed and took the rest of her with them.

"They went for a run at daylight. How--?"

"We don't know. We came here immediately. Our concern was your safety."

"Me? But--" Her look didn't waver. Her expression didn't change. It was as if somewhere inside a switch had shut off. She stared straight ahead. Did not move.

Shack stood in the front door, ill at ease, looking at the floor.

I went to her, put my arm around her shoulder.

Slowly her eyes refocused. In her stare I saw for the first time the furtive reptilian glitter of her soul.

She looked up at me, and in a voice that would shake hell itself to its foundation, asked, "Who--?"

"We don't know."

"Hegewood?"

"Probably not."

"The one from Venezuela?"

"Most likely."

"Take me to my daughter."

"Rose, you do not want to see Alella the way she is."

"No! You take me to her."

Shack looked up. "Jay, she needs to see. Let's do it before the field fills with people."

These were hard country folks, used to the harsh realities of life. Who was I to argue?

She held her daughter for a long time. Then she lay her gently in the grass. She ran a finger through the black hair of Alicia. Rubbed her fingers over her cheeks. Finally, she stood, stared at me intently. My guilt was so deep, I wondered if she was blaming me for these deaths. It was true; all this was my fault.

"Get the sheriff, Jay. I do not want her to lay in this field all day."

We went back to my place and phoned John Quincy Adams.

"I'll be there in twenty minutes, Jay."

"Thanks, John."

Rose made a pot of coffee. We moved as if sedated, not knowing what to do or what to say.

Pouring me a cup, Rose put a hand on my arm. "Do not start blaming yourself. This goes way beyond your control."

"I did not see this coming. The Venezuelan had no knowledge of anyone in this part of the country but me. Why the girls? Saunders, I can understand, but not Alella and Alicia."

. . .

True to his word, Sheriff John Quincy Adams arrived twenty minutes after we hung up.

"Sheriff, I want my daughter out of that field. I don't want gawkers seeing her like that."

"I'll take photographs and get an ambulance to move them immediately. I'm not supposed to do this, but if it were my daughter, I'd want the same thing."

He went to the phone and dialed the ambulance service.

"This is Sheriff Adams. We need to transport three deceased as quickly as possible. The Jay Leicester place. Yes, the same location as before. Thank you." He hung up.

Rose nodded. "I appreciate that, Sheriff."

"Leicester, you and Runnels come with me. Ms. English, you okay to stay alone?"

"I'll be fine."

"Let's go, men."

Shack looked at Rose. "You sure?"

"Go."

We rode out to the bodies.

It was still a shocking sight. Shack stood off to the side. John Adams carefully examined all three, took photos from all angles and close-ups. The ambulance arrived and took them away.

"We have to do autopsies. There is no choice."

"We understand, John."

"Let's sit in my car, go over all that we know."

"Saunders said he wanted to work the perimeter, wait for the Venezuelan to appear. Something about waiting at the trap for the trapper to appear."

"It's an old technique we were taught in Vietnam. A lot of paramilitary groups use it."

"Rose said the girls went for a run at daylight."

"That explains why they were dressed in jogging clothes. I can assure you these three killings were not done by Will Hegewood. This was a professional. What I can't explain is why the two innocent women."

"What about the note?" Shack said.

"What note?"

"I'm sorry, John. I completely forget about it. Whoever did this pinned a note to Saunders' chest with a K-bar. It was postmortem. There was no blood on it."

"You think maybe I could see the damn thing?"

Shack took it out of his pocket. The sheriff held it with his handkerchief.

"It's Spanish. That rules out Hegewood. He can't even write in English."

Adams read the note several times.

"I'm rusty with my Spanish, but here's what I think it says. I'll read it in Spanish, then translate.

Demasiado malo cola caballo no es un adversario mas digno.
Las mujeres nos hace incluso.
Todo termina aqui.

Too bad ponytail was not a more worthy adversary.
The women makes us even.
It all ends here.

He carefully folded the note and placed it in an evidence bag.

"We'll run it through the lab along with the knife."

"The K-bar belongs to me."

"You? Then how did it end up buried to the hilt in the Key West guy?"

"Hebrone gave it to me. He saved my life with it years ago. Saunders took it and an AR-15."

"Where's the assault rifle?"

"I don't know."

John Quincy Adams shook his head.

"We better get back," Shack said. "Rose don't need to be alone."

Riding back, the sheriff said, "This killer is on the way back to Venezuela. We'll never get a shot at him."

"I will find him."

"Killing him won't bring these three people back to life."

"No, but that's not the point."

"I wish we could catch him here." Shack said.

We found Rose talking on the phone with a local mortuary, making arrangements for Alella's funeral.

"When can I have my daughter's body?" She looked at Sheriff Adams.

"As soon as the pathologist is finished. I'll instruct the lab to have her done first. A couple of days, at the most."

"Thank you. Would one of you take me home? I must go through Alicia's things, try and find a contact for her parents. They must be notified."

Shack stood up. "I'll go with you and help look."

"You two can ride with me. I'll drop you off. There's nothing I can do out here." He looked at me. "This place will be crawling with investigators looking for clues. You may want to disappear."

After they left, I called Hebrone. No answer. Damn! Alec Aardwolf did not answer, either. I sat at my desk trying to absorb the deaths. B.W., my cat, jumped in my lap, smelled my hands, then leaped down with an alarmed cry. The blood--my hands were still covered with the blood of Alella, Alicia, and Josie Saunders. In the bathroom, I scrubbed them clean--the blood wouldn't come off. I washed them again, tears running down my face. "Get hold of yourself, Leicester. Now is not the time to lose it."

The phone rang.

"The wolf welcomes you."

"He killed Alella and another girl. He killed Saunders."

There was silence. Then: "Rose?"

"No."

"Maybe he will take another run at me?"

"He left a note. Says we are even, and that it is over."

"It's never over."

"No---."

"Did he do'em quick?"

"The girls, yes. No so with Saunders."

"Is there enough of him left to bury?"

"Garroted."

"I'll tell Skinner. You send the body to him."

"Okay."

"I'll be in touch in a couple of days. Are you alright?"

"Fine. We can plan a trip to Venezuela."

He hung up.

Aardwolf returned my call. I told him everything. After I finished he said, "The limo driver, I believe his name was Willie Whitten, the one drove Carmen Cicogna from Jackson hunting you, gave up Ms. English's home address. The Haverstein woman's boyfriend told us."

"How long have you known this, Aardwolf?"

"We never thought they'd do something like this. Not civilians."

"That's the trouble with you people, you never think." I slammed the phone down.

It was a childish thing to do, but anger built up in me and burst forth. I had never thought they would attack innocent people, either. I remembered Aardwolf saying days ago how inane minutiae ran through all of his operations. Some of it happened to turn out relevant. You just never know which part of it gets your loved ones killed.

Sheriff John Quincy Adams was right. By one p.m. my fields were once again filled with crime scene investigators. Their search of my farm and surrounding areas would be fruitless. The Venezuelan was too much of a professional to leave clues. By the time night fell, all of them were gone and God's country once again returned to its rural splendor, a little sadder, but wiser.

. . .

It was a restless night and as dawn broke, I lay in bed listening to a rare winter thunderstorm rumbling down from the northwest ahead of a cold front. In weather like this, I remember an old Captain who would push his seat back against the cockpit bulkhead, light a Picayune cigarette, turn the flying over to me and, with a sly grin, comment that this was an *"anomalous propagation of atmospheric phenomena and therefore good experience for a young aviator."*

He would stare out the side window, unconcerned, as I fought our way through the turbulence. But I knew that this ancient pelican, even though he appeared half-asleep, did not miss a thing happening with the thunderstorm or his airplane.

At nine a.m., I drove to Rose's house. She seemed to be handling the deaths with her usual stoicism. Alicia Atienza's parents had been notified. Subsequent phone calls had resulted in the decision to have her body shipped to Spain for interment. I volunteered to handle the arrangements and used the phone to call Carl Haverstein. He would pick the body up from the state crime lab and prepare it for shipment.

Rose arranged for Alella to be brought to a local funeral home as soon as the body was released.

"What about the man from Key West?"

"I talked with Hebrone. We will send the body to Miami. From there it will be transported to Key West for burial."

"Does he have family there?"

"I don't know."

Rose had a disgusted look on her face. "The man comes to help, gives his life, and you don't know anything about him. Did he have a wife, children? Is someone going to mourn his death?"

"I'm sorry. Hebrone knew the man, sent him here to help."

"Hebrone--you and Hebrone Opshinsky. It's always something with you two."

"Yes. Maybe I should leave this part of the country. Go back to the capital."

"Oh no, Jay. I'm sorry. I didn't mean to blame you. It's just that I'm so sad. Forgive my anger. If you left, I don't know what I'd do. You and Shack are the only two true friends I can count on. Promise me."

"Sure."

She was angry, but she realized that she must accept me with all my complexities, especially since tending to me included much that made her happy. Once she said to me, *"A man like you should be irreproachable in every respect, but nature does not behave that way. What she gives extravagantly, she takes away extravagantly. The good and bad have to be accepted as a whole. I have to look at you as all of one piece. God has given you much, and I find you wonderful, although life with you is exhausting and complicated, and not only in one way but others."*

My cell phone rang.

"It is finished."

"What happened?"

"The man should have gone on back to Venezuela."

"He's dead? But his note said it was over?"

"His body will be found with a K-bar in his chest. There was no garrote."

"Understood. Are you in any trouble?"

"None I can't hide from."

"Can you come to Alella's funeral?"

"No. This phone number will no longer be usable. I have to go away for a time."

"Contact me as soon as you can."

"Tell Rose I love her."

"Say hello to the wolf for me."

"Keep your wings level, Leicester."

The phone went dead.

"What happened?"

"The Venezuelan went back to Florida. Tried to kill Hebrone. Big mistake."

"But I thought he said all was even? He left that note."

"For my part, we were finished. Hebrone killed two of his team. Maybe he wanted to avenge those deaths. At any rate, it's over now."

"It's going to rain all day. Will you stay with me? I don't want to be alone."

"Yes. I will stay with you."

Epilogue

Three days after Shack found her dead in my field, John Quincy Adams arranged for Alella's body to be released from the state crime lab. The funeral was scheduled for one o'clock this afternoon.

Shortly before noon, I closed up the cottage and went to pick up Rose and drive her to the funeral home. The weather was clear and crisp. A good day to be buried, I thought. It is a fact that most airplane pilots killed in a crash are buried on clear days. Bad weather plays a major part in aircraft accidents.

Shack and his wife joined us at the funeral home for a private viewing.

Alella looked as if she was asleep. Her head was tilted slightly forward on the pillow, concealing the wound to the neck. The people at the funeral home did an outstanding cosmetic job covering it up.

Rose had been uncharacteristically outgoing this afternoon. But as she stood looking at her daughter, her eyes changed. It was like two windows slamming shut. Death affects all of us in different ways.

She leaned down close to Alella and said something of which I only caught parts: "For wherever you go, I will go--when you die, I will die, and there I will be buried." I thought it some biblical quote.

She raised up, looked at me. "I am okay now."

My relief was immense.

There was a long line of cars following the hearse from the funeral home to the cemetery. Many more than I expected. The preacher from the little old church in the wild wood was brief with the graveside service. As the pallbearers placed their boutonnieres on the casket, I noticed a lone figure standing on the far side of the graveyard under an oak tree. It was almost in the exact same spot a man stood at Smash's memorial. A man I thought was

Hebrone Opshinsky. The preacher came by shaking hands. When I looked back, the figure was gone.

I asked Shack if he saw the man. He did not. Maybe it was my imagination.

We started from the gravesite back to our cars. Missy Applegate stood with Will Hegewood and his mother. The young man did not dress appropriately for the occasion. He wore overalls and muddy boots. The bruises around his eyes had turned a sickly green. The smirk that he gave me said that our trouble was not over.

I spoke to Missy Applegate and Mrs. Hegewood. As I passed Will, he whispered under his breath, "I heard the dead girl was a Mexican whore."

His mother heard him and gasped, putting the back of her hand to her mouth. Rose heard it and stopped in her tracks.

It was a straight, short jab I'd been working on for years in Frank Hugh's gym. The jab I'd been saving for a special occasion. I felt all of me go into the jab. I felt it in the wrist, up my arm and into my chest and shoulders and back. I felt it in my soul. Solid like a bat on a ball, a golf ball hit in the center, the sweet spot on a tennis racket.

Hegewood folded like a cheap accordion.

His mother looked at me. "Thank you, Mr. Leicester. He deserved that."

John Quincy Adams took me by the arm. "Go on home, Jay. I'll take care of this."

From somewhere far off, I thought I heard Alicia Atienza yell, "Ole!"

· · ·

At ten o'clock the next morning, I sat on the front porch enjoying the unusually warm weather, listening to Christmas music on the radio. It was that season. B.W. lay at my feet digesting an unlucky mouse that had also been out enjoying the day.

I watched a UPS delivery truck turn onto the terrace row and make its way down the drive.

"You Leicester? I have a package you need to sign for."

I had a vision of the Union Post Office and Will Hegewood.

The driver handed me the box, looked at the signature. "Merry Christmas, Mr. Leicester."

"Yeah. Merry Christmas."

The box originated in Miami. There was no return address, but in one corner someone had hand-written the word "Wolf" under a child-like drawing of what could resemble the profile of a canine. Hebrone.

Opening the box, I found two packages. In one was my AR-15 and a note in Hebrone's handwriting. "Nice jab."

The other package was from Alec Aardwolf. It contained his well-worn Oakland Raiders cap with a note: "I'm officially retired. If you'll root for the

Raiders, I'll do the same for the Saints, except when we play each other. May we meet one day crossing the bar at Green Turtle Cay. I'll buy the first drink. "A"

I put the Raiders cap on my head, pushed the box aside, propped my feet up on a cedar post, looked out across the brown fields. A flock of turkeys fed their way through a nearby hollow.

Rose English came to mind. She was doing okay. I once heard her hum a tune, a high lonesome song that held me still by its beauty. Seraphic, her voice. Cold and pure as spring water. It was a lament of broken vows and lover's betrayals. The murder of her daughter, Alella, came to mind. Murder is the sort of thing that's easy to talk about, but few people can actually do it. I seem to meet an inordinate amount of them.

Whatever the manner, death has everyone's number. But we don't have to answer when the phone rings. Too soon most of us will listen to some medical doctor speak the name of our killer.

Picking up my cat, I sat him in my lap. He started to purr. Rubbing him behind the ear, I thought about the mystery of life. Some of the mysteries of the past have been fathomed by science. Others still bewilder mankind. All of the garnered wisdom of the ages is only a scratch on the surface of man's search for the knowledge of the universe.

For the most part, God has retained his secrets, and man standing on his intellectual tiptoes can comprehend only a small fraction of his doings.

I once read that a "mystery" in scripture is a previously hidden truth now divinely revealed, but in which a supernatural element remains unknown despite the revelation.

B.W. growled, jumped down, looked back at me, then padded away. I wondered about the future of my fate. An old Dottie Rambo song, God rest her soul, popped into my mind.

Too many miles behind me
Too many troubles are through
Too many tears help me to remember
There's too much to gain to lose.

I crossed the hot burning desert
Struggling the road to choose
But somewhere ahead I see cool clear waters
And defeat is one word I don't use.

I got up, looked across those fields, those fields of blood, and went inside.

Printed in the United States
131197LV00004B/8/P